DIXIE DANDELION

AND THE

White Doves

R. H. BURKETT

Publishing Coordinator – Clarissa Willis
Book & Cover Design – Sharon Kizziah-Holmes
Cover Art – Kashif Qasim

CWL INDIE PRESS

Springdale, Arkansas

ISBN: 978-1-959548-83-6

DEDICATION

Dedicated to the memory of Joe, King, Prissy, and million-dollar horses worldwide.

Other Publications by R. H. Burkett

Soldiers In the Mist
The Rook and the Raven
Bad Moon Rising
Moon Child Rising
Broomflyer's Tales & Spells

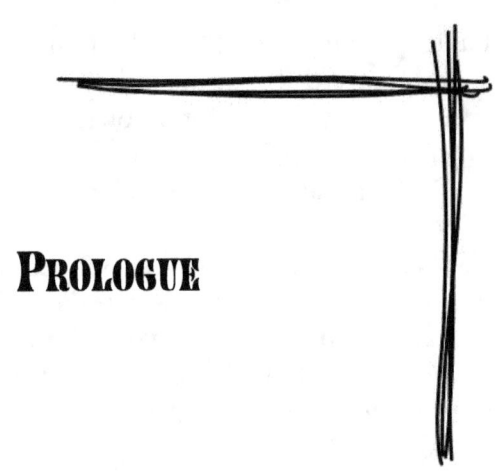

PROLOGUE

"I should've shot the low-down mangy polecat when he first rode into town."

"Watch your mouth, young lady."

Desperate to make Mama listen, I grabbed her arm and pulled her from the mirror to face me. "Mama, I beg you. Don't marry him."

She jerked loose from my hold and tossed the lacy wedding veil on the bed. Her emerald eyes shot bullets at me. I backed against the wall, closed my eyes, and braced for a slap. It never came.

"Margaret. I'm sick and tired of dealing with your rudeness and won't tolerate it for another minute. This is my last warning. I am marrying Nathanial Payton today and that's all there is to it."

She picked up the veil and turned back to the mirror.

"I would've thought you'd be overjoyed for my happiness," she added.

A deep breath shook my body. *Stay quiet,* my head screamed. But my heart never listened to my head and the words poured out.

"Mama, if for one minute I thought you were truly happy, I'd turn cartwheels in the street. We both know it's

Payton's *money* you love. Not him."

"Margaret!"

In for a penny, in for a pound. I rushed on. "What about Papa?"

On hell and damnation. Her jaw clenched and it chilled my heart.

"What about him? He abandoned us to run off and fight in the War of Northern Aggression. He selfishly gave no thought to how hard life would be for me without him. I'll never forgive him. I hope he died in that war. Hope he's rotting in a grave under some God-forsaken piece of Yankee dirt."

She knew I adored Papa. Her cruel words were in retaliation for what I said earlier.

"I am marrying Nat regardless of your approval and moving to California as soon as he can make arrangements."

What? My insides went numb. "California? Why?" My knees trembled as much as my voice.

"Nat is quite influential in California. He's destined to become the next governor, and I'll be the First Lady. "We'll travel by wagon train to Sacramento in a few days."

I snorted like a boar hog. "Wagon train? Delicate you? I've read stories about how awful wagon trains are. They take months to reach California. The weather is stifling-hot one day and bone-chilling cold the next. Torrential rain. Mud and snow up to the hubs. Dust thick enough to choke a pig. Wild Indians. Putrid water."

"Enough! I won't have you ruining my special day with your rudeness. For your information, Nat has gone to a great deal of trouble to ensure … *our* comfort. He's purchasing two wagons and drivers as we speak. One will carry more supplies that we could use. The other will be a makeshift home on wheels with comfortable chairs, dressers, and a bed. He and I will sleep in the first wagon, of course."

Of course.

"You can have the second wagon all to yourself." She turned to me and smiled. "Won't that be grand? That's what money can do for a person, Margaret. Comfort. Convenience. Everything can be bought."

Even you, Mama.

"I gotta' hand it to you, Mama. You fooled everyone. Even me. I thought you were a delicate flower, evidently, however, you're more than capable of surviving, especially when money and prestige are concerned."

This time the slap did come. Hard and quick. It burned like a brand.

"How dare you speak to me in that manner! I am moving to California with my husband with or without you."

Maybe I deserved the slap. But my disrespectful words didn't warrant this. Talk about selfishness. Was Mama so self-centered as to choose money over her only child? Abandon me?

"You'd go without me? Leave me here?"

"The choice is yours." Her smirk brought tears to my eyes.

One week later, I sat perched alongside Mama on a padded wagon seat, leaving my beloved land of cotton, heading towards the Promised Land.

Mama and I hadn't spoken to each other since the day she looked Nathanial Payton straight into his beady eyes and said, "I do." She glanced over at me and sighed.

"I declare, Margaret Kate. That sullen, Irish attitude of yours will be the death of me yet."

She was wrong.

3

CHAPTER I

Feelings have color.

Sorrow: Deep purple and indigo. The same as the stormy sky that spread across the plains like a giant bruise from horizon to horizon.

Grief: Slate gray. The drizzle that fell. Stones heaped upon a grave.

Sorry for your loss. False sympathy: Dirty dishwater brown.

Fear: Black as pitch.

The wagon master flipped the ragged-edged Bible shut with a snap. Impatient and grumbling, he stomped back to the train. A day wasted. Damn fool woman. Stupid accident.

Mama wasn't dumb.

Murder was no accident.

A spindly arm wrapped around my shoulders. I pushed back. "Get your hands off me."

The slap came so fast I couldn't block it. One minute, I was standing. The next, I lay crumbled at the foot of Mama's grave. The bitter taste of blood on my tongue.

"Don't sass me, girl! You're all mine, now." He gave me a leer so sinister, my stomach lurched. "And I got big plans for you."

No one witnessed the blow. Even if they had, nothing would've been done. Family business, none of theirs. My stepfather, a slick, dressed-up dandy in fringed trousers, laughed and swaggered back to camp. No doubt to meet with his partner, Ike Morgan, the wagon master, for a night of drinking, gambling, and scheming. Lead the sodbusters west. Earn their trust. Take their money. Then, lose them.

Mama overheard their deception.

They killed her because of it.

Hate is the color of blood-red meat.

"He your pa?"

A hand reached to steady me. The scout for the wagon train, Jackson Wayne, stood solid as an oak before me and just as tall.

"No. Papa never raised a hand to me."

"Against your ma?"

"Her, neither."

"Huh. How'd y'all get mixed up with a varmint like Payton?"

Why the hell did he care? None of his business anyway. Yet, the need to explain burned in my throat.

"The damn war. Papa was a huge Irish man with twinkling blue eyes and a laugh that could shake walls. Rode off to join the Confederacy one day, and never rode back. Mama is . . . was . . . a real looker but fragile as glass. Couldn't fend for herself or me."

I rushed on unaware of walking by his side. "Nathanial Payton is a man who always gets what he wants. He set his snake eyes on Mama. Promised her a land of milk and honey if she'd marry him and go west. Wealth. Society. All the things she dreamed of. The stars in her eyes blinded her to his shortcomings. Whiskey. Cards. Hair-trigger temper."

Talking about Mama and Papa brought fresh tears to my eyes. I kept my head down and tried to keep up with the scout's long stride. Didn't need his pity. We walked away from the wagons to the picket line.

The sound of a low whinny stopped me short. A buckskin horse stretched out his black- velvet nose and nudged Wayne's arm. The scout reached into his pocket and pulled out a ripe fruit.

"Persimmons?" I asked.

"Yep. He's crazy about 'em'."

A low nicker came from the Paint Gelding tied next to the stallion.

"Him, too?"

"Yep, afraid so."

"Why two horses?"

He walked over and shook the saddle on the buckskin. Hooking a stirrup over the horn, he tightened the cinch. "Buck is big and strong. Dependable as sunup and sundown. But there are times when speed is more important than strength." He reached over and patted the Paint's neck. "Joe, can pick 'em up and put 'em down faster than most."

"You always keep both of them saddled?"

"When necessary. Extra Colt in the saddlebag, too."

"Why?"

He winked. "Never know when I might need to make a fast getaway."

I smiled. "You some kind of outlaw or something?"

"Something."

"Then you know."

"Know what?"

"Morgan and Payton. They're in cahoots. They cheat honest folks out of their life savings. Leave them lost, wagon-wheel-deep in the snow. Mama found out about it and threatened to tell. That's why she's dead. They killed her. Made it look like an accident."

"Sounds about right," he mumbled. "I hear the Pinkerton Agency got complaints on Morgan's outfit."

"Somebody ought to arrest them."

"Whoa, hold on there, Dixie Belle. Knowing and proving are two different things."

"My name isn't Dixie."

He chuckled.

The laugh irked me almost as much as the pet name.

"Stop it! My name's Margeret Katelyn O'Shea."

His bourbon-colored eyes traveled up and down my body. No one had ever looked at me that way. Half of me liked it.

Desire: rosy pink.

"Huh. Scarlet hair, snappy blue eyes, soft southern drawl, creamy skin. Nope. Don't look like a Maggie. Sorry, darlin'. Dixie fits ya' too good."

My fists clenched. "Go to hell."

Loud laughter rolled out of his tight belly, and he doubled over, holding his sides. Buck threw his head and snorted. I turned to go. Lightning fast, he reached out and caught my arm. Spun me around to look up at his chiseled face, now serious and stern.

"You got any idea just how much danger you're in? How old are ya' anyway? Fifteen?"

"Sixteen."

"You ever been with a man before?"

I gasped. How dare he. Lips flattened in a straight line, I reared back and swung with all my might. He caught my fist in midair. Amusement flickered in his eyes.

"Didn't think so."

Damn the man.

"Simmer down and listen. The point I'm making is this. Payton is your step-pa. Family. Ain't no one gonna interfere with anything he does. I heard him tell you he had plans. You know what that means?"

Fear shot an arrow into my heart. My mouth dry as sand, I wilted like a daylily. "I got some idea."

"A buck, no matter how mangy, is a dangerous, strong animal in rut. Savvy?"

Panic: Puke green.

"You wouldn't let anything happen to me."

Broad shoulders sagged, and he removed his hand. "Don't saddle me with that burden.

Besides, I'm not always gonna' be around. Fact is, I'm riding out today."

"Where to?"

"Six Shooter Siding, a railroad town two days north of here."

"Won't Morgan be suspicious if you're gone too long?"

"Well, Dixie Belle." He winked again. "That's the beauty of being a scout. Can come and go as much as I please. Not being here for a few days won't be unusual."

Reined-in emotions made my voice tremble. "He killed Mama."

"And he'll swing for that. I promise." A muscle quivered in his square jaw. "But you need solid proof. It looked like an accident. Said so yourself."

Dropping to one knee, he pulled a knife from his boot. He straightened with a loud sigh. "Take this. Got the guts to use it?"

Thoughts of Payton's slimy hands on my skin and waxy lips on my mouth made me shiver. My hand tightened around the blade's elk-horn handle.

"I'll skin the son of a bitch if I have to."

"Darlin', of that I have no doubt." His laughter came easy and fullhearted.

"You're a wild prairie dandelion, Dixie gal. Good thing. Gotta' feeling you're gonna' need all that fire before this is all over with.

He untied Buck and swung a long leg over the saddle. "Watch your back, Dixie Belle. See ya' in a few days." With a gloved hand, he touched the brim of his Stetson and spurred the buckskin into a slow lope.

Heaviness laid a hand on the top of my head and pushed me to the ground. I was on a wagon train in the middle of nowhere heading for a place I never wanted to go. California was Mama's dream, not mine. My life depended on the very man who killed her.

Despair: black as soot.

Free to roam, my tears broke and splashed the dirt. I raised my gaze to the horizon and whispered a silent prayer to the distant disappearing dot.

"Hurry."

CHAPTER 2

Finished with the evening chores, I crawled into the wagon. The yellowed thumbnail moon played hide-and-seek with the clouds, and my eyes grew heavy. On guard for Payton, I refused to rest and sat rigid and upright. Waiting. Sleep pulled at my eyelids. I struggled against the pull but finally succumbed to it.

The bitter scent of cheap whiskey covered me before Payton did. A slimy tongue licked the side of my face like a cow slurping a salt lick. Sweaty hands pawed the front of my dress. Someone screamed—me.

He threw me to the floor like a rag doll. The full weight of his body crashed down on top of mine. Another scream ripped from my throat. His hands, grimy and tasting of stale tobacco, clamped down hard on my mouth, cutting off my breath. Terror grabbed my heart with a cold fist. He hissed in my ear.

"Ain't no one coming to help ya' girl."

A picture of Mama surrendering night after night to the brutal attacks of this slobbering pig flashed in my mind and cooled the wildfire of fear and panic to frosted water.

Revenge is colored ice-cold blue.

I forced my body to go limp.

Payton relaxed.

My teeth clamped down on his fingers like a wolf and I bit plumb to the bone.

Crying out, he yanked his hand away from my mouth and gawked at the blood trickling down his wrist.

Lungs filled with blessed air. Strength returned. I kicked free from his grasp.

Wayne's knife lay within inches of my hand. Payton lunged across my body to grab it.

Too late.

I drove the blade deep into the small of his back and ripped it across his skin like gutting a fish.

He let out a howl a coon dog would be proud of.

My fist hit him hard, square on the nose.

Blood poured and covered me in a blanket of snot and gristle.

Struggling to stand, he fell backward. His head hit the side of Mama's mahogany dresser. He crumbled to the floor, twitched, then lay still.

Satisfaction: Golden.

God almighty. How much blood does a body have? Buckets of the stuff spread across the floor quicker than soft butter on warm biscuits.

Stunned, I watched crimson inch ever so slowly toward the toe of my boot. Every nerve in my body danced like I'd been hit by a lightning bolt. Bile squirmed in my belly and crawled up my gullet. I clamped both hands over my mouth and choked it down.

My temper flared. Bad enough the son-of-a-bitch killed Mama, but now he'd forced me to become a killer.

Anger: Hot, poker orange.

I drew back my foot and kicked the body beside me.

One.

Two.

Three times, until sweat rolled down my neck and nausea started to march up my throat again.

"Bastard!" I yelled and kicked him once more for good measure.

What was I going to do? Payton and Morgan were partners. No one would believe my story. Only one thing to do.

Run!

Money. Where could I get money?

Payton's silk vest lay in a rumbled heap on the floor. I rummaged through the pockets and pulled out a wad of bills that made me gasp. For once, I appreciated his gambling. Where to put it? My dress had no pockets. Remembering Wayne's hiding spot, I tucked the bills into my boot.

Get the knife.

Using the vest, I wiped the blade clean and eased the sharp edge into my boot between the tanned leather and the greenbacks.

Widow Sawyer did laundry for the bachelors and widowers on the train. In my haste to get to the picket line, I forgot about the makeshift clothesline she'd strung between the trees. I ducked just in time to avoid being throttled.

Men's and boy's clothes flapped in the soft breeze, laughing at me. My dress, soaked with blood, sticky and smelly, went flying over my head after I ripped it off. It took only a second to wiggle into the smallest pair of breeches hung on the line. Snug around the hips, but not too bad. My fingers trembled buttoning the plaid shirt. Had to hurry. Better take another pair. As an afterthought, I pulled a few bills from my boot and pinned them on the line.

Wasn't a thief, just a murderer.

Joe let out a soft nicker and nudged my pockets for persimmons. I patted his brown-and-white shoulder and whispered into his flicking ears. "Get me out of this mess, and I'll pick you a bushel full."

I crammed the extra clothes into the saddlebags. My fingers brushed against the cold, smooth steel of a gun barrel. Even if I couldn't hit the broad side of a barn, it was comfort knowing it was there. *Wait. What was this?* A badge. Wayne was a lawman. Why hadn't he told me? No time to think about it now, I had to hurry.

Oh hell and damnation! The stirrups were too long. I adjusted the length and wondered if my hands would ever stop shaking. Odd. Wayne took good care of his horses, so much so, he spoiled them. Why would he leave Joe fully saddled knowing he was going to be gone for days? He wouldn't. Unless . . . unless he figured someone would need to make a fast getaway. I smiled and led the gelding away from the wagons before stepping up into the saddle.

I had more in common with Papa than his red hair and blue eyes. He could ride like a wild Comanche and so could I. Full of piss and vinegar, Joe fought the reins, begging to run. I fixed my gaze on the North Star and nudged him with my heel. Six Shooter Siding was two days away. Judging from the way Joe flew across the prairie, we'd be there in one. Leaning low on his neck, I surrendered all thought and listened only to the wind whistling in my ears.

CHAPTER 3

The Siding stank like a drawer full of dirty socks and looked like a stomped-on ant hill. Folks, mostly men, crawled out of every nook and cranny and swarmed the boardwalks and streets. I weaved Joe through the crowd and searched for the livery stable.

The bowlegged stable master spit a stream of tobacco between Joe's front hooves. "Ain't seen no Buckskin horse. Talk to Big Finn. Nothin' goes on in this town he don't know about."

Except for the mustache that drooped like a soggy haystack around his upper lip, Finn Donovan could've been Papa's twin. I liked him on the spot.

"No, lass, I haven't seen a man nor horse that fits that description. Sorry."

Disappointment color: wilted, leafy brown.

Worry must have crawled across my face because he cocked his head to one side and studied me hard.

"Need a job?"

Didn't see that coming. "What kind?"

"The honest, hardworking kind. Cooking. I ramrod a rail crew. We work in shifts around the clock, which means we eat twenty-four hours a day. Two of me biscuit-rollers got in a gunfight over a crooked poker game. Shot themselves full of holes, they did, and straight into Boot Hill. Left me in a hell of a mess. You interested?"

I couldn't go back to the wagon train and had no place to go. Why not? Yet, I hesitated.

"You can cook, can't ya'?

"Sure."

The color of guilt over telling a small white lie: eggshell white.

"Good. It's settled, then. By the way, what's your name, lass?"

I was a murderer and a horse thief, but no fool. Either one could get me lynched with no questions asked. Sure wasn't going to tell my real name.

"Dixie. Dixie Belle Dandelion."

He removed his hat with an exaggerated gesture and bowed at the waist. I laughed.

"Well, welcome to Six Shooter Siding, Miss Dixie Dandelion."

Hope is colored bright, jonquil yellow.

CHAPTER 4

Jackson tossed another log on the campfire. Sparks of orange and yellow spit at the blackness then disappeared with a snap. He leaned back against his saddle and drank the last cup of Arbuckle's before turning in. Doubt he would sleep well. Bluebonnet eyes would haunt his dreams.

Margaret Katelyn O'Shea. Name was bigger than she was. Very pretty. Feisty. A rebellious spit-in-your-eye kind of spirit as proud as Dixieland itself.

"Like it or not, little darlin', Dixie is the only name that suits ya."

His voice bounced off the trees and brush, echoed small in the prairie's vastness. A falling star darted across the heavens. He followed its trail. Felt a loss when its brilliance flamed out. His thoughts returned to her . . . just like her namesake, the Old South, Dixie had fallen into big trouble.

Payton would come for her. No doubt about it. It was only a matter of time.

He'd never cottoned to Payton or Morgan and believed all the complaints received by the Pinkerton Agency about their bamboozling sod busters headed to California. Now he could add murder to the list. Always figured of the two, Payton was the brains and the worst. But how to prove it?

He should've stayed. Watched over her. He couldn't take the chance. He had to meet Donavon in Six Shooter before the big man came looking for him, blowing his cover as undercover Pinkerton. Maybe he'd get back before Payton made his move. But just in case, he'd left her an ace-in-the-hole—Joe.

Joe was a scrappy bangtail who could run the legs off a deer. He would get her to Six Shooter safe and sound. He'd warn Donovan to keep an eye peeled for her.

Cup empty, he settled in for the night. Wasn't like him to get mixed up in something like this. He'd sworn never to care again. To never allow himself to get close. But he found himself wanting to wrap this girl in his arms. To shield her from all harm. Why? He tipped his Stetson forward over his eyes and grumbled.

"Because I'm a sucker for bluebonnets and prairie dandelions, that's why."

CHAPTER 5

"Choppy, choppy. Choppy, choppy."

I stared at the little man, not understanding a word he said. Behind me, Big Finn laughed.

"Stop ye yammering, you dang fool Chinaman. This here be Miss Dixie Dandelion. She'll be working the morning shift." He turned to me. "Miss Dixie, meet Chow Ling, me number one cook."

I extended my hand. Chow Ling bowed low at the waist. My hand dropped, and I gave a slight nod.

"Berry busy, Big Boss Man. Must hurry. Chop. Chop."

Chow Ling was the strangest man I'd ever seen. His face looked as if someone had taken a piece of charcoal, drawn a thin line of hair on either side of his nose, and curved it around his mouth to frame a sketched-in scraggy pigmy-goat beard. He scurried around like a tiny mouse with slippers on its feet. A tight pigtail running the length of his back wagged from side to side, reminding me of a black cougar tail switching back and forth.

"What sort of Indian is that?"

Loud laughter boiled out of Finn. "Hey, Chow! Miss Dixie thinks you're some kind of Injun."

Scampering back to us, Chow Ling grinned up at me.

"Ah, Missy Dixie, you funny rady. Chow no Indian. Chow Chin-ee."

Still confused, I scratched my head. "What tribe is that?"

"A Far Eastern one," Finn said between guffaws.

Chow's laughter sounded like a barnyard full of chickens. His upside-down teacup hat fell to the ground and rolled to my feet. A snip of a nose wrinkled when he picked it up.

"Missy Dixie smell like horse. No work for Chow until clean."

Embarrassed, I stepped away and turned my back. On the sly, I took a whiff of myself. Whew! He was right. I turned back. "Uh . . . been on the trail for days. Didn't have a chance to wash or change clothes. Was gonna do that straightaway but got sidetracked with this job offer and things."

"Don't worry about it," Finn said. "Chinese are always washing something."

"Oh," I said, grateful for his casual manner. But I did need to wash up. Maybe I could find a creek nearby.

"I pay $35. a month. Best rate going. All me employees, except for the coolies, room at Mildred Atkins' boarding house."

"Coolies?"

"Chinese workers. They stay to themselves."

"Millie runs a respectable place. Very clean." He winked. "Think she has ideas about making me husband number four. She has a bathhouse too. Cost two-bits.

"Don't worry about that good-lookin' paint horse of yours. Got me own stables and corrals. Feed is free so long as you work for me and try hard. So are your meals. Be here at four in the morning. Chow will tell ya what to do." His lips pursed. "That's all I can think of. Got any questions?"

Questions? I had a bucket full. Things were moving fast. Why was Donovan so nice? What had that livery owner said? "Big Finn knows everything that goes on in this town?" Could he be Wayne's boss? If so, it would make sense he'd deny seeing him. Jackson left Joe saddled and waiting. Maybe he'd warned Finn that I might be riding in and told him to be on the lookout. Sure would explain the sudden job offer. Huh. For someone not wanting to be burdened with my welfare, the scout sure was blazing an easy trail for me.

"Which way to the barn? I need to get Joe bedded down, then get that room."

CHAPTER 6

About an hour later, with saddlebags clutched tightly to my chest, I searched for Mildred's place. I wished Finn had come with me. My heart pounded. I'd never seen a place as wild and woolly as the Siding. Gambling halls and saloons lined the sidewalks. Loud, boisterous laughter crawled under their batwing doors and galloped rampantly up and down the street. Ever-so-often what sounded like gunshots popped in the air. Gamblers, gunslingers, a lot of those strange, squinty-eyed Chin-ee Indians, noises, and smells were thicker than fleas on a hound dog. I hugged the storefronts and tried to stay out of everyone's way and remain unseen. Just missed being slammed into by a long, lanky cowboy pulling on a brown shirt with patches on the elbows.

"Donny Ray, you get on now! Told you a hundred times, no money, no service."

My mouth flew open. A woman with bosoms so large you could eat breakfast off of 'em, poked the cowhand's shoulder with a fingernail painted deep red. A yellow beehive of hair wobbled and threatened to topple over with every word. Wide hips jiggled and swayed with every menacing step she took toward the unlucky fella.

"Daggett might own most of this town, but not The White Dove." She jabbed him again. "You tell that boss of yours, my girls don't work on credit. Now, git!"

"Bye, Donnie Ray," a syrupy voice called down from the second floor. "Come back with a dollar. Ask for Abby."

Headed back to the door, the big-busted woman caught sight of me. "You all right, hon?"

The mole on her cheek looked like a brown tick and I couldn't help but stare. "I . . . fine," I stammered.

She looked at me up and down. Felt like a horse up for trade. A slight smile tugged her ruby-colored lips and made her moss-green eyes crinkle at the corners. "New in town, hon? Lookin' for a place to stay?"

"I . . . I work for Big Finn. Trying to find Mildred Atkins' place."

She waved her hand. "Follow me, I'll show ya' where it is. My name's Della Williams. Most everybody calls me Mama Della. I own the White Dove."

I fell in beside her. "My name's Dixie. Is the White Dove a hotel?"

A low raspy chuckle came from deep in her throat. "Of sorts." She pointed across the busy dusty street. "That's Mildred's boarding house, there. I'd introduce ya' but that uppity, bluenose Yankee don't approve of me. Best go in by yourself."

"Why doesn't she like you?"

Her chuckle grew into a loud snort. "Because I'm a soiled Dove and so are my girls."

"Soiled Dove?"

She gave me that crinkly-eyed look again. "Prostitutes. Prairie Nymphs." She shook her head. "Innocent as a lamb, ain't ya'? We entertain men—for a price."

The way she winked and stressed the word "entertain" made me think hard. Her meaning finally dawned on me. Eyes wide, I gawked. "You mean men pay for *that*? Thought they just took it."

A funny look crossed her features, and she studied me. She broke into a motherly smile which made her features soften. Bet before life and time had worn her down, Della had been a beautiful woman.

"Some men do. Not all. Don't judge the lot by the actions of a few."

She squeezed my hand. "Good luck to you, Dixie. If you need anything, ya know where I am."

I watched her sashay down the street, head high, green skirts and black petticoats swinging from side to side. Men smiled but didn't tip their hats.

Soiled Dove or not, Mama Della had a kind heart and was probably the best friend a girl could ever have.

Mildred Atkins, on the other hand, was a raw-boned, cold, hard strip of dried jerky with frown lines and big feet.

CHAPTER 7

"**R**ent's due the first of the month. Don't be late. Won't tolerate excuses. No drinking. No swearing. No men. I keep a God-fearing establishment." Her nose stuck even higher in the air. "Seen you talking to that . . . that . . . woman, Della Williams. Word to the wise, don't associate with her kind."

Irritated at her holier-than-thou manner, my mouth overrode my head again. "And what *kind* would that be?"

The sour look she shot me would've curdled milk. "Hussies! No good heathens." She banged a key down on the polished desktop. "Room five top of the stairs, to your right."

"Mr. Donavan said I could get a bath here."

"Most certainly can. Cleanliness is next to Godliness, I always say. The bathhouse is around back. Cost ya' a quarter." She looked down her thin nose and darting sparrow eyes narrowed. "In advance."

On purpose, I slapped the coin down and picked up the key. "Thank you," I said and headed for the stairs. Three husbands? God bless 'em. Bet they'd shot themselves.

Room five was clean alright but only because there was nothing for dirt to cling to. One window facing north, a bed, a scarred dresser with a lamp and wash basin, and a straight-backed chair. Home, sweet home. A sign posted on the wall caught my attention.

No Relieving Yourself out the Window

The meaning became clearer when I noticed the rusted screen. Bet that was one stain Mildred would never get out. No Relieving? Doubted any tinhorn dumb enough to pee out a window would know how to read.

Weary, I flopped on the edge of the bed and wiped at the tears that sprang up from out of nowhere. My insides felt as empty as the room. *Oh, Mama, I miss you.* Missed Papa even more. What would he say?

"Life isn't fair, lass."

I jerked around, expecting to see Papa standing right behind me. But no. Must've been the wind and wishful thinking that carried his voice to me.

Everything had turned upside down in three days. Buried Mama, killed a man, stole a horse, and got a job—as a cook. A fit of giggles nudged the tears aside. Me. A cook. Barely knew how to boil water. Pretty sure that news would send Chow-Chow into a fit of squirrel chatter. A deep sigh shook the bed. Better get that bath. Paid too much for the darn thing to waste it.

CHAPTER 8

The next morning, Chow tossed an apron to me and pointed to a large table. "Missy Dixie. You make biscuits. Hurry. Chop. Chop."

The sack of flour glared at me in silent ridicule. Somewhere Mama laughed. She tried to teach me to cook, but Papa and horses were more fun. Lard. Buttermilk. Sugar. Was that all I needed? Damned if I knew. How much of each should I use? Oh hell and damnation. It can't be that hard.

I threw all the ingredients into a bowl deep enough to fall into and stirred until my arms ached. I remembered Mama kneading dough with her hands. Lifting the sticky blob onto the table, I beat it senseless. Rolling it flat, I cut out circles with the rim of a tin coffee cup, placed them on a baking pan, and shoved the whole shebang into the oven on a woodstove big enough to cook a longhorn steer, horns and all.

I pulled them from the oven a few minutes later and placed the pan on the stovetop. What a mess. Flat, burnt, and hard as bricks. Before I could throw them away, Big Finn reached over my shoulder and took one.

"Chow? What the hell are these?"

I winced. He banged the roll against the edge of the table and grinned. Chow-Chow jabbered away in his singsong talk saying something about "Missy Dixie berry pretty. No good cook."

"Sorry," I murmured. "Guess I forgot something."

Finn chuckled and clapped me on the shoulder. "Chalk it up to first-day-on-the-job jitters. Tomorrow will be better." He and Chow walked out of the cook tent shaking their heads and muttering something about river-rock biscuits.

I needed help.

CHAPTER 9

"**D**ella, they were awful. Chow called them river-rocks."

She held her sides and laughed until tears ran down her face making tiny trails of dusty-rose rouge. "You forgot the baking powders, that's all. Don't worry about Chow Ling, hon. I know him. He'll throw buckets of gravy over the mess and serve it up. Those rail-crew boys are so hungry and worn out, they'll never notice."

I gasped. "You know Chow Ling? He comes to the White Dove?"

"No." She winked. "But Finn does. Waltzed in here last spring and said Chow Ling and his family were sick. My girl, Abby, lost her ma to the fever. Got powerful upset when she heard. Made up a big pot of soup and took it to Chow. Helped nurse them all back to health. Chow never forgot her kindness. He stops by every now and again with baskets full of Chinese vegetables. Can't pronounce any of the names, but that don't spoil the taste any."

I smiled. "Chow said I was pretty."

"Well, that's because you are, hon." She put her arm around my shoulder. "Sure you don't want to work for me?"

Four days ago, I would've died at the suggestion. Today, I laughed.

"Didn't think so."

She sighed. "Pity. We could make a lot of money. Come on into the kitchen. I'll get Abby to show you how to make the best biscuits in the territory."

CHAPTER 10

Six women sat at a round kitchen table drinking coffee, talking, and joking. They looked up when Della cleared her throat.

"Girls, this here is Dixie."

"She a new Dove, Mama Della?"

"No, just a friend. Cooks for Big Finn. Needs a little help. Abby? Can you whip up some biscuits? Show Dixie how it's done?"

Tall and willowy with skin as smooth as cream, Abby twirled her wheat-spun hair around one long, slender finger and smiled. "Why, sure. Be happy to." Southern to the bone, her accent was thick enough to cut with a knife.

Making biscuits wasn't the only thing I learned that morning. Della and her girls were one big family. The White Dove, their home. I sat in the golden sunlight that streamed through the big kitchen windows, listened to their talk, joined their laughter, and drank in all the coffee and warm love I could get. I wondered about all of them.

Dominique's bronzed skin glowed like glazed honey in the sunlight. Deep chestnut eyes hidden under thick lashes, caught every move and blinked mysteriously at me like a sleek, sable-haired cat.

Pearl and Rosie were solid, corn-fed twins with strawberry curls and freckled faces. Looked so much alike that I couldn't tell them apart, except Pearl's nose was crooked as a dog's hind leg. Must've been broken at one time.

Sassy lounged, wrapped in a peacock-green gown with white feathers around the collar and cuffs. So lively and funny, she made me laugh until my facial muscles hurt.

Mary Louise twittered like a tiny Jenny-Wren songbird.

Then, of course, there was Abby.

"Well, whatcha think about my girls?" Della asked when they'd gone upstairs.

"I like them. If I didn't know better, I'd think they were your daughters."

I was surprised to see a sad smile slide across her face. "That's how I think of them. Never could have young'uns of my own. They filled the void." She snorted. "Funny how life works. I moved to Six Shooter to escape righteous, judgmental folks only to end up with a brood of girls that no one else wanted."

Her faded palomino hair fell into her face. She brushed it back with a ring-jeweled hand. "Dominique hails from Cajun country. Half Creole. That little French accent of hers drives the men wild. She showed up at my door starved as an abandoned puppy. Didn't have the heart to turn her away. Then, just like stray kittens, the rest came along."

"Abby was only ten when her mama came with her in tow. Meg Brown didn't want to have anything to do with men. Been mistreated and beaten up by too many I suspected, so I hired her as a cook. It was only natural to take Abby into the business when her mama died. She cooked for me until she was of age then, despite my objections, she became a Dove." A heavy sigh.

"God blessed Abby with the looks of an angel and a heart bigger than Texas. But, bless her, she's simple-minded as a goose. Can't separate business from emotion. Falls in love with every client who smiles at her. Someday, one of them will do her wrong. All of us try to look after her."

Speechless, I drank the rest of my coffee and got up to leave even though it was the last thing I wanted to do.

"You're easy to talk to," Della said and walked me to the parlor.

Eyes wide, I gawked at the room. Bright, cheery, with thick rugs, soft couches, and chairs, even a piano. Made Mildred's place look like a cave. Abby sat at the piano bench running her fingers across the keyboard. I walked over to her. "Do you play?"

"Naw, we got a darkie grandpa who comes in at night that does. I just like to run my fingers across the keys. Feels smooth, like silk."

I sat beside her and picked out *Old Susanna*. She smiled. "You play good."

"Not really." I shook my head. Another thing Mama had tried to teach me that I didn't have time for. "My mama did though."

"My mama's dead."

A lump rose in my throat. "So's mine."

"Miss her a lot, sometimes."

"Yeah, know what you mean. If you'd like to learn to play, I could teach you."

A wide smile lit up her face and eyes the color of robin eggs almost popped out of their sockets. She clapped her hands like a little girl and squealed, "Oh, Dixie, would you, for certain?"

"Sure. You teach me to cook, I'll teach you some simple music."

Della smiled. "You're good for the soul, Dixie. Stop by anytime." She winked. "Better come to the back door. Not as awkward."

And that's what I did.

Every morning after work, I'd spend time with Abby. First in the kitchen then at the piano. Della and her Doves plugged the hole in my heart that Mama's death had made. Everything settled into a nice routine, and I started to relax.

The easy feeling didn't last long.

CHAPTER II

"Dixie! Dixie! It's awful, just awful."

Mary Louise's white face scared the liver plumb out of me. "What?"

"He took her."

"Who? Took who?" I eased her into the chair and poured a glass of water. "Who's he? Took who?"

"Abby. Daggett's goon took her."

"What?"

"That gawky kid, Donnie Ray." She took a deep gulp of water. "Knew he was no good. All of us warned Abby to stay away from him, but she wouldn't listen. Said they *loved* one another. The no-good desperado grabbed her tonight."

"Why?"

"Reese Daggett owns most of this town. Been after the White Dove for as long as I can remember, but Mama Della won't sell. He had Donnie Ray steal Abby. Told Della if she didn't hand over the deed to the Dove, he'd kill all her girls, starting with the stupid one."

Oh my God. My heart flopped over.

"Mama Della is beside herself. Refunded everyone's money, shooed them out the door, and locked it behind them. The only other time she done that was when Abby's mama died, five years ago." She turned her teary face to mine. "What are we going to do? They can't kill Abby. They just can't."

"Get the law. They'll stop it."

Mary Louise laughed, short and hopeless. "Oh, Dixie, you ain't been here long enough to know, but the only law in the Siding is whoever can draw their .45 the fastest and shoot the straightest. Even if there was a sheriff, Daggett would have him in his hip pocket."

"Big Finn. Go tell Della I went to get Big Finn. He'll help, I'm sure."

In a hurry to get to camp, I took the stairs two at a time. I pushed past the men lined up for supper and looked for Chow. Found him out back chopping up a side of beef. I grabbed his arm. "Where's Finn?"

"So sorry, Missy Dixie, Big Boss Man not here."

My knees buckled, and I slumped against the table.

"Missy Dixie no look good. Look white, like flour."

"Really? That's because I'm scared to death. Reese Daggett kidnapped Abby and is gonna' kill her."

Chow-Chow's almond-shaped eyes grew into circles as big as pie pans. "Missy Abby?" His hand tightened around the meat cleaver, and he turned toward the front of the tent. "Daggett berry bad. Missy Abby berry good. Chow not let him kill her."

I grabbed him by the jacket sleeve and whirled him around. "Go to the White Dove and wait. I'll be there quick as I can. Gotta' do something first."

He blinked.

"Go. Hurry." I pushed him toward the door. "Chop! Chop!"

Running hard, I weaved around the drunks and stragglers on the sidewalk. Street lanterns blurred into yellow streaks. The door of Mildred's boarding house slammed so hard behind me Jesus almost fell off the crucifix hanging on the sitting-room wall. I took the stairs two at a time. Abby was more than my friend, she was family. Already lost Mama because of a no-good excuse for a man. Damned if I'd lose a sister to one. If the men in this town didn't have the guts to stand up to Daggett, to hell with them. By God, I did. Didn't need anyone's help, either.

I checked Wayne's Peacemaker hoping it was loaded. Good. Five rounds. One empty chamber. His leather gun belt could wrap around me twice and the holster would still hang past my knees. I slung it across my right shoulder and under my arm then hurried downstairs. Mildred stood at the bottom, arms crossed, big duck foot tapping like a woodpecker.

"Miss Dandelion, need I remind you, yet again—"

I brushed past her. Had more important things to do than listen to another lecture on how to conduct myself as a proper, God-fearing lady.

"Dixie!" Della yelled when I burst into the sitting room. "I got a half-loco Chinaman in my kitchen swinging a meat cleaver big enough to chop up a horse. Now you rush in here with a gun large enough to shoot one with. What the hell are you doing?"

Mary Louise and the girls gathered around Della and gawked at me. Without batting an eye, I stared them down.

"Takin' the law into my own hands. You gonna' help me or stay here and hide like helpless women?"

"Yee-haw!" Sassy yelled and headed for the stairs. "Don't leave without me."

"We're with you, Dixie. Tell us what to do."

Chow Ling shuffled into the room. "Need guns."

Della's back stiffened. She walked over to the closet and opened the door. A collection of pistols, rifles, and shotguns littered the floor. "Some of the boys leave these here for collateral." She pulled out a 10-gauge shotgun with round barrels as big as telegraph poles. "Take your pick, girls."

Sassy returned with a scattergun bigger than a cannon. "Never been a helpless female in all my life. Ain't gonna' start now."

Della looked at us and shook her head. "A cook, a flock of soiled Doves, and one crazy Chinaman. God help us."

I grinned. Yep. Mildred Atkins would throw me out on my ear for sure.

If I made it back alive.

CHAPTER 12

"What's the plan, Dixie?" Sassy asked.

Plan? Didn't have one. I looked at Della for help. "Got any ideas on where Daggett would hide Abby?"

"Daggett owns over half the buildings in this town." Her brow furrowed for a moment then smoothed. "But his pride and joy is the One-Eyed-Jack. He lives in a gaudy suite on the second floor and his office is downstairs off to the side of the bar. Most likely he'd stash Abby there."

Even though the night was black as pitch, I didn't think it would be a good idea to march boldly down Main Street. Six Shooter Siding wasn't a stranger to gun-toting outlaws and gamblers. Still, the sight of rouge-painted, red-skirted, bosom-showing women armed and loaded for bear might cause a few too many eyebrows to arch. Not to mention an ax-wielding, slanty-eyed, Chin-ee Indian.

"Can we get to the One-Eyed-Jack using the back alleys?" I asked.

"Good idea," Della said. "Follow me."

We stepped out the Dove's back door. Cool air slapped me full in the face. A purple-violet circle surrounded the moon and grabbed at the clouds with bloody fingertips. Blood on the moon. Danger not far away.

Ah, lass, ya be just like your papa. Can't resist a good donnybrook, now, can ya?

Papa? I whirled and looked behind me. This was the second time I'd heard his voice in my ear. I'd never given much thought to ghosts. Was Papa haunting or watching over me?

Slow and steady we slipped through the night. How Della could walk so gracefully wearing her high-heeled slippers was a mystery to me. I'd be flat on my butt with the first step, yet she weaved down and around the nooks and crannies of the back streets like a silent, black-petticoated panther cat.

On tiptoes, I peeked in the kerosene-smudged window of Daggett's back office. Della stepped beside me. Her lilac-scented perfume wrinkled my nose, and I stifled a sneeze in the crook of my arm. Abby sat in a straight-backed chair, arms tied behind her. Honey-gold hair plastered to her sweat-drenched skin. An imprint of a hand on the side of her face glowed red like a brand.

"Damn that Donnie Ray," Della hissed. "Didn't have to slap and hogtie Abby that way. She ain't no threat."

"But I am." Sassy's lips flattened into a hard line. "Ain't got no use for a woman beater."

With a wave, I motioned the girls and Chow to gather around me. "Here's what we're gonna do," I whispered. "Della, you, Sassy, and Mary Louise go around front and waltz into the One-Eyed-Jack like you own it. Keep Daggett busy talking about the sale of the Dove. While you're distracting him, me, Pearl, and Rosie will sneak in through the back door and get Abby."

I tugged the knife from my boot.

Dominique gasped. "Ah, Dixcee," she said in her soft French accent. "You are full of the surprise."

With a quick flip, she hiked her skirt up over her thigh and pulled a thin-bladed knife from her lace garter. "Stiletto," she explained. "We think alike, do we not?"

"Looks like Abby is alone," I said and took a deep breath. "I'll cut her loose then hightail it back to the Dove." I nodded at Della. "Give me about ten minutes then get out of there."

Della handed her shotgun to Mary Louise and hurried off to the front of the saloon. Sassy followed, scattergun hid in the folds of her dress.

Oh, Papa. Protect me.

I counted to twenty then eased through the back door with Pearl and Rosie nipping at my heels. Dominique and Chow Ling stood guard outside.

The stink of stale cigar smoke and cheap beer met me at the door. Abby's eyes widened in surprise, and I clamped my hand over her mouth before she could say anything. "Be quiet," I whispered into her ear. I removed my hand, bent down, and started cutting the ropes.

"Dixie," she whimpered.

Oh hell and damnation. "Abby, shut up before Daggett and his men hear ya' and come bustin' in here."

"But, Dixie—"

A low growl sounded to my left. My hands froze. Slow and easy, I turned my head. A black-and-gray, half-wolf, half-dog big enough to throw a saddle on stood stiff-legged and bushy-haired not more than three feet away from me.

"His name is Lobo. I tried to warn you," Abby said.

Lips curled, teeth barred, the wolfdog leaped from the floor, headed straight for me.

Shit. Why did I think this was going to be easy?

A blur of gray flashed by. With no time to think, I covered my head with both hands and braced for the pain of teeth ripping flesh from bone. Someone let out a rebel yell. Not me. I lifted my gaze. Lobo had a death grip on a long, lanky cowboy—Donnie Ray.

A loud boom sounded from the front—Sassy's scattergun. All hell busted loose. While Lobo mauled and Donnie Ray howled, I sawed through the ropes on Abby's wrists, jerked her from the chair, and flung her into Rosie and Pearl's arms.

"Get her out of here," I yelled.

Before I could pull the Peacemaker from its holster, Dominique bolted through the door. "Dixcee! Get down!"

A whoosh of air whistled past my ear followed by a scream. I turned. A cowboy dropped his pistol and clutched at the black-handled stiletto stuck in the middle of his chest. He crumbled to the ground. Dead. Dominique walked over and pulled the knife from his heart, cool as ice. She acknowledged my look of gratitude with a nod of her head.

"Hurree, Dixcee. Abby is safe."

With pistol drawn, I charged into the barroom only to stop dead in my tracks when I heard Della yell, "Let her go, Daggett."

A rail-thin man with a pencil-line mustache had his arm around Mary Louise's neck, pistol pointed at her head.

"Tell that big heifer of yours to drop that hog leg or I'll put a bullet through this one's head."

"Let her go first, then I'll put the gun down," Sassy countered.

It was a Mexican standoff. Neither Sassy nor Daggett had any intentions of backing down. Better think of something, fast. I stepped to the middle of the barroom floor and shot into the air.

Eyes burned from the bitter gun smoke. A blue-gray fog swirled ghostlike in the air. My chest ached with every choppy breath I took. The metallic click of the Peacemaker's hammer being pulled back echoed through the high rafters.

"Drop it, Daggett, or I'll put a hole between your eyes big enough to ride a horse through."

My voice bounced off the walls, raspy and tough. I sounded mean. Good. It was a bluff. Couldn't hit fish in a barrel.

"Dixie, no," Della yelled. "You might hit Mary Louise."

One glance at Della told me she'd run through the fires of hell and back. Blouse ripped. One shoe missing. Hair tousled wild around her gun-smoke-streaked face. Sassy didn't look much better, but the fight was still strong in both their faces.

Daggett wasn't buying any of it. He loosened his choke hold, grabbed Mary Louise's hair, and dragged her toward the batwing doors. She squirmed away from his shoulder, giving me a clear shot. Tears streamed down her cheeks, but no sound came from her lips. Big doe eyes sent a silent message to me to shoot the bastard and be quick about it.

What the hell? Surely to God, I could hit a man.

I pulled the trigger.

The bullet went wide. Clipped an antler off a ten-point buck hanging above the bar. A crooked smirk crossed Daggett's rat face. I cocked the hammer and fired again.

This time, the shot ricocheted off a spittoon and hit the mirror in the back of the bar. The crash of shard glass deafened my ears.

Teeth clenched, I took aim yet a third time and let fly. The window behind Daggett shattered.

"Mother of God, Dixie. Quit farting around and shoot the son of a bitch," Sassy yelled.

Just what the hell did she think I was trying to do?

This time, Daggett laughed out loud. Big mistake. The blood howling in my ears turned to frosted water. I pointed the pistol at the middle of his chest and pulled the trigger.

Shot the toe off his boot.

Shocked, the yellow coward yipped in pain and hopped to one foot. Mary Louise struggled out of his hold and darted behind the bar.

I pulled the trigger.

Click.

Out of bullets.

Shit.

Mouth turned to cotton.

Breath stopped.

Daggett took dead aim.

A loud boom shook the walls.

Bright crimson spread across his vest.

Daggett pitched forward. Dead as a mackerel.

Smoke from Sassy's scattergun circled the room.

Dazed, I watched her stand over the body, cross herself, and whisper, "May God have mercy on your soul. And I ain't no heifer."

Her gaze lifted to meet mine and a small smile touched her lips. "A whore who's got Jesus in her heart is a powerful woman."

If I wasn't about ready to faint, I would've laughed myself sick.

CHAPTER 13

Legs shaking, I slumped into the nearest chair. Stunned, I looked at the destruction around me—shattered glass, holes in the ceiling, overturned tables and chairs, a body sprawled on the floor. The stink of blood oozed out of every board and slat.

"Don't fall apart on me just yet, hon."

Della's voice jarred me back into the moment. "We got work to do. Gotta get rid of the evidence."

"Why?" I asked. "Thought there wasn't any law in this town."

"Not any *official* law, but Daggett was in cahoots with a lot of sidewinders who may not take kindly to his death. Gunshots at night are a common thing in Six Shooter Siding. No one's gonna' investigate till morning, but we need to get a move on. Besides, I don't want my girls or the White Dove implicated in any of this. Bad for business."

Huh. I could well imagine. Knowing the woman ya paid good money for could shoot a hole plumb through ya, might make a fella think twice before he crawled between the sheets with her.

A rustling noise came from the back room.

Wide-eyed and tense, I glanced at Della. Mary Louise

flew from her hiding spot behind the bar and grabbed the shotgun off the floor. Even though my pistol was empty, I cocked the hammer anyway and turned.

Chow Ling scampered into the room like a curious little mouse—a mouse with a meat cleaver clutched in its paw. Relief flooded through me, and I let out my breath.

"Dammit, Chow. Ya scared the liver out of me."

On silent feet, Chow Ling crossed the room and stared at Daggett's body. He tilted his round face up to meet my gaze. "Chow Ling help Missy Dixie bury the dead."

"Bury?" Della snorted. "Don't intend on burying nothing that could be dug up later. To my way of thinking, we'd be better off carting the bodies up into the mountains and throwing them over a cliff. Let the vultures and coyotes finish the job."

Chow Ling shook his head and looked at Della. "You must go home. Missy Abby berry upset." He eyed all three of us. "Missy Abby need all of you. Go. Chow Ling fix mess."

Suspicious, I looked at the small man standing so calm and sure. "What's going on in that head of yours?"

"Chow family not be alive if not for Missy Abby. Chow owe her. Now is time to repay debt. No one find bodies. No one ever know what happen."

"How's that?" Della asked.

Chow carefully ran his thumb down the edge of the cleaver. "Berry sharp." He glanced at me with a mischievous glint in his almond eyes.

"Choppy. Choppy."

Blood rushed from my face to the soles of my boots in a split second because the room spun like a top. Rooted to the spot, I watched Sassy and Mary Louise move toward the back door like they hadn't heard a word Chow had said.

Della found her lost shoe and crammed it on her foot. "Come on, Dixie. Let's get outta' here."

My mouth opened, but no words came. The touch of

Chow Ling's hand on my arm made me jump.

"Missy Dixie. You brave rady."

"Yeah?" A nervous giggle made my voice shaky. "And you're one crazy Chin-ee."

The four of us melted into the night like ghostly shadows. We slipped back to the White Dove and into the kitchen.

CHAPTER 14

Pearl, Rosie, and Dominique sat gathered around Abby. All of them looked up when we bolted through the door. Abby jumped up and threw her arms around my neck. "Dixie," she gushed. "I owe you my life. Thank you. Thank you."

Embarrassed, I pried loose from her grip. A low whoof sounded from under the table. Fear stabbed my heart with a frosted dagger. I grabbed a butcher knife from the counter and whirled, ready to plunge the thick blade into Lobo's big throat before he chewed my leg off. How the hell did he get into the kitchen anyway?

"Dixie. Wait," Abby yelled. "He won't hurt ya'

In disbelief, I watched Abby call the big dog to her. He lumbered over, head low, tail wagging like a goofy hound dog pup. Knees weak, I leaned my back against the wall. My nerves were shooting higher than Mexican jumping beans in a hot skillet.

Sassy collapsed into a straight-backed chair. "Mother of God, Abby. I about peed down both legs. What's that . . . that . . . animal doing in here?"

"I need a drink," Della said.

"Coffee is a good idea," I said.

"Coffee, my hind leg. Need something stronger than that."

Della fixed Abby with a stern frown. "Explain why that smelly beast is in my kitchen. And it better be good."

"He was Daggett's, although I don't know why he wanted a dog. Keep him tied up most of the time. Hardly ever fed him. Donnie Ray . . ." Her voice caught. "Donnie Ray kicked him every chance he got. Should've known then what a mean cuss he was."

She looked up at me. Tears glistened in the corner of her eyes. "He slapped me. Hard. Never did love me, did he?"

"No," I said, feeling lower than dirt.

"Daggett was right. I am stupid."

"No, Abby, that isn't true," Mary Louise said and put her arm around Abby's shoulders. "You're just blind to the bad in people. Nothing's dumb about that."

"What about the dog?" I asked, changing the subject.

"I guess Daggett forgot to tie him up. When he caught Donny walking through the door, I reckon he saw his chance to even the score for all them kicks." A deep breath. "Donny's dead, ain't he?"

"As Judas Iscariot himself," Sassy said.

"Amen to that." Della shoved a bottle full of amber-looking liquid into Abby's hand. "Take a swig. Make ya feel better." She glanced at Lobo lying peacefully at Abby's feet and sighed. "I suppose the next thing you'll be asking is if you can keep this hunk of fur."

"Oh, Mama Della, can I?"

Abby's voice sounded so much like a little girl's that all of us smiled. I looked at Della and shrugged.

"I ain't never had a pet before. He's really sweet ifn' you treat him right. Besides, dogs are loyal." Her small back straightened in her chair. "I'm never gonna trust a man, ever again. From now on, I'm going to be just like Dixie—hate every man I see."

Whoa. My head jerked up and I gawked at her like she

had six ears. Why did she say that?

"I don't hate men," I said. "Just don't have much use for most of 'em, that's all."

"Anyways," Abby babbled on. "This dog *loves* me. I can tell by the look in his eyes."

"Mother of God," Sassy groaned. "Break out another bottle, Della. This has been one hell of a night, and it ain't over yet."

Mouth dry as baled cotton, I took the bottle from Abby, tipped it to my lips, and took a giant gulp.

Della gasped. "Dixie. I wouldn't—

Her warning came too late.

Good God All Mighty! I swallowed liquid dynamite. A hole burned through my gullet and my innards exploded.

CHAPTER 15

Doubled over, spitting and hacking up everything but my toenails, I struggled for breath. "What *is* that stuff?"

Reared back in the chair, long legs stretched in front of her, dainty feet propped up on the table, Dominique raised her bottle. "Tequila. Golden elixir of the handsome, bronzed Aztec gods. Is good. No?"

Didn't know any Aztec deities. Probably because their magic cure killed them all.

"No, is not good," I mimicked. "Is nasty."

"Ah, Dixcee, don't be so hasty. You must try again."

"Dominique's right," Sassy chimed in. "You're one of us now, and . . ."

"What do you mean, one of you? I'm not a Dove."

"Ohhhh, but you are, hon," Della said and took my hand. "Dixie, no one in this town was willing to help us tonight. No one. Except you and one crazy Chinaman."

"And you didn't think twice about it," Mary Louise said.

Della smiled. "It took a lot of guts to do what you did. The bravest thing I ever did see."

None of them understood. It wasn't bravery so much as it was survival. Had a bad habit of acting first and thinking second. Papa's Irish temper didn't help, neither.

"Della, stop. Most of the time, I'm scared of my own shadow. I get into messes before I realize then have to fight my way out. Courage doesn't have anything to do with it. I'm only scrambling to save my neck."

Della chuckled, poured a shot of honey-colored lava into a small glass, and handed it to me. "That's what every hero says."

She glanced around the table and her features softened. "You saved my girls tonight, Dixie. That makes you one of us. From now on, you're living here. You may not be a Dove in the flesh, but you are in spirit. Now drink up."

Dominique reached across the table, grabbed my hand, and sprinkled salt on the back of my palm. "Lick first, then drink. It cools the fire."

This time, only one eye watered and twitched like a fish on a string. Warmth slid down my throat and spread across my belly smooth as melted candle wax. Not bad. I giggled.

"Voila!" Dominique laughed.

I pushed the glass toward Della. "Hit me again."

"Now you're talkin'," Sassy said.

I gasped at the cigarette dangling on her painted lips. "Oh my God. Are you smoking?"

"Can't drink without a smoke. They're called cheroots. Have one."

Another giggle rippled from my throat, followed by a hiccup. I placed the cigarette between my lips and puffed. The sweet tobacco circled my head and made the perfect companion for the tequila, like coffee and cream.

I waited for a lightning bolt to zig-zag through the door and strike me dead. Drinking and smoking. Somewhere Papa laughed while Mama rolled over in her grave.

My mood sobered. Tears sprang up out of nowhere and stung my eyes. Poor, pitiful, Mama. If only she'd had the gumption to stand on her own two feet, she'd be alive today. By God, I wouldn't make that mistake. Wouldn't be depending on any man, ever.

I swiped at the tears. Damn Aztec joy-juice. It did funny things to my head. One minute, I was flying high, the next, wallowing in sadness. Maybe another drink would chase the blues away.

"Dixie," Sassy shouted. "I'm talking to you. Can't ya' hear?" Laughter circled the table. Why was everything so funny?

"I hear fine." I drained my glass and slammed it down on the tabletop. "This stuff bucks like a bucking bronco."

"Yep." Della laughed. "It's thrown many a good man to his knees."

"Damn good thing we ain't men then, ain't it?" Sassy said and slapped the table with her hand.

Pearl and Rosie brayed like lop-eared mules.

Abby giggled.

Mary Louise twittered.

Dominique grinned like a possum.

Della almost fell off her chair.

I gawked at all of them.

The liquid in the little crystal glass called out to me. I said hello and tossed it down.

"I got a bone to pick with you," Sassy said. She pointed a smoldering cheroot at me. "You can't shoot worth spit."

Mary Louise came around the table and draped her arm around my shoulder. "There isn't anything wrong with the way Dixie shoots."

Thankful for her support, I puffed out my chest and gave Sassy a smug look. "It's just hitting what she's aiming at that's the problem."

Again, Pearl's hee-haw joined with the other guffaws and shook the floor.

Dear, sweet Mary Louise. How could she betray me so?

"Where you'd get that pistol anyway? Belong to your daddy?" Della asked.

Wayne's big brown eyes swam in front of me. Tall. Strong. Sinfully charming, Jackson Wayne. Wonder where he was? Melancholy pulled a chair up beside me, and I sighed. "Belongs to a man who doesn't want to be burdened with me."

Dominique's eyebrow arched. "A past lover, perhaps?"

Not liking where the conversation was headed, I changed the subject. "Della, what happened in that barroom tonight? How did you lose your shoe?"

"I yanked it off and threw it at Daggett."

The mental picture made me giggle. Or maybe it was the tequila. "Why?"

"Because of me," Mary Louise said. "It was a trap. Daggett was going to kill all of us. I panicked and showed the shotgun too soon. He ripped it out of my hand and then grabbed me. That's when Della threw her shoe at him."

"It was the only thing I could think to do," Della said.

I laughed so hard tequila squirted out my nose. Burned every hair to a crisp.

Della's voice lowered and she looked hard at me. "Do you really think that loco Chow Ling hacked Daggett and Donnie Ray into tiny pieces?"

I swallowed another drink to drown the thought. Pretty red roses on the kitchen wallpaper danced and twirled.

"Let's put it this way," I said. "If Chow-Chow serves anything in the next couple of months smothered in loads of gravy, I ain't touching it."

Laughter bounced off the walls so hard the dishes rattled. This time, *I* about fell on the floor.

"Well, well, what do we have here?"

Even though my brain was pickled, I recognized the velvet-smooth voice. I jumped from the chair and whirled. The room spun like a roulette wheel. My eyes crossed.

"Dixie? Della?"

Jackson Wayne, all three of him, stood a step inside Della's kitchen. Broad shoulders filled the doorframe. He pushed his Stetson back off his forehead and a slow grin spread from dimple to dimple. "Howdy, darlin'."

"Ooo-la-la!" Dominique's exclamation sounded a mile away.

Whew! Shouldn't have stood up so fast. My stomach bucked and pitched.

Ears ringing, heart pounding, head spinning, I took a step toward him.

Big mistake.

Never made the second one.

Passed out cold into the arms of an Aztec god.

CHAPTER 16

If it wasn't for the herd of horses thundering through my head, I'd swear I'd died and gone to heaven.

Everything was blue. Like bows on Christmas packages, sky-blue curtains wrapped around three floor-to-ceiling windows. Three. Not one. Didn't know how much I'd missed the sun's golden rays until I saw them spill cheerfully across the thick, dark-blue carpet. Pictures of wildflowers—instead of Jesus bleeding from the cross—graced the turquoise walls. I snuggled into sheets that were cloud-soft and stared at the creamy-white lace canopy above my head. Where was I?

"About time you woke up."

The blankets flipped back, and Della sat on the edge of the bed. With a firm hand, she forced me to a sitting position and pushed a cup into mine. "Drink this."

Had to admit the coffee's strong, rich aroma smelled wonderful. A small sip stripped the buffalo robe off my tongue. Eyes closed, I sighed and leaned back against billowy pillows.

"Am I dead?"

"No. You're in your new room. Hope you like it. Abby insisted you have the Peacock Suite because the colors match your eyes." Her tongue clicked. "That girl thinks you hung the moon. Made a friend for life with that one."

Over the rim of the porcelain cup, I gazed at the rest of the room. Fragile glass oil lamps, a rocking chair, a dressing table, mirrors, and a fireplace. Mildred's place looked like a mud hut compared to this little slice of paradise. I ran my hand over cool cotton sheets. A canopy bed? Didn't know such things existed. "This beats anything I've ever seen."

Della laughed, got up, crossed the room, and opened the window. A fresh breeze flavored with pine drifted through. "Well, a good bed is a must in our business. I see the color came back to your cheeks. Feel better?"

I nodded. Owed Arbuckle's my life.

"Good. I had the maid fill the tub with hot water. Get washed and come downstairs."

A tub in my room? Impossible. "I have a bathtub? Here? Don't have to go to a bathhouse and wash in lukewarm water?"

"Or pay a quarter for it, neither." Della laughed. "All my girls have tubs in their rooms." Her back straightened and a pinch of pride seeped into her voice. "You think The White Dove is some seedy, south-of-the-border chicken ranch? I take good care of my girls and clients. The Dove has the reputation of being a clean, luxurious, pleasure palace with classy, elegant girls. I can afford the best, and I only serve the best. Now hurry up, you got a visitor downstairs."

"Me? Who?"

"That long tall drink of water by the name of Jackson Wayne."

Coffee spewed from my mouth.

A teasing look crossed Della's face. "He carried you up the stairs last night as easily as if you were a gunny sack full of feathers. Put you in bed. Pulled your boots off. Even smoothed the hair back off your face, nice and gentle, like you were a fragile doll."

"I made a complete ass of myself, Della. Send him away. I'll never be able to look him in the face again. Tell him . . . tell him . . ."

"I ain't telling him nothing except you'll be down shortly. Abby went through her wardrobe. Found a pretty meadow-green dress for you. It'll go good with your scarlet hair."

"What?"

"Well, ya can't parade around a man looking like a dusty cowpoke all the time." She took my hand and pulled me from the bed. "God blessed ya' with curves in all the right places, hon. Show 'em off." A quick swat on the butt sent me toward the closet. "Get a move on. I think that cowboy is sweet on ya'

Stunned, I walked to the little room off to the side of the dressing table and eased into the tin tub. Thought about drowning myself in the warm, lavender-scented water. I picked up the soap instead and started to scrub. My mind whirled like an Oklahoma twister. Why did she think he liked me? And why did it matter if he did? He'd left me high and dry to face Payton alone. But he'd left Joe for me. Or, did he? And if he liked me so damn much, why was he just now showing up? Where he'd been for the past few weeks?

By the time I was dry and dressed, anger had squashed the butterflies in my stomach. Didn't care if I'd drank too much and fell dead in his arms. Served him right. I marched down the stairs to the kitchen ready to fly all over him.

"Howdy, darlin'."

Oh hell. How could I stay mad at a man with a voice smooth as butter and dimples the size of dimes?

"Good morning," I mumbled and sank into the kitchen chair. Never seen him without his wide-brimmed hat pulled low across his face. Tried not to wonder how good it would feel to run my fingers through his thick, chestnut hair.

Didn't succeed.

Della refilled his coffee cup and poured a mug for me. He slid a plate of biscuits and gravy across the table.

"Hungry?"

My belly squirmed. Wasn't ready for food yet. "Ah, no. Coffee is all I need."

He chuckled like he knew my stomach flipped and flopped like a turtle on its back.

Not ready to meet the amusement in his deep brown eyes, I looked around the kitchen and peeked into the parlor. We were alone, except for Della. "Where is everyone?" I asked Della. Wayne answered instead.

"Sleeping in, I reckon. Quite a shindig you had last night."

Heat raced up my neck, and I knew the tiny freckles across the bridge of my nose danced in its glow.

Della grinned. "I need to wake them up, and get ready for business."

My heart leaped, and I shot her a pleading look. Wasn't ready to be alone. She ignored me. "Jackson, stay as long as you want. You're always welcome."

I gave him a weak smile and raised the cup to my mouth. Banged the rim against my teeth. Coffee sloshed on the linen tablecloth. Dammit!

"Kill any men lately?"

Fear and surprise fanned the heat into a prairie fire. How did he know about Daggett? Nerves snapped. "What's that supposed to mean?"

"Easy, gal. It's a logical question considering what you tried with Payton."

He was talking about Payton. Not Daggett. Be calm. Wait. What did he mean, try?

"Try?"

"You didn't kill Payton, darlin'."

I didn't believe him. "That's impossible. The blood. He hit the back of his head—"

"Oh, you came close, but he's still kickin.' 'Course his nose is as crooked as a dog's hind leg. What did you hit him with anyway?"

"My fist."

He pushed back from the table and grinned. "Dang, darlin', remind me never to make you mad."

A tiny sense of pride swelled and gave me the confidence to look him in the face. Wished I hadn't. His eyes bore a hole straight through my heart into my soul. Unflinchingly, I stared back. Took all the nerve I had.

"Widow Sawyer found him. Said she heard some commotion outside and went to check her washing. Found a bloody dress and some clothes missing."

"Did she mention the money I left for those clothes?"

His grin widened. "Nope. Not a word."

"Huh. Didn't think so."

"Payton lost a lot of blood, but he's on the mend. Doc Webster on the train patched him up. Said he'll walk with a limp the rest of his mangy life. Payton told everyone you ambushed him, stole his money, and left him for dead. You wounded his pride and ruined his pretty face, darlin'."

"Should've shot the yellow dog."

"Yeah, well, from what I hear, you were better off stabbing him."

Who had he been talking to?

"I noticed Joe was gone when I got back to the train. Figured Payton had tried something. Got asked if I'd seen you on the trail. They were going to come after ya, but I told them since it was my horse you stole, I'd ride into Six Shooter Siding instead."

"You know I didn't steal Joe, just borrowed him. Isn't that why you left him saddled?"

He skirted the question. "Guess you got yourself a horse. I can't go back with him and without you."

The hardwood chair creaked when he leaned in closer to me. All playfulness left his face, and his words came so low I struggled to hear them. "Dixie, did Payton hurt you?"

Wasn't expecting the raw emotion in his voice. My heart shivered.

"No," I whispered.

A sigh so soft I thought I'd dreamed it came from deep inside him. His hand reached for mine but pulled back before our fingers touched.

"Dixie, listen to me. That man spits on the ground you walk. He'll hunt you down until he either finds you or until the end of time, whichever comes first."

"Let him come. I ain't scared of him."

His features turned to granite. "You should be. If he finds you . . ." A deep breath. "Just don't let him find you."

Once more his concern made my insides stir. For a heartbeat, time stopped and all that mattered was the compassion that smoldered in the warmth of his dark eyes. His look quickly turned mischievous. "Thought you didn't like being called Dixie?"

Heat rushed up my neck for the hundredth time that morning. Damnation. If I didn't stop blushing at his every word, he'd be calling me Strawberry Nellie next.

"Didn't figure it be wise to give my real name. Dixie just popped out of my mouth."

"Uh-huh. Guess the same thing happened with dandelion?" Before I could think of a smart answer, he asked, "By the way, where *is* Joe?"

Irritated that he suspected I liked the nickname, I snapped, "Big Finn's barn. Thought that would be the first place you'd look since he's your contact man."

"What gave you that idea?"

"I found your badge. I just assumed. I mean, that's why he offered me a job, wasn't it? Didn't you tell him I might be riding in?"

"Darlin', I didn't tell Donovan anything."

"But you are a lawman, aren't ya'?"

Two breaths went by. Thought he wasn't going to

answer. He sighed.

"Pinkerton Detective. But I don't know Donovan."

More confused than ever, I sipped my coffee and tried to figure out where I'd gone wrong. Someone was keeping him informed, but if it wasn't Finn, then who? I cleared my throat. "Guess you want your knife and pistol back."

He shook his head, and a crooked grin made his dimples flash. "Nope. You keep 'em. But I do need my saddlebags . . . and that badge."

I squirmed in the chair. I had to ask him for a favor. I would rather walk barefoot through a cactus patch. Not looking at him, I played with the delicate lace on my dress collar.

"I . . . ah . . . been told I don't shoot that well. Think you could teach me?"

His lips twitched. By God, if he dared laugh at me, I'd pound his Stetson flatter than a snake's belly.

As if reading my mind, he reached for the hat and stood. Almost got a kink in my neck looking up at him.

"I'll make you a deal. You stay quiet about who I am, and I'll teach ya to shoot."

"Deal."

He walked to the kitchen's back door then turned. "Tell Della thanks for breakfast. I'll be around."

In one fluid move, he crossed back to the table. With a swift touch, he lifted my chin with his finger and smiled deep into my eyes. Stood so close, the clean, fresh scent of his shaving soap washed over me.

"Good to see ya' again, darlin'." A small chuckle told me he knew damn well my heart fluttered like a wounded bird. "You look mighty pretty in green, Dixie Belle Dandelion."

Before I could stop the redness from circling my neck, he was gone.

CHAPTER 17

"Whoo-wee! Takes your breath away, doesn't he?"

Sassy leaned against the parlor door dressed in a flowing, white robe with delicate feathers at the cuffs. Wondered how long she'd been there and just how much she'd seen and heard.

"I hadn't noticed," I said.

"Oh, Dixie." She chuckled. "If God loved a liar, He'd squeeze you to death."

"That obvious?"

"Yep."

She poured a cup of coffee and sat down beside me. Sunlight captured the rings on her fingers with its rays and threw tiny rainbows of light across the shiny mahogany table. "But don't feel bad. You're not the only woman who's slobbered over him."

Slobber? "I never salivate over any man, no matter how good-looking." Her don't-try-and-fool-me look stopped me cold. Okay, maybe I did drool . . . but only a little.

Wide-eyed, I watched her pour half the sugar bowl into her cup. She met my stare with faked innocence. "What? Sugar's good for the soul."

Couldn't help but grin, but a nagging thought tugged at

me. How did she know Jackson? Couldn't explain why, but I didn't want him to be her client.

"Don't worry, he's not." She smiled at my gasp. "Don't ever play poker, Dixie. Your face is an open book. And, in answer to the next question rattling around in that mighty pretty little head of yours; he isn't a customer of The White Dove."

She took a sip of coffee, winced, and added yet another spoonful of sugar. "Oh, he could hang his spurs on any one of our bedposts that's for sure, but he chooses not to."

"Then, how do you know him?"

From the pocket of her robe, she pulled out a cheroot and lit up. A twinge of vanilla smoke circled the cozy kitchen. Still floored me to see a woman smoking. Long stork-like legs crossed, and she took a deep drag. Acted like she was trying to make up her mind on something. Whatever it was, the satisfied look on her face made me believe she had come to terms with it. She smiled.

"We work together."

"You? You're his contact man . . . ah . . . woman?"

"Well, who better to keep her finger on the pulse of a town than a soiled Dove?"

"So, you're not really one of Della's girls? You're a Pinkerton Detective?"

"Let's just say I'm a woman of many talents."

"Does Della know?"

"Of course. In our business, it's always helpful to have the law owing ya a favor or two."

She flicked the ashes off the cheroot and grinned. "You didn't have it figured all wrong. Big Finn is a Pinkerton. The railroad hired him to keep peace between the Chinese and the town folk. He's what they call undercover. Masquerading as a supervisor."

Good God Almighty. For a place that wasn't supposed to have any law, Six Shooter Siding was crawling with lawmen.

"Donovan and Wayne are partners. Been working together as Pinkerton Agents ever since—" She paused.

"Ever since what?"

A slight smile pulled her painted lips, and she shook her head. "Ever since Jackson lost his family."

My breath caught. "What do you mean, *lost*?"

With a quick look around, she stubbed her cigarette out in a China saucer. Wasn't sure Della would like that.

"Dixie, I ain't sure I should be talking like this. That handsome cowboy has a lot of secrets bottled up inside him, and if he knew Finn spilled his guts and told them to me in a moment of . . . ah, let's say, passion, well, I'm just not sure what would happen."

Curiosity burned. Had to know. "I won't tell anyone, Sassy." I crossed my heart and spit. "I promise."

She stirred her cup and frowned. How she could drink that much sweetness was beyond me, but then again, anyone who could down tequila easy as water could handle anything poured into a mug. A heavy sigh broke the silence.

"Jackson was sixteen when his pa died. Promised him on his deathbed that he would always protect his mother and younger sister. The family moved from Ohio to Kansas to live with his aunt. Everything settled nice and easy until four years later when the War Between the States broke out."

The war. Its evil made me sick.

"Dixie, you all right? Look peaked as milk toast."

"I'm fine," I lied. "Still queasy from the tequila."

She leaned back in the chair and grinned. "Well, you ain't supposed to guzzle it like a pig in swill."

Now was a fine time to tell me.

"Jackson didn't want to have anything to do with the fighting. His pa hailed from Ohio, but his ma and aunt were raised somewhere in the South. Virginia or Georgia. Don't recall which. Don't matter. The point is, he had kin and friends on both sides. Then there was the promise he'd made to his pa. Joining the war would force him to break that vow, and Jackson Dallas Wayne never goes back on his word."

She pulled another cheroot from her pocket. Could practically taste the sweet tobacco on my tongue.

"Anyway." She blew out a lung full of smoke. "He decided he wasn't going to join any side. Not a popular decision with most, but he ignored them." A thin eyebrow arched. "He shouldn't have."

CHAPTER 18

Something in Sassy's tone of voice froze my butt to the chair.

"He was gone hunting when the marauders attacked. Came back to find his house and fields on fire."

Her voice caught.

My body tensed.

"Found his ma, aunt, and little sister dead."

"They killed them?" I gasped.

"And worse."

I tore out the back door like my hair was on fire. Puked my guts in the bushes lining the split-rail fence. My weak knees buckled, and I slumped to the dirt. No wonder his face turned so ashen when he asked if Payton hurt me.

Anger boiled inside me. Frustration simmered alongside it. So unfair. Life was so unfair. I wanted to cry. To scream. To shoot something. I grabbed a rock hiding in the dirt and threw it a country mile. Hated the war.

The *war* took Papa away and turned my life upside down.

The *war* forced Mama to marry Payton. A fatal mistake.

The *war* tore me from home and put me on a wagon train in the middle of nowhere.

The *war* came within a frog's hair of turning me into a killer.

The *war* cost Jackson his family.

That stupid damn *war*.

A soulful whine made me turn. Lobo stood beside me peering at my face with eyes the color of slate. Itching to touch something alive and real, I reached for him and buried my face into silky fur that smelled strangely of lavender.

Damnation. What was I doing? This dog could gnaw my face off. But he didn't. Instead, he curled beside me and laid a heavy paw in my lap. Acted like he'd claimed me for his own and that he understood the torment flooding my heart. Sorry, Abby, but I'm gonna' steal your dog.

The strong scent of lye soap made my eyes tear. Wash day. Chinese laundry girls no bigger than matchsticks, wrestled Della's sheets and pillowcases into a cast-iron kettle. They sent curious looks my way as they scrubbed. I stared back without seeing them. Couldn't shake the picture from my mind of Wayne kneeling beside his dead family while fire and brimstone burned behind him.

A low growl rumbled in Lobo's throat, and I saw Sassy walking my way. She hesitated. I smoothed the dog's ruffled fur and yelled, "It's okay. He's just warning me someone is around. He won't hurt ya'."

With a the-hell-he-won't look on her face, she tiptoed to my side. "For crying in a bucket, Dixie. Better not drink any more tequila for a while. Stuff makes ya' too puny."

She settled down beside me and wiped my face with a cool washrag. I brushed a tear from my eye and rested my head on her shoulder. Didn't have the heart to tell her my being sick had nothing to do with what I drank. The three of us must have made a strange sight sitting underneath the oak tree. Again, the faint scent of lavender wafted on the breeze, and I wrinkled my nose.

"Why does Lobo smell so good?" I asked her.

"Oh hell. You know Abby. She insisted on bathing him. Used all of Della's swanky-smelling bath salts. He's lucky she didn't put ribbons in his hair."

That explained his sorrowful look. How degrading for a half-wild wolf to be treated like a child's rag doll.

"She wanted to name him Gumdrop."

We broke out into a fit of giggles. Felt like a yo-yo on a string. One minute, crying, angry, and depressed, the next, comforted and laughing. My mood sobered. Had to know the rest of the story.

"What happened after . . . after, you know, he found his ma?"

With a large sigh, she gathered her robe under her. Didn't seem the least bit worried about the grass and dirt that stained the elegant dressing gown. Absentmindedly, I weaved my fingers in and out of Lobo's fur, listened to the birds chirping, and the drone of her voice.

"There ain't that much more to tell. Guilt ate a hole in his heart. Blamed himself for the whole mess. Said if he had been home, they'd still be alive."

"That's loco. He couldn't have stopped those bloodthirsty hoodlums. They'd shot him dead."

She picked up a twig and drew circles in the dust. "Oh, hon. Don't you think he's been told that a hundred times?"

The singsong talk coming from the laundry girls drifted past us on a gentle breeze. The air still carried the cool of the night. By afternoon, it would be too hot to sit in the grass. Such a peaceful morning to be talking about such violent things.

"He buried all of them, then found the Pinkerton Agency and became a detective. I think tracking down outlaws is like a penance to him. Each arrest is an atonement. Swore he'd never be responsible for any life other than his own."

Words from weeks past came back to my memory. *Don't saddle me with that burden.* He'd made me angry then. Now I understood.

"He built a wall around his heart that none of us thought could ever be torn down." A deep breath jiggled her bosoms. "But something happened that changed all that."

Curious, I glanced at her. "What?"

"You."

My heart leaped so high into my gullet, I almost choked. "Me? How?"

"Have no idea. All I know is the Jackson Wayne that sat across from you at the breakfast table this morning is a changed man." She squared around to look me in the eye. "Mother of God, Dixie. Ain't never heard him call anyone darlin'."

"He's always called me that."

"My point exactly. That cowboy keeps his mouth shut tighter than a bear trap. Never heard him talk as much as he did this morning." She stood and pulled me from the ground. "I think he's met his match. And: —she winked — "I think he's yours for the taking."

I laughed.

"Dixie, I'm serious. He's in love with you, only he don't know it yet. It's like you and him are one half of the other." She scoffed at my snort. "Think about it. Your lives run side-by-side. You're from the South. So was his ma. You lost all your family. So did he. You're alone. He is too. He locked up his heart. And so have you."

"I don't know what you're talking about."

"Oh, don't play that card with me, Dixie." Green eyes snapped with frustration and a touch of anger. "You may not hate all men like Abby said, but it's plain as the freckles on your nose that you don't trust any of them. Got a stubborn streak a mile long. Wouldn't ask a man for help if you were on fire and he carried the only bucket of water."

"I can't."

The pout on her lips would've been funny if I wasn't so riled. My outburst hushed the birds and ruined the peace of the day. She didn't understand. I wouldn't be like Mama, weak and depending on someone else for support. It's what killed her. Had to be strong in order to survive. Trusting a man with my heart would only lead to trouble. In a huff, I whistled to Lobo and yelled back at Sassy as I stomped to the house.

"Won't never love a man. Ever."

Her laughter followed me and before the door slammed, I heard her yell, "Never say never, Dixie. It has a way of coming back to bite you in the butt."

CHAPTER 19

I climbed up the stairs cussing a blue streak. Didn't need no damn man. Why did everyone think I did? So what if I was the only one Wayne called darlin' and my insides turned to jelly every time he did? Didn't mean I belonged to him like some horse or steer.

A picture of me wearing a big DARLIN' brand on my hip flashed in my mind. I tore at the buttons on my collar. Couldn't get that mighty pretty green dress off fast enough. Didn't need him. His gun. Or his horse. Well, maybe his horse. I really did like Joe.

It felt comfortable to be in britches and a cotton shirt again. A worn Stetson, found in the back of the closet, completed the outfit. With saddlebags thrown over my shoulder, I marched down the steps and out the front door. Lobo followed at my heels. Time to end this nonsense once and for all.

A slight breeze stirred the dust in the street and coated my throat with grit and grime. Sure would like to stop at the cook tent for coffee but skirted around it on my way to the stables. Felt guilty for laying out and not helping Chow with breakfast. I wondered if the shootout at the One-Eyed Jack would spoil my relationship with him. Hoped not. I liked Chow-Chow and all his funny Chin-ee ways.

Deep, masculine voices drifted from the barn and stopped me before I busted through the big doors. Wasn't my nature to eavesdrop, but the sound of my name made me curious. I ducked behind the stacked bales of hay and listened. Big Finn's lilting voice sounded amused. Wayne's didn't.

"Judging by your silly grin, I'd say you found that sorrel-haired filly of yours."

I peeked around the edge of a square bale. Always loved the scent of fresh hay but not crammed up my nose. I stifled a sneeze. Jackson's dimples hid behind a scowl, and he brushed Joe's coat with quick, short strokes.

"Dixie ain't *my* anything. She's nobody's woman but her own."

"Oh, is that so?" Big Finn heaved his meaty butt up on the feed bin and grinned. "Didn't sound that way a few weeks back when you warned me she might be riding in, and to watch over her, give her a job, and a place to stay." He clicked his tongue. "Sure hated to lie to the little lass about not knowing you. Took the blue shine right out of her eyes, it did."

Why, that overgrown, red-nosed lying Irish rascal.

Wayne shot him a look. "That's just between you and me. Don't want her knowing I had anything to do with her welfare."

He threw the curry comb to the straw floor with disgust and whirled. Joe tossed his head in surprise. "And that reminds me. I told you to get her a safe, decent place to live. And where did I find her last night? At a bordello."

Finn didn't back down. "Ah, don't bow up at me, laddie. From the way ye talked, I expected a shy, wee snip of a girl to come dragging in. Ye neglected to tell me she'd be a stick of dynamite with a fuse of wild, scarlet hair. I fixed her up at Mildred's place right proper, I did. But she's got hot Irish blood running through her veins and a mind of her own. Couldn't stop her from falling in with Della and her girls."

He cocked his head to the side and gave a quizzical look. "And what's wrong with that, I ask ye? Sassy works for us and has a good soul. Got more compassion in her big toe than that dried-up piece of leather, Millie Atkins has in her whole body."

Wayne's stern look dissolved into a grin. Gleaming white teeth flashed. "Didn't say Della and her Doves weren't good women, just don't care for their line of work. Sounds like you and Sassy have more than a working interest in common."

Donovan stroked his walrus mustache, and a blush ran up the back of his thick neck. "Aye, and what if we do? Love's a funny thing. Finds ye' when least expected. Have a mind to make an honest woman out of her one of these days. A man doesn't live by bread alone, lad.

What about Dixie?"

"What about her?"

"Ah, lad, ye needn't play stupid with me. I've known ye' far too long. Every farmer's daughter and schoolmarm have pranced and danced around ye. Ye' never gave them a second look. But this Dixie lass has ya tied up in knots. What's different about the girl?"

Lobo whined. I bent down and put my hand around his muzzle. "Shh," I whispered in his ear. This I had to hear.

Wayne gave Joe a final pat on the shoulder. Not finding anything to sit on, he squatted on his heels and leaned his back against the stall door. Finn waited patiently for his answer. I, on the other hand, wanted to dart across the barn floor and yank the words right out of his mouth. Of course, it didn't help that the coffee I drank earlier had worked its way through my innards. Had to go—bad. Maybe if I sat down and crossed my legs, the urge would go away. Finally, Big Finn broke the silence.

"Didn't know it was that hard of a question."

A slow, easy grin spread across the lawman's sunburnt face and made those damn dimples of his deepen. He pulled a stem from a nearby haybale, put it between full lips, and chewed. His brow furrowed, deep in thought.

"Those schoolteachers and daughters who paraded around never once looked me in the eye. They were too busy batting theirs and pretending to be something they weren't. But Dixie holds my gaze with a look so deep it rattles my soul. She is who she is. And if you don't like what ya see, to hell with ya'."

"Aye, noticed that about her. What else?"

He chewed thoughtfully on the stem until it splintered. With a soft pouf, he spit it out into the sunlight that streaked through the high windows of the barn and spilled across the dirt floor. Barn sounds closed in around me—the chomp-chomp of horses eating oats, chickens clucking. My gaze never left his face.

"Isn't an easy thing to put it into words."

Good God Almighty. Am I *that* bad?

Big Finn shifted his weight on the feed bin and hooked his thumbs into his suspenders. "Laddie, ya got to be doing better than that."

Yeah, laddie. Explain.

Wide shoulders shrugged. "All right," Finn said. "There's more than one way to skin a cat. Let me ask ye this way. If ye' could only use one word to describe the lass, what would it be?"

"Passionate."

Yeehaw. I liked the sound of that.

"When life slaps her down, she jumps up, spits in its eye, and dares it to hit her again. She rushes headfirst into the day and gives it everything she's got. Lives every moment like it was her last."

Warmed up now, his deep walnut eyes flashed, and his words ran faster. "She's on fire all the time. Burns with a passion for seeing justice done. Right the wrongs. Every little thing that makes life worthwhile and beautiful she notices, not even aware she's one of them. When I'm with her, I catch that fever. Fills my heart with joy plumb near to overflowing. Makes me feel wild. Free. Alive."

I about wet my pants.

Big Finn cleared his throat, and I glanced at him. The serious way his thick lips puckered together made me take a second look.

"Sounds to me like you're in love, lad."

"Love? Not me."

"Oh, is it now? A man wouldn't be giving up his horse and gun without a fight. You handed both over to the lass without even a whimper. And ya can't deny the way that mug of yours lights up with just the mention of her name." He leaned back and jabbed the air with his finger. "Ya can't hide from love, laddie boy. Trust me. I know."

The silence was deafening. I could hear every peck the scrawny banty rooster made on the hard, dirt floor.

"I got one more question to ask ye."

"Promise?"

"Oh, I be certain there won't be any others after this one. But I need your word that you'll answer it."

"If it will shut you up, I give my word."

A huge sigh made Big Finn's belly shake. He hesitated for a moment like he was about to do something unpleasant. Then he fixed his partner with a dead-on stare.

"Do you think all this heat and passion that is the essence of Dixie would be hot enough to sear closed that wound across your heart that's been weeping ever since that bloody day in Kansas?"

I nearly bit my tongue in half.

Jackson leaped from the floor. Even though out of sight, I scooted back and waited for fists to fly.

"Damn it, Donovan! I told you never to speak of that day."

"Aye, that ya did," Finn thundered back. For the first

time, I sensed the power that hid under the man's huge coat. "But ya gave me your word. I be expectin' an answer."

Jackson paced. Three steps one way. Three another. He turned his back, gripped the top of Joe's stall gate, and leaned hard into the wood. Wide shoulders that could carry the sins of the world slumped.

"Jackson! I be needin' that answer."

Soft. So soft I struggled to hear.

"Reckon she might."

Hell and damnation. If it started raining pitchforks, I couldn't be more stunned.

"Satisfied now? Why's it so damn important for you to hear this anyway?"

"It wasn't so important that I heard it, lad, as it was for you to say it."

A slight chuckle. "Finn Semus Donovan, you're as tricky as those little green leprechauns you talk about."

"Aye that I am. And damn proud of it."

"I doubt you could fool Dixie. She's got too tight a rein on her heart."

"Aye. Noticed that. Because of Payton, I suppose."

"Reckon that's most of it. She didn't volunteer too much information about that night except to say he didn't ruin her. But just the same, undeniable damage was done. Wouldn't be surprised if she has nightmares about the whole thing. Ain't likely she'll be trusting of any man for a very long time—if ever."

The big Irishman climbed off the feed bin and rubbed his butt. "Aye, I agree with ya there, lad. She's made it more than plain she don't have any use for men. Almost bolts and runs when one gets close enough to touch her. Ya can imagine what a stampede I had on me hands when the boys heard I hired a new woman. They act silly enough around a beefy one. But when they saw Dixie, what with her silky crimson mane, upturned nose, flashing blue eyes, and womanly shape."

"Donovan!"

"Sorry, lad. Thought I'd have to beat them off with a shillelagh bigger than a redwood, but Dixie took care of it herself. Micky Doogan, the blithering idiot, made the mistake of grabbing her arm." A huge laugh boiled out of Finn. "Damn near pulled back a stub, he did."

Wayne laughed. "Of that I have no doubt."

"Aye. But 'tis a sad thing for one so young to hate so. Be an awful lonely future for the lass if she doesn't learn to forgive." He grinned. "'Course the right man could—"

"You playing matchmaker now?"

"Ah, laddie, 'tis as plain as the nose on your face that you and she belong together. Both your souls were linked before the beginning of time. Both of ya have the strength to heal the other."

I'd heard enough. Been holding my breath so long my lungs hurt. I'd done made up my mind to tell Jackson thanks for everything but to take his gun and horse and hit the trail. Now I wasn't so sure I wanted him to go. To know that out of all the women in the world, he thought I was the one who could stop his suffering made me feel special yet overwhelmed at the same time.

The stink of horse manure added with fragrant sweet hay and saddle leather closed in tight and smothered me. I needed time to clear my head. If I could back out nice and quiet, they'd never know I'd overheard the big confession.

Unfortunately, at that exact moment, Sylvester the barn cat strolled through the door. Lobo took one look and leaped. Growls and howls, spits and hisses hit the air. Dust flew. Horses threw their heads and snorted. Matilda the milk cow let out a bawl loud enough to wake the dead.

Big Finn swore. "Sweet Mother Mary! What manner of beasty is this?"

"Dixie?" Wayne's roar shook the dust and hay from the rafters.

I jumped from the floor, brushed the straw and dirt off my butt, and walked casually toward him. Every nerve danced, and my stomach flip-flopped.

"How long you been here?" Jackson asked.

His dark look edged on dangerous, and the ice shooting from his eyes froze me to the spot.

Sure hoped I didn't pee all over his boots.

CHAPTER 20

The secret to telling a good lie is to convince yourself you're telling the truth. By the time I reached the two men, I believed the sun rose in the West and set in the East.

"I just got here," I said and matched his frosty glare with one of cool indifference and wide-eyed innocence. "Came to give you your saddlebags."

His clenched jaw relaxed. He took the bags and even managed to smile.

And Sassy said I couldn't play poker. Ha!

"Miss Dixie," Finn said and doffed his bowler hat. "Would ya mind calling off that woolly beast of yours before me cat suffers a fit and dies?"

Sylvester killed and ate copperheads for breakfast. Doubted he'd die of anything but old age. Peering over the edge of the hay loft, the wily tom twitched his scarred tail and watched in amusement as Lobo tried everything but standing on his head to get at the want-to-be cougar.

"Lobo. Come."

Surprised and a little miffed that he obeyed Wayne's commands so willingly, I swatted the dog on his rump when he walked past.

"Traitor," I mumbled when his gray eyes gave me a

confused look.

"Miss Dixie, I found this man eying your horse. Says he's a friend of yours. Is that so?"

I nodded. "It's okay. Big Finn meet Jackson Wayne."

It was all I could do to hide my grin when I watched the two shake hands, acting like strangers. Still playing the game.

"Well, then all is well. I be needin' a smoke." He tipped his hat again. "Be seeing ya in the morning, lass. Good day, Mr. Wayne."

Joe nickered. I turned away and patted the horse's shoulder.

"He's getting a hay belly."

I bristled. Finn wasn't fat, just round. Then it dawned on me. Wayne was talking about Joe.

He leaned casually against the stall gate and fixed his gaze on me. "Joe's the kind of horse that needs to run." He winked. "A soft horse won't carry ya far if you need to make a fast getaway."

I smiled.

"I'm riding up in the mountains today to see an old friend. Why don't you saddle up and come with me?"

Oh hell. No. No. No. How could I back out of this? Had to admit, a ride in the fresh mountain air sounded good. Would give me time to think. Only alone. Not riding beside the very person I needed to clear my head about. No. I wouldn't go. I raised my gaze. He grinned. White teeth flashed.

My head shouted no, but I heard my mouth say, "Sure. Be right back."

Coward, I told myself as I made a beeline to the outhouse.

Joe was already saddled when I returned. "I'll return your saddle," I said.

"Nope. You need it."

Good God Almighty. First his knife then his pistol, and

Joe. Now his saddle. If he gave me his Stetson and boots, we'd be as good as married.

"I can't accept all of this," I said. "I have money. I can buy my own horse and rig."

He threw a long leg over his saddle and settled easy on Buck's broad back. "Already told you, I can't go back to the train with my horse and not you. Besides, Joe and the saddle are gifts."

"Horses are a dime a dozen."

"Not like Joe."

"Yes, but—

"Dixie. My horse. My decision."

His stern tone told me there was no sense in arguing. Okay, Mr. Pinkerton Detective, you won this one, but I'll find a way to get even.

The feisty mustang pranced and danced down Main Street. When we got clear of town, I gave him his head. The painted gelding streaked across the flat, hard trail like a lightning bolt. From the corner of my eye, I caught sight of Wayne and Buck. They stayed even for about a quarter of a mile then dropped back. I melted into Joe's shoulder and forgot everything except the sound of pounding hooves and the wind biting my face.

When Joe settled into a lazy lope, I circled around and rode back. Jackson leaned forward on his saddle horn and watched me ride toward him. His warm bourbon eyes blazed and glowed in the sunlight. A half smile pulled at his lips.

"What?" I asked.

"Joe fits you."

The sun played tag with the clouds and lost its bite the farther we rode into the hills. With each hoof beat, the tightness in my shoulders eased. "Who's this friend we're going to see?"

"You'll find out soon enough."

CHAPTER 21

The fresh scent of pine needles and honeysuckle circled our heads. I took a deep breath. Wondered why he was so quiet. I tried again. "Cat got your tongue?"

"What?" His scowl surprised me.

"Why so quiet?"

"Been thinking, that's all."

"About what?"

A huge sigh shook his wide shoulders. He turned in the saddle and pushed his Stetson back off his head. "Horses. Been thinking about horses."

I didn't like his tone. Felt like a child being scolded for asking too many questions. My temper simmered.

"Keeping up with two horses is a waste of time. What I need is one horse with the speed and agility of Joe and the strength and dependability of Buck. Hope my friend has just what I need."

I couldn't believe it. Was he going to trade Buck for another horse? He loved Buck. My insides twisted. It was my fault. If I hadn't taken Joe, he wouldn't have to get rid of his faithful, persimmon-eating buckskin.

As if he heard my thoughts, he said, "Been thinking of trading horses for a while. Buck's carried me many miles, but he can't clear those six-foot fences as easily as he once could." He patted the horse's tanned shoulder. "He's earned a rest."

Still didn't make me feel better. My mood turned sour. Wished I hadn't come. The bubbling sounds of a nearby creek gurgled through the air. We reined to a stop. "We'll hold up here for a bit."

He dismounted and strolled off through the woods. Reckoned his coffee had run its course too. I stepped down and led Joe over to the water's edge. He and Buck drank with long, slurpy gulps.

A bloodcurdling shriek tore through the still wooded air. Spit froze in my mouth. Both horses snorted. The yell came from the direction Jackson had walked.

With my heart about to burst, I scurried to the top of a large boulder and looked down. Below me. Wayne and a huge, black-haired Indian rolled on the ground. Damn! If I only had a gun. On second thought, maybe it was better I didn't. Another war-whoop ripped through the trees. Fighting panic, I searched for a weapon. My hand found a good-sized rock. I threw it at the Indian's head. Hit Jackson in the back of the neck instead.

Damnation!

Where was Lobo when I needed him? That mutt picked a fine time to stay behind and hunt for a mangy tomcat.

The Indian pinned Wayne to the dirt. Think, Dixie. Better do something fast before that Indian kills him. Without a second thought, I leaped from the rock and landed on the savage's back.

I wrapped tight around his waist. I beat his head with my fists. The smell of rancid bear grease almost made me puke when I grabbed a hold of his braids and yanked. He shook and roared like a crazed grizzly. Teeth clenched, I stuck to him like a cocklebur to a saddle blanket. I heard Jackson yell.

"Dixie!"

A glance made blood roar in my ears. Wayne was bent over clutching his belly. Oh God. This heathen must've stabbed him in the stomach. Anger and fear spurred me on.

Legs squeezed tighter.

I yanked and pulled his greasy hair.

Fingernails scratched his thick neck like cat claws.

I bit his ear.

With a howl, the Indian pitched forward. I somersaulted over his head and landed square on my butt.

The hat flew from my head.

Hair spilled onto my face.

My teeth rattled and air left my lungs.

I'm gonna' die.

Always knew a man would be the death of me.

CHAPTER 22

Through tousled, curly locks I caught sight of Jackson lunging past the Indian in an effort to reach me. Damned if I'd let him die for me.

Grabbing anything I could find, I flung dirt, rocks, and twigs at the Indian.

"Dixie. Stop." Jackson laughed.

Laughed?

In disbelief, I watched him slap the Indian on the shoulder and walk toward me. "Dixie, this is the friend I was telling you about." He offered me his hand.

His friend? Oh, how stupid of me. I should've known.

Thoroughly pissed, I ignored his gesture and struggled to my feet. I tore at the buttons on his cotton shirt and searched for the gaping cut the Indian's knife made. "You mean he didn't stab you?" I pushed the hair back out of my eyes with trembling hands.

"Is that what you thought?"

"What else was I supposed to think? He pounced on top of you, yelling and screaming."

A slow grin spread across his square face, and he slapped his knee. "Aw, darlin', that's just Flying Eagle's way of saying howdy."

The Indian inched toward us. So mad I could chew nails, I shot him a look of pure death. He stopped in his tracks.

"Dixie, this is Flying Eagle, my blood brother."

Not feeling very hospitable, I stood and gawked at the red-skinned man. He was short with arms and legs the size of tree trunks. Black eyes stared back at me, but he said nothing. Smart man.

Still chuckling, Jackson threw his friend a grin. "We'll get our horses and catch up with ya'.

He rubbed a purple bump on the back of his neck. "Why'd you throw that rock at me?" he asked.

"Didn't mean to hit you."

"Good God, woman. Sassy was right. You can't aim worth a hoot."

The chuckle in his voice infuriated me. "Well, excuse me for trying to save your hide. Next time, I'll let him scalp you while I run for help."

"You *really* were trying to save me, weren't you?" He mounted up. "Dang, darlin', I'm touched."

He was making fun. I whirled ready to fly into him, but the fire burning in his dark eyes wilted my insides. He was serious. A quiver tickled my stomach. I couldn't meet his smoky gaze.

"It's your fault. None of this would've happened if you told me your friend was an Indian in the first place."

He rode over to Joe and held him by the bridle while I climbed into the saddle.

"Yep. You're probably right."

Damn the man. How could I argue with that?

CHAPTER 23

Wayne fell in beside Flying Eagle. I rode a few paces behind them. Solid as granite, the brave kept staring at me like I had spots and four ears. When he turned and gawked at me for the hundredth time, I had enough. A slight nudge from my heel put Joe into canter. Heard the Indian grunt when I rode by.

"Wayne's woman not happy."

Wayne's *woman*?

"Dixie?"

I slowed to a trot but refused to turn around. It wasn't long before Buck's shoulder came even with Joe's. "What's got you so riled?"

"Why's he looking at me that way? Doesn't his tribe have women?"

"None with fiery-red hair."

"Why does he think I'm *your* woman?" I asked and tucked stray wisps under my hat.

"Because you're with me and you're riding my horse."

"And that just naturally makes me yours?" He ignored the sarcasm dripping from my tongue.

"In his eyes it does. And it would be best if you let him keep right on thinking it."

Everything in me balked against that line of reasoning, but his words carried a warning. He and Flying Eagle acted like loyal friends but maybe only to a point. Being Wayne's *woman* offered me protection. From what? I didn't know and hoped I didn't have to find out.

"How does he know I'm riding your horse?"

"Who do you think I got Joe from?"

"So Flying Eagle's your horse-trading buddy."

A slight frown creased his smooth forehead. "Naw, not him directly. Gotta trade with the medicine man, or rather the medicine man's son."

The slow chuff, chuff of hoof beats came up behind us. This time when Flying Eagle cast a curious glance my way, I managed a weak smile. He answered it with a toothy grin. Maybe he wasn't such a big, bad man after all.

"Don't you like the medicine man?" I asked.

"It ain't that." He rubbed his square jaw. "Snapping Turtle is old and crank—"

"Wait!" I laughed. "Snapping Turtle? You're joshing."

The serious look on their faces told me I'd made a mistake making fun of the name. The Indian's smile disappeared. Ebony eyes narrowed. His deep, rough voice rumbled like thunder. "Not every warrior called Grey Wolf or Crazy Horse."

Hell and damnation. I done pissed off the Indian. Embarrassed, I stammered, but the grin pulling at Wayne's lips stopped me from a lame apology. A mischievous glint in Flying Eagle's eyes let me breathe again.

"I fool Wayne's woman."

I didn't laugh quite as hard as they did at the joke, but I couldn't help but smile at the two hee-hawing like silly schoolboys. Besides, the smile crinkles around Jackson's brown eyes were cute and made a perfect partner for the dimples that danced in his square face. He should laugh more often.

"Is the medicine man's name really Snapping Turtle?"

"Yep. Wasn't pulling your leg about that. Promise to keep a straight face when you see him."

I'd try. But I swear if the medicine man's son was named Chirping Cricket, all bets were off.

Chapter 24

A thin trail surrounded by trees and their leafy canopy magically opened into a valley rich with green, wavy grass and the sight of horses and tipis planted beside a cheerful singing creek. Bronzed-skinned, half-naked children shouted our arrival. Black, oily braids bobbed from side to side as they scurried to their mothers. With dark eyes that loomed large and round in their small faces, they watched us ride past. I waved and smiled when a small boy ducked behind his mother's back only to peek up at me with a shy grin.

A leathery Indian who looked older than dirt, shuffled toward us clutching a red blanket around his shoulders even though the sun rained down warmth. Jackson stepped down from Buck's back and greeted him with a firm handshake.

"Great Chief, the winters have been good to you."

"Um. Come. We sit. Smoke. What bring Tall Warrior back to our village after so many moons away?"

"I need a horse."

The old Indian shifted his beefy rump to look back at Joe. "Spotted pony not to liking?"

"Joe's perfect, but I gave him to Dix . . . my woman for a gift. I'm looking to trade the buckskin."

"You have woman?" He put his pipe down and struggled to his feet. "I must see."

By this time, the tribe had us surrounded in a large circle. Every eye trained on me. Felt like a lonely peppermint stick in a candy jar being slobbered over by dozens of sweet-toothed young'uns.

I climbed down from Joe. A gust of wind blew my hat off. My hair flew about my face and streamed down my back. Brushing the wild curls away, I heard the whole tribe gasp. I didn't understand. One minute, I was a piece of sweet candy. The next, the big, bad wolf. A shiver of fear zipped up my spine. Wayne stepped to my side and placed his hand on my shoulder. Never thought I'd be so relieved to feel his touch.

Thought Snapping Turtle's eyes were gonna pop out of his head. What had I done now?

"Woman is fox spirit."

Another intake of breath came from the crowd. A broad-shouldered brave charged like a raging bull. Hell and damnation, I wanted out of there.

"Dixie, meet Roaring Bear. Snapping Turtle's only son."

Like his father, Roaring Bear's name fit like a hand in a glove. Tall, sinewy, and strong, he walked quick and silently stopping so close to my face I could smell his wild, gamey body odor. Eyes the color of pitch stripped the courage plumb out of my bones. My innards shriveled up like a piece of overcooked bacon from the heat of his stare. Damn near gagged when he ran strands of my hair through his bear-paw hands. Legs shaking, I clenched my jaw so tight thought my teeth would crack. Jackson felt my trembling.

"Easy, darlin'. He doesn't mean any harm. You should be honored. Fox medicine is powerful to these Indians."

Honored? Oh, hell, yes. That's exactly how I felt as Roaring Bear petted my head like I was a prized coon dog.

"Woman's hair like foxtail."

Wow, he could talk. I'd expected roars or grunts. He lifted his gaze from my head and grinned. "Tall Warrior lucky man."

The grin changed him from a fierce grown-up bear into a cute cub. The starch came back into my legs, but I wasn't going to let my guard down. Cute or not, a bear is a bear.

Wayne stepped from my side. "Roaring Bear, I need a good horse. Can you help me out?"

His smile widened. "Have many horses. Come. Look. Foxtail Woman come too."

Foxtail Woman?

Oh well, it beat the hell out of Chirping Cricket.

CHAPTER 25

Roaring Bear ran in front of us. Jackson looked down at me and smiled. "You all right?"

"Sure. Why wouldn't I be?"

A muscle in his square jaw jumped. I said something wrong. All sense of humor left his eyes. His usual velvet-warm voice turned chilly.

"Dixie, you've got grit. More than a lot of men I know. But you don't fool me. I felt your legs shake when Roaring Bear touched you. He's fierce, big, and wild. If ya weren't spooked by him it wouldn't be normal. Why do you feel the need to deny that? Especially to me?"

He didn't wait for an answer. Felt lower than dirt when he stomped away. Don't think I'd ever forget the hurt in his voice.

Tears stung my eyes. No one understood. Papa was dead. Mama, murdered. I was alone in a wild territory on the run from a man so evil the devil would spit him back to God. Fear followed me like a shadow. It walked beside me on the streets and curled by my side at night. Nothing or no one, not even Della or her girls, could ease the black worry that gnawed at my gut day in and day out. Like the runt of the litter, if I didn't act brave and fearless, I'd be eaten alive, especially in a town as lawless and immoral as Six Shooter Siding. I couldn't let my guard down. Show weakness. Couldn't give off the scent of a helpless female. I'd be prey for varmints like Payton and Daggett. I had no one to turn to. If I didn't protect myself, who would? Even as I asked the question, my heart knew the answer.

Jackson Wayne would.

Not if you keep pushing him away.

Get out of my head, Papa.

A loud yell dried my tears. The ground shook. Excited, I ran toward the sound. I stood and watched horses of every size and color cover the prairie like a living blanket of browns, sorrels, grays, blacks, and whites. Roaring Bear stood proud amid the herd. He turned and gave a sharp whistle.

When I was a young girl, Papa told me stories of a white-winged horse of the gods. I loved the notion, and believed it too, except he got the color wrong. A horse, dark as midnight, glided across the prairie so silently and smooth, I searched for black wings. Mane and tail flowed like onyx ribbons in the warm breeze.

Roaring Bear reached into his buckskins and pulled out a persimmon. The black one slowed and plucked the treat from his palm gently and soft. So, the sweet fruit hadn't been Wayne's idea at all. With a smug look, the young brave took a handful of mane, swung onto the stallion's back, and nudged him toward us.

"See, Tall Warrior? Thundercloud tame. You like?"

Stupid question. The black was big and strong enough to carry two men the size of Wayne all day with jackrabbit speed. A blind man could see how much he wanted this black horse birthed by thunder and lightning.

He ran his hands over the horse's silky withers and down his long legs. Thundercloud stood calm under his touch. Roaring Bear slid to the ground.

"You like?" he asked again.

Wayne rubbed the black's nose and chuckled when the horse nuzzled his pockets looking for more persimmons. "You take the buckskin in trade?"

"Have many horses. No need for another."

A large sigh. "Thought you'd say that. What do you want?"

I thought Roaring Bear's thin lips would split from his wide, possum grin. He pointed his finger at me.

"Trade horse for Foxtail Woman."

Holy hell! My stomach twisted into a knot. My head swam, and I stumbled. Didn't know what scared me more. An Indian buck wanting me or the look on Wayne's face. For an instant, I thought he'd hand me over, no questions asked.

"Sorry," he said and rubbed his whiskered jaw. "She's my woman. I can't do it."

A dark look flashed in Roaring Bear's eyes and his nostrils flared. Chills marched up my spine. The scent of danger caused Thundercloud to throw his head and paw the ground. When Roaring Bear turned and walked away, my legs folded like a newborn colt's. I sunk to the dirt.

"Scared now?" Wayne asked.

My mouth was so dry I could barely manage to croak, "Yes."

"Come on." He helped me to my feet and put his arm around my waist. We stumbled toward the creek. "You could use a drink."

He knelt by the creek's edge, dipped his bandana in the stream, and held it against my forehead. The cool water helped ease the dizzy feeling. I took the neckerchief from his hand and asked, "Why does Roaring Bear want me so much?"

"Well, darlin', he doesn't want *you* exactly. It's your hair he's after."

"My what? I don't understand."

He pulled a reed from the creek bank and sat cross-legged beside me. Chewing on the stem, he sighed. "I told you. Fox medicine is powerful to these Indians. Because your hair looks so much like one, he wants it for its magic."

I must have looked blank because he explained slowly. "The Navajo believe that since the fox can be seen at dawn and dusk, it walks between the spirit world and the real world. Fox hide and hair are believed to have great healing powers. Anyone who has a fox as a totem has the power of shapeshifting."

A turtle slid off a log into the water with a dull plop, and the smell of minnows and crawdads tickled my nose. I dipped the cotton neckpiece into the stream again and held it against my neck. "What's that mean?"

He leaned back on his elbows and spit out the wilted blade. "Being able to take the shape of any animal or bird, is a great advantage over your enemies. Snapping Turtle is old and the tribe is looking for a new medicine man. Roaring Bear is the obvious choice, but he's young. Has a burning itch to prove himself. Having the power to shapeshift and the magic of fox medicine to boot would go a long way in gaining the tribe's respect and confidence."

Never heard of such a notion. Didn't know what to think. I changed the subject. "What are you going to do now?"

He lowered his head and studied the ground. "I'll go back to the herd again. There might be one or two horses that would serve my purpose. If not, Buck has a few more years left in him."

"We both know you won't find any of them better than that stallion. He beats any horse I've ever seen." I laughed. "Thought for a minute you just might take Roaring Bear up on his offer."

He uncoiled his long legs and stood up. "It was damn tempting. That black is one in a million for sure. But, darlin,' so are you."

Heat raced up my back and crawled up my neck so fast I

almost started to pant. But I held his smoky gaze without wavering. The soft sound of bubbling water, chirping birds, and wind playing with the trees mixed with the smells of green grass, wood, and creek water. Time hung sultry and heavy between us.

Don't push him away, lass.

"Thank you."

My voice was a whisper, but he heard. A slow smile inched its way across his strong face. Thought my heart would bust.

"Coming with me?"

My heart still hammering hard in my chest, I didn't trust my legs. I shook my head. "Think I'll just sit here for a while."

He tugged a knife from his boot and handed it to me. "I want this one back. He winked. "Watch out for snakes in the grass."

I didn't know if he meant the ones what crawled on their bellies or the ones who walked on two legs.

CHAPTER 26

A few deep breaths finally slowed my stampeding heart, but the joy of Wayne's words lingered with every beat. I watched him amble away. For such a tall man, he walked with deer-like grace with long, smooth strides giving the illusion he floated across the grass. My face still burned from the heat of his bold compliment. I'd never forget that moment. Thank God I didn't ruin it with my big mouth.

I sighed and leaned against the weeping willow surrounded by branches that dipped gracefully to the ground. A happy calmness settled next to me. For the first time in a long time, my innards didn't rumble like thunder. The feeling didn't last long.

Guilt tugged at my sleeve. I hadn't been fair or even nice to the wagon scout. How could he understand my worry and fear if I didn't have the guts to confess it to him?

Until this morning, he'd never said a cross word to me and had put up with my temper tantrums with amused patience. Even though he'd deny it, he protected me from my time on the wagon train until now. He gave freely of his knife, gun, and saddle, not to mention his horse. He even confessed after a long, tortured look deep within himself, that I could heal his wounded heart.

What had I given in return? Suspicion, mistrust, and sarcasm. I took his horse, for Pete's sake. Oh sure, I told myself I would give Joe back, but deep down inside, I counted on him giving the painted gelding to me. Because of my selfishness, he had to find a new mount. Even then, he tried to spare my feelings by making up a story about two horses being twice the trouble.

He deserved better. I'd acted like a spoiled kid, yet he overlooked my shortcomings because, of what? Love? Could Sassy and Big Finn be right? Did Jackson Wayne love me?

Eyes squeezed tight, I swallowed hard. Did I love him? Too afraid of that answer, I took the coward's way out and ignored the question.

I pushed away from the tree, knelt by the creek's edge, and stared at my floating reflection. A frog jumped off its pad and stirred up the strong scent of green pond scum. I waited for the ripples to settle then studied my face in the water.

What did he see in me anyway? I had nothing to offer him. Wasn't even pretty. My nose was a snip covered with freckles. My ears were too big and my cheekbones too high.

I tossed my hat aside. Silk ribbons loosened and tangled hair spilled around me. My hair was a mass of wild, unruly curls that always needed a brush and barbed-wire ribbons instead of silk to hold them in place. Curls streamed down my back almost to my waist in ringlets that were always in my way, blowing about my face and getting into eyes. God, I would love to cut it. But without its mass, my head would look too little for eyes bluer than robin eggs.

I dipped my fingers in the water and slicked tousled curls that were too hot in the summer and too heavy in the winter. The image in the steam laughed. It was plumb crazy to think this mop held any magic.

A twig snapped behind me. I whirled. Roaring Bear

stood not more than two feet away. His dark eyes glowed like coals and never left my face. I'd just gotten my heart slowed down to a brisk walk, and now it was at a full gallop again. I clutched the knife in my hand and stood ready to plunge the blade deep into the man's chest. Roaring Bear's white teeth flashed in a little boy's grin, and the cute bear cub came out to play.

"Not fear. I not harm you."

Oh, sure, and a rattlesnake was just a piece of rope with jingle bobs on the end.

He walked toward me. My hand tightened on the knife, and I lifted my chin in defiance.

"What do you want?" Damn the tremor in my voice.

"I see much love in Tall Warrior's eyes for his woman."

I cringed when he reached to touch my hair. "But maybe Foxtail Woman not feel the same for Tall Warrior? He would not want her if she desired another."

The full meaning of his words lit the fuse on my temper and burned away the fear stored up inside me. How dare he! I'd come closer to crawling in a cave with a real bear then between the sheets with this . . . this . . . son of a Snapping Turtle.

"Go away."

I wasn't prepared for the disappointment and hurt that flashed across his chiseled, red-rock face. Wide shoulders slumped. He dropped his hand and backed away like a whipped pup with its tail between its legs.

Oh God. I felt sorry for him.

In a way, Roaring Bear and I were alike. Both of us desperately wanted to prove we could stand on our own two feet and not depend on anyone. All he wanted was to show his father he was worthy and strong enough to be the next Medicine Man. I understood that need. If he thought my fox-red hair could gain his father's approval, then what was the harm?

"Wait!" I couldn't believe what I said next.

"I will give you powerful fox medicine if you give the black stallion to Tall Warrior."

Excitement polished his dark eyes to glazed ebony. He stood silent and waited.

I leaned over at the waist and brought all my hair forward. With short, choppy strokes from my knife, I sawed through the strands. I straightened, tied the severed curls in a ribbon, and handed him the bundle. With great care and respect, he placed it in his medicine bag as reverent as if he were Moses being handed the Ten Commandments.

Standing tall and proud, he lifted his gaze from the prize and stared me straight in the eyes.

"Fox spirit will make Roaring Bear powerful Medicine Man, a great protector to his tribe. Heal many people. He will never forget this gift from Foxtail Woman. I give Thundercloud to Tall Warrior. I give loyalty and friendship to his woman."

He turned to go, but I stopped him with a shout.

"Don't tell him about our trade."

His thick eyebrow arched, but he nodded with a grin. "Foxtail Woman *do* love Tall Warrior as much."

Well, I'll be damned. Maybe I did.

CHAPTER 27

Oh, Hell and damnation!
 Was I loco or just plain stupid?

I almost slipped and broke my neck on the wet rocks, scrambling to the water's edge to gawk at my reflection. With trembling fingers, I pulled at the choppy strands and tried to stretch them longer. I twisted and turned side to side, looking at the watery image. If I had pointed ears and a green face, I'd look like one of Donovan's little leprechauns.

"You worry Wayne not love his woman with little hair?"

I jumped at Flying Eagle's raspy voice. "How long you been standing there?"

"Long time. I see Roaring Bear come to stream. I follow in case Foxtail Woman need help." A grin played at his lips. "But Foxtail Woman take care of herself. I hear and see much. How you explain no hair to Wayne?"

Huh. Good question. I needed time to think up a good answer. Until then, this beat-up dirty brown Stetson and me were going to become close friends. I jammed the hat on my head. Without a bushel of hair crammed under its cover, it slid plumb down over my eyes. Struggling to see, I tilted my head back. Flying Eagle laughed. "Foxtail

Woman now Peeking Turtle."

Wonderful. Yet another nickname.

Before I could tell him to "go to hell," he plucked the hat off my head, bent down on one knee, and pulled reeds from the creek bank. Sitting cross-legged in the grass he worked the stems under the inside hatband. I eased down beside him.

Bright sunshine on my back and the warm breeze on my face, melted nerves strung tighter than a bowstring. Flying Eagle's nimble fingers laced the soggy shoots in and under the leather band with a spellbinding rhythm. My eyes grew heavy. I glanced away from the weaving and studied his profile. Sharp features chiseled out of hard red rock. I wondered about him and Jackson.

"Why do you call him Wayne instead of Tall Warrior?"

Without lifting his gaze, he grunted, "Was first name I know."

"How did you meet him?"

"Two winters past, he save Flying Eagle's life. Much snow cover ground. Little food. I go hunting. My pony too weak from hunger and fell. Broke my leg. Couldn't move. I lay in snow until I could feel no more cold. I made peace with Great Spirit and waited for death."

He shook the grass from the hat, reared back, and looked at it. A small grunt. He picked more stems and stuffed the brim.

"Wayne find me. He carry me to cave, made fire, and splint for leg. When storm passed, he take me home to village. We became blood brothers. He good friend to tribe. Make peace between white men in town called Six Shooter Siding and my people."

"How'd he do that?"

Broad shoulders shrugged. "Don't know. But Wayne promise white man would let us live in peace as long as we stayed in mountains, and it is so. Tribe named him Tall-Warrior-That-Speak-True."

With a grunt, he turned toward me and placed the Stetson on my head. A perfect fit. His tobacco-stained lips split into a grin. I smiled back. Never would have thought something as simple as a hat could start a friendship.

"Why are you helping me?"

The toothy grin changed into a serious line, and he gazed across the stream. "Know Wayne long time. Loyal brother. But sadness always walk with him. Bad memories haunt dreams." His glance returned to capture my eyes. "But Foxtail Woman chase bad spirits away. You give him laughter. He love Foxtail Woman."

I held his gaze for a few seconds before I ducked my head and mumbled, "Can't figure out why he does."

His soft chuckle made me look up from the ground. "Because Great Spirit made it so from beginning."

"What?"

With a sweep of his hand, he cleared away the creek pebbles. Picking up a twig, he scratched two straight lines in the damp dirt, one for the ground and another for the sky. He drew two stick figures. "When Great Spirit make all that is, He not only breathe life into man, but locked His soul into man's heart. When man dies, the soul returns to the Great Spirit."

I grinned at the small dots he made in the dirt. Stars, I reckoned.

"Little pieces of Great Spirit's soul shine forever in night sky. Sometimes Great Spirit sends one back."

"You mean a shooting star?"

He nodded his head in agreement. "Umm."

Fascinated with the story, I couldn't turn away from his crude dirt drawing.

"But when two souls fall together, it is said Great Spirit has blessed them with everlasting love. These souls walk the earth together again. Over and over. Many lifetimes. This why Wayne love Foxtail Woman. And why she love him."

I stared, open-mouthed. "You think that he and I were two falling stars that happened to streak across the heavens at the same time, and because of that, we were destined to fall in love? That's hogwash."

His dark eyes crinkled at the corners in a silent laugh. "White Man never understand. But still, is true."

Trying to poke holes in his story, I asked, "The sky is awfully big. What happens if one soul dies before the other?"

"First soul search every star until it find the second."

"That could take forever."

"Time not matter in the land of the Great Spirit."

"Dixie?" Wayne 's voice rang out across the stream. My breath caught.

Flying Eagle stood and brushed dirt from his buckskins. "I go. Give Foxtail Woman time to think." He winked. "But have no reason to worry. Wayne love you even if bare-headed. Is written in the stars."

I watched him limp away until he disappeared around the bend of the creek. Flying Eagle had many years to go before he would be a grandpa, yet he sure could spin yarns like an old man.

The dirt picture stretched out before me. I lightly traced the figures with my fingertips. Was it such a silly notion, this legend of the star-soul lovers? Deep down inside, I wanted to believe.

"Dixie?"

Time had run out.

Taking a deep gulp of air, I stepped over the picture and walked toward the village.

Sure hope Flying Eagle was right about having nothing to fret over because underneath this hat, I looked like a skinned jackrabbit.

CHAPTER 28

Jackson's grin stretched for a country mile.

"Darlin', you not going to believe this, but Roaring Bear changed his mind. He traded Thundercloud for Buck after all."

His joyful smile pulled one from me, and I had to laugh, even though I wondered what reason the brave gave him for the sudden change of heart. I walked over to the stallion and stroked his velvet nose. Already wearing Buck's saddle and bridle, the horse pawed the ground, impatient to run.

"Wonder why he did that?" I held my breath waiting for the answer.

"Said the Great Spirit sent him a message." He mounted up. "Thought it funny, but I wasn't gonna ask any questions. Get Joe and meet me on the trail. I must take the edge off this rascal before he busts wide open."

He relaxed his firm hold. With a flick of his tail, Thundercloud bolted. I half expected to see flames shooting from his hooves as he tore across the grassy plain. A shrill nicker sounded behind me. I turned. Flying Eagle walked toward me, leading a side-stepping Joe. "Painted pony wants to run too," he said and handed me the reins.

My off foot had just slipped into the stirrup when Joe

took off after the black. It would've been easier to rope the wind than hold the feisty Mustang in. I settled deep into the saddle and gave him the bit. Wind whipped tears to my eyes. Trees whizzed past in a blur.

It wasn't long before the black's muscled rump came into view. Joe never slowed. The distance shortened. When we were only a few yards away, Jackson slowed. Both of us knew Joe would never give up. He'd chase that stallion until his heart burst. I heard Wayne's laugh when we shot past and his shout to circle and come up beside him.

After he passed the big horse, Joe let me check him and ease him down to a walk. His sides heaved. My ears rang from the sound of the wind. I reached to tug my hat lower. I felt only hair. Short, choppy hair.

Oh, hell and damnation.

Trying not to panic, I searched the trail. I couldn't hide my boyish hair for too long, but I counted on having more time. Damn the wind. Maybe I could find the bruised and battered Stetson before he saw me.

No such luck.

"You lookin' for this?"

I think my heart leaped into my throat. Either that, or I swallowed my tongue. It was hard to tell since the lump lodged in my gullet was as big around as a tree stump. Feeling like a condemned man walking up the steps to face the hangman, I forced myself to take the hat from his hands, but I kept my gaze fixed on the ground.

"Dixie. Look at me."

Anger flared. But not at him. I was mad at myself. Why did I feel so ashamed? It wasn't like I'd killed my firstborn. It was just hair. My head shot up, and I stared him square in the eye, daring him to say anything.

He said nothing, which was worse. A shocked expression crossed his tanned face, followed by a puzzled look, then understanding. His square jaw tightened.

We rode in silence. Two feet separated us but it felt like

a mile. I heard him sigh.

"You shouldn't have."

"I wanted to. Besides Thunder is a gift."

"Horses are a dime a dozen."

"Not like Thunder."

"Dixie—

"Jackson. My hair. My decision."

His jaw muscle twitched.

The dull clop-clop of horse hooves sounded too loud in the strained silence. Each squeak of saddle leather backlashed the rocks and trees. Purple and orange streaks painted the sky, and the sun sank lower. The wind blew cool matching his mood. He cleared his throat.

"A lot of folks think it's a sin for a woman to cut her hair."

I snorted. "No doubt they're the same people that think it's a sin for a white man to have an Indian for a blood brother."

Tinged with amusement, his voice sounded resigned. "Yep. No doubt."

A quick glance at his face told me the storm had passed. Taut shoulders relaxed and swayed in rhythm with Thunder's smooth stride. He reined in closer. Stirrup to stirrup, we rode back to town in comfortable, peaceful companionship.

CHAPTER 29

The last rays of sunshine vanished when we reached the barn. I held Thunder while Jackson lit a lantern. We unsaddled the horses in the dull yellow glow. I hooked a stirrup over the horn and tugged at the saddle girth. A question about something he'd said on the trail burned on the tip of my tongue. I drew a deep breath and asked, "Do you?"

"Do I what?"

"Think I'm sinful for cutting my hair."

He chuckled. "I think you're a lot of things, Dixie, but sinful ain't one of 'em.

I couldn't help the grin from inching its way across my face or the flutter of my heart. His answer made me feel like a giddy schoolgirl whose beau had just grabbed her hand.

Strong hands around my waist made me gasp. He picked me up and sat me on top of the feed bin like I was no heavier than an empty tow sack. Eye-to-eye, we stared at one another, so close I could see the pulse beating in his neck and a tiny scar above his eyebrow that I never noticed before. His scent of sun and wind washed over me. Barn noises of chickens and cows faded. Wood slats and beams closed in around us. It was just him and me, all alone in the glow of the soft light. The serious look in his eyes stole my breath.

"When I turned eighteen, Mother gave me an elk-horned handled knife that I'd been admiring for weeks in the window of ol' man Grayson's dry goods store. It cost two dollars. Every night for a month, she'd ride into town to dust, sweep, and mop the store to pay for it. That knife was the last gift I ever got."

He hesitated for a heartbeat that seemed to last forever.

"And it was the last time anyone thought I mattered enough to make that kind of sacrifice for—until today."

I didn't dare breathe, twitch, or blink.

His large hand, strong and hard enough to break a man's jaw, reached and smoothed the jagged strands of my hair into place. Inches from my face, his voice came soft. "Hair don't make the woman, darlin'. It's what's in her heart that does."

He winked.

I wilted.

"And you, Miss Dixie Belle Dandelion, stand head and shoulders above 'em all."

Good God. I wanted to throw my arms around his neck and kiss him till my lips fell off. I leaned toward his warmth. His breath, a mere whisper on my skin, sent chills racing up my spine. And his scent. Wild, untamed. I could do it. Just a fraction of an inch and I'd feel those full lips on mine.

Payton's face flashed in my mind.

I pushed back on the bin and stared at the floor.

"Dixie?"

The wonder in his voice made me want to explain. He'd expected a kiss. Sassy said a man could always tell when a woman wanted to kiss. I owed him a reason for my sudden coldness. But none came. I jumped down and reached for the water bucket.

"Gotta get Joe some water."

I shot him a forced smile when I walked past and headed for the door. "See ya' tomorrow. Maybe you can teach me how to shoot?"

I didn't wait to hear his answer, just kept walking away. Papa's voice shouted behind me.

Margret Katelyn O'Shea, you be nothing but a coward.

CHAPTER 30

The revolver sat heavy in my hand.

Yesterday, learning to shoot seemed like a sure-fire good idea. But today, after running off and leaving Jackson flat-footed and all confused looking the night before, the excitement of guns and bullets had waned.

"Put linen cartridges in the chamber. Ram the ball down tight against the powder. Cap the nipples."

Jackson's voice sounded a mile away. Half-hearted, I listened to his instructions on how to load the six-shooter. For the hundredth time that morning, I tugged at my short hair. Doubt I'd ever get used to it.

"Are you ready?"

I jumped at his voice. "What?"

He cocked his head and shot me a puzzled look. "We need to do this another time?"

"No. What do I do first?"

He pointed to tin cans he'd lined up on a boulder. "Bring your gun arm up like you were pointing a finger at that second red can there and squeeze the trigger."

First shot went wide.

Second shot hit dirt.

Third shot chipped a piece off the rock.

Fourth shot went only God knows where. Good thing the horses were tied behind us.

Fifth and sixth were closer to the target, but the tin cans stood free from holes, mocking me.

Thoroughly disgusted, I swore under my breath. "Hell and damnation."

"Darlin'? Stop." He took the pistol from my hand and reloaded it. I watched every step of the complicated process. "It's a wonder anyone gets around to shooting someone. Takes too long to load one of these things."

"Yep. That's why I carry extra guns and loaded cylinders. Saves a lot of time."

"Guess it doesn't matter anyway. I can't hit nothing."

He came up beside me. "That's because you're pulling the trigger instead of squeezing."

I scoffed. "Pull. Squeeze. What's the difference?"

He whirled me around so quickly my eyes crossed. Fast and heartless, he gave me a peck on the mouth hard enough to crack walnuts. To top it off, the rude smack missed my lips entirely hitting their edge instead.

"That's pulling," he said.

Before I could slap the fire out of him, he folded me into arms strong enough to crush a small grizzly. Lowering his mouth to mine he kissed me full.

A hint of firm yet tender salt-flavored lips made my head swim. Knees weak, I surrendered to feelings I'd be hard-pressed to describe. Hot. Chilled. Dizzy. He didn't attempt to pull away holding me steady against him. His scent of shaving soap, horse, and morning coffee wrapped me inside a cocoon of fringe and buckskin.

Sounds of wind and birds, leaves and grass hushed.

My heart leaped from my chest, met his halfway, and melted into one.

He backed away. Brown eyes twinkling. Dimples dancing.

"That's squeezing."

He winked. "Now you tell me. Which one hit the mark?"

Hit the mark? Which one? Was he loco?

At the moment, I couldn't even tell him my name.

CHAPTER 31

His kiss boiled my insides. The need to say something . . . anything lay heavy between us, but I struggled to catch even a whisper of a breath. Talking was out of the question. A mixture of confusion, humor, and a hint of a blush raced across his strong face. For a minute, I thought he was close to apologizing, making heat creep back into my bones. I'd slap him silly if he did. It would cheapen the moment.

Reckon he heard my silent warning. He turned back to the box of ammunition and cleared his throat.

"I think that's enough," he said. "You get the idea. All you need to do now is practice."

Still weak in the knees, I managed to pull my way into the saddle and watched him slide his new gun and holster back into his saddlebags. That's when I noticed how heavy the bags were packed.

"You're leaving, aren't you?" My voice cracked.

"Yep. Got to get back to the wagon train. Been gone far too long. I don't want them to come looking for me and finding you. I need to show you something before I go."

If I hadn't been trying to start my heart again, I would've asked him a bushel basket full of questions. First, a kiss that sucked the wind out of me, and now, the news of him riding away made me dumb as a post.

About a mile's ride through woods and brush, he stopped on a ridgeline and pointed down at an old ranch house surrounded by corrals, a barn, and a bunkhouse that had seen better days.

"I wanted you to see this," he said.

"Why?"

"I think you should buy it."

"What?"

He rushed on ignoring my snort. "I saw this place a while back. It used to be a working ranch but when the owner died, it went to seed. I've been asking around. I don't know how much money you *borrowed* from Payton, but you could get this place for a song. 'Course you'd need to fix it up. But you could hire some hands darn cheap. Build back the corrals and barn. Shore up the house."

"Whatever for?"

"Well for your own horse ranch, darlin'. The railroad is gonna'be finished in a few months. That means the Army will be moving west. They're gonna' need good mounts. People will start moving in. Good horseflesh will be in demand. Roaring Bear will give you mares and foals. Heck, for what you did for him, I'd wager he'd throw in a good stud. Probably ol' Buck."

"And just why would I do this?"

He looked at me then.

"To get out of Six Shooter Siding and the White Dove."

Anger flared. *He* didn't want me living there? He'd ask around? He didn't want? He. He. He. What right did he have telling me what to do? I spit back at him.

"Well pardon me, sir, but the last time I checked, my welfare was none of your concern. In fact, you made it more than plain you didn't want to be burdened with me. Besides, I thought you liked Della."

"I do like her. Admire her grit. Like all her girls too. But

I don't like the business they're in." He twisted in the saddle. "It's —

"Not respectable enough for ya'? Didn't think you were a snob."

Dark eyes flashed like black lightning.

"I didn't say that. Their life is bitter, Dixie. Hard. Dangerous. Often violent. Della does her best to protect her girls. Keeps them and The Dove clean. But the cold, hard truth of the matter is most Doves die young. Either from disease or some cowboy who gets too rough with them. Remember how Donnie Ray slapped Abby around? That's tame compared to what some men do."

I thought about Payton, and my voice lost its bite.

"I'm not a Dove."

"I know that and Della knows that. But some dusty cowpoke who's been on the Santa Fe for months don't know that. Face it. You live at a whore house, Dixie. You associate with soiled women. I don't want some drunk yahoo kicking down your door in the middle of the night, pawing, fondling, and taking advantage of you."

The raw emotion in his voice pinned me to the saddle. His gaze returned to the ranch.

"I've seen you with horses. You have a special way with them. You're smart. And just stubborn enough to build this ranch up into something big." He turned back to me.

"True, there are things out here that can harm too. Wolves. Cougars. Snakes. Cold winters. Hot, dry summers. I have no doubt you can hold your own with them. But men are a different kind of animal. Deceiving. Ruthless. Cruel."

Once more, my thoughts turned to Payton then jumped to the outlaws who had raped and killed Jackson's family. I swallowed hard.

"Dixie, I'm not trying to run your life or tell you what to do. I'd just sleep better knowing you were away from all of that. Promise me you'll think about the ranch."

Well hell. How could I stay angry at him for caring so

much?

"I'll think on it."

Satisfied, he sighed deeply. Heavy, uncomfortable silence hung in the air between us. Truth be known, I didn't want him to go. I'd gotten used to his strength and calm ways. His steadiness tamed the panic always lurking under my skin.

"Guess you'll be leaving now?" I asked a little too cool.

"Reckon so."

Papa's voice whispered in my ear. *Ask him to stay, girl.*

I couldn't.

"Well, I'm burning daylight." He touched the brim of his Stetson. "Take care of yourself, darlin'."

And just like he rode away. Again.

CHAPTER 32

Jackson resisted the urge to turn back.

He had a mission to complete. A duty to see the wagon train through to California. To keep folks safe.

But he would've stayed.

Morgan and Payton had to answer for their crimes. He was a Pinkerton. Hired to bring outlaws to justice. Besides, he needed to get proof Payton murdered Dixie's mother. He'd promised her he'd hang, and he wasn't going back on his word.

But he would've stayed.

He was a lawman. Sworn to uphold the law.

Didn't matter.

He would've stayed. For her.

All she had to do was ask him not to go.

He would've stayed.

But she never said the words.

Chapter 33

I leaned back in the saddle and gave Joe his head. He placed one careful hoof in front of the other and picked his way down the ridgeline. The sharp crack of iron shoes against rock echoed through the quiet woods. I patted his brown and white neck when we reached the flats for a job well done. Wished I had a persimmon to reward him with.

We trotted through the gate and under a sign with faded letters. I strained to see the name of the old ranch. The Double D. Ghosts of wild mustangs and leathery wranglers floated past like feathers in the wind.

I stepped down from Joe's back and led him to a well that stood by the house. Surprised to find a good rope and bucket sitting on the rocked edge, I dropped the pail into the blackness. A loud splash followed. The old pulley squeaked and groaned but drew smooth. I tasted the water. Cool and clean. Joe drank with long slurps while my gaze traveled from the house across the yard to the barn and corrals.

What a shame. A once-proud outfit left to rot in the wind and rain. Papa's voice rang out so clearly, I expected to see him standing before me.

Can still be a fine ranch, lassie. With a little elbow

*grease and good stock, ye can build it back grander than
ever.*

"Oh, Papa. I can't. Not alone."

I said his name out loud. Feeling foolish I glanced
around. Only phantoms of chaps, spurs, and lariats heard
my cry. A feeling of great loss and self-pity washed over
me. I sank to the dust. Why did all the men I cared about
ride away from me?

Stop your moaning, lass. Papa came to me again. *'Twas
your mother's selfishness what pushed me out the door and
your stubborn pride what chased that fine boyo down the
trail. You're never alone. I be by your side always.*

I could almost see his wink.

My back straightened. What was wrong with me? Damn
kiss scrambled my thinking. Softened my resolve. I didn't
need Jackson Wayne or anyone else to save my hide. I was
strong enough to take care of myself.

I stumbled to my feet. Fate was a funny thing. Papa lost
his dream of a horse ranch only for it to land right back into
my lap. I would do this. For Papa. For his memory. His
love.

My boot found stirrup leather. I touched spur to flank.
Needed to hurry.

I had a ranch to buy.

CHAPTER 34

Hubert Lee Rutherford of Rutherford Land Bank gawked at me from behind his polished desk, with a look of amusement on his puffy face so severe it teetered on ridicule. I wanted to spit in his eye.

"Let me get this straight, Miss . . . um . . . Dandelion, is it? You want to buy the old Double D? A worthless, once-upon-a-dream horse ranch in the hopes of restoring it to its former owner's unrealized potential?"

"That's right."

"May I ask what experience you have with horse ranching?"

"I helped Papa with his."

"And when was that?"

"A few years ago."

A tiny smirk pulled his lips. "I see. That would have made you all of what? Ten? Eleven years old? Miss Dandelion, I'm truly sorry. But I don't see how this institution can help you. We simply can't afford to loan money to someone with no business experience or creditability. I'm sure you understand."

The urge to condemn him to hell itched something fierce. Instead, I asked myself what would Mama do? I smiled brightly and gushed sticky sweet.

"Well of course I do, Mr. Rutherford. After all, it's only sound business practice, and I can tell you are an intelligent businessman. Furthermore, I'm sure that me being an unmarried woman has nothing to with your decision at all. Does it?"

Faking a false look of offense, he shot back, "I assure you, Miss Dandelion, it does not."

Bullshit.

Still oozing warmth and politeness. I continued.

"I am so relieved to hear this as I did not come to borrow your bank's money but instead to pay for the property outright. In addition, I do not expect to pay one penny over seventy-five dollars for let's see, how did you so elegantly put it? A once-upon-a-dream horse ranch?"

Whoa. That got the ol' sidewinder's attention. His sneer vanished.

"Seventy-five dollars? That's ridiculous. That ranch consists of fifty acres of prime pastureland, not to mention a creek of the purist water that has never been known to go dry even in the hottest of summers."

"And yet you called it worthless."

"Well, I . . . I . . . was confused. Had it mixed up with another piece of land. I apologize. I misspoke."

Pompous jackass.

"Quite understandable, Mr. Rutherford, as I assume this institution is responsible for numerous properties as it's the only bank within forty miles of here. Nevertheless, it is well-known the property in question has been vacant for two years with nary a nibble of an offer to buy. In addition, it will require quite a lot of attention which will strain my pocketbook. I can't possibly go any higher than seventy-five dollars."

"And I can't go any lower than two hundred."

On the sly, I pulled a hundred-dollar note from my boot. I called his bluff.

"One hundred dollars. Cash money. Take it or leave it."

His bushy eyebrow twitched. But only for a minute. He stood and offered me his hand.

"Congratulations, Miss Dandelion. You just bought yourself a horse ranch."

I shook with him.

Papa wasn't the only one kissed by the blarney stone. I would've paid three hundred.

CHAPTER 35

Signed deed in hand, I walked until I was out of eyesight from the bank then ran full bore to the White Dove. A few skips away, the sight of Dominique being carried down the street in the arms of the biggest, darkest man I'd ever seen stopped me dead in my tracks.

Unable to open the back door of the Dove with Dominique and all her fluffy petticoats in his arms, the giant banged the wood door with a boot large enough to sail the Mississippi in. I rushed past and swung the door open. Abby jumped backed up with a tiny squeal. Sassy grabbed her by the arm and yanked her out of the way.

"What's going on here?" Della asked calmly as an afternoon nap. As if seeing Goliath standing in her kitchen was a common, everyday occurrence.

"Now, don't y'all frets none. The little lady just turned her ankle is all."

I expected a small twister to come roaring from his mouth and bust all the windows out, but his voice purred velvet smooth like a spoiled mama cat.

"Bring her into the sitting room," Della said. She fluffed the pillows on the settee. "You can put her here."

Gentle as setting down a basket of eggs, he eased

Dominique onto the sofa.

"'Tis nothing, Mama Della," Dominique said. "Do not worry so."

Della was having none of it. "Must be serious if you had to be carried here."

Dominique's face took on a strange expression. All sappy and tender. Her eyes threw off a funny look too. Helpless-like. She smiled up at the large man. "Ah, Della, I told this gentleman not to carry me, but he wouldn't hear of it."

By this time, the rest of the girls crowded into the room. Sassy came from the kitchen with hot water and a washcloth. Steam rose from the pan and dampened Della's rouge as she eased Dominique's shoe off and dabbed at her foot.

"It don't look bad at all. How did this happen?"

"It was my fault, ma'am." The giant removed his hat and twisted the brim in his grizzly paws. "We was walking toward one another and she turned her ankle trying to keep from running right smack into me. Everythin' been all right ifn' I'd kept on walking, but I couldn't.

Ain't seen no woman so beautiful before. Her beauty froze me to the spot."

"Mon Cher, it was I who was stunned. Never have I seen a man so handsome."

If Sassy's eyebrow arched any higher, it would've jumped right off her face. Mary Louise twittered. Abby giggled. Della grinned like a possum. What was going on here?

Della got to her feet. "Name's Della Williams. Thank you, Mr. . . ?

"Abraham Hayes, ma'am."

"You a Buffalo Soldier?"

It was then I noticed his faded blue cavalry jacket.

"Not anymore, ma'am."

His gaze traveled the room, drinking in the stylish

furniture, elegant rugs, and thick curtains. Shifting his weight from one foot to the other, I sensed his uneasiness. So did Della.

"These here are my girls, Mr. Hayes." She pointed to each one. "Sassy, Mary Louise, Abby, Pearl, and Rosie. And, of course, you already met Dominique."

He flashed a wide grin. "Yes, 'em. I know her all right."

I swear all of them sighed as one.

"You understand my meaning when I say *my* girls?"

It's not easy to see a blush on skin blacker than midnight, but a tinge of dark red traveled up his neck. His gaze never left Della's face.

"I do."

"That bother you?"

"Ain't no business of mine. The world's a hard place. Gotta make your way through as best as ya'can."

Della ushered him to the door. "Thank you again, Mr. Hayes, for your kindness. You're welcome at the White Dove anytime."

Judging how fast that dark-red color had spread, I'd bet good money Abraham Hayes wouldn't be stepping back into the Dove any time soon. Then again, the grin he shot Dominique on his way out and the shy smile she gave in return might cost me.

The door hadn't closed all the way shut before Sassy gave Dominique a playful punch on the arm. "You can stop pretending now, Little Miss Innocent."

"He's a keeper for sure." Della chuckled. "I'd throw a loop over him right quick before someone other gal snubs him up tight."

Confused, I didn't understand their laughter. After everyone except Dominique left the room, I sat down beside her. "Your ankle isn't hurt, is it?"

Long stocking legs swung to the floor. "Only, how you say? A teeny bit?"

"Then why did you let him carry you?"

"Oh, Dixcee, you have much to learn in the ways of men."

What the hell did that mean?

She patted my hand and sighed. "A man needs to feel needed."

"You're sweet on him, aren't you?"

"Oui."

That quick? "Why? How? I mean, you've been with . . .seen . . .um . . . met a lot of men. What makes this one so different?"

Little shoulders shrugged. "It is not so easy to put into words, Cheri. Is true. I've had many paramours. This is good. No?"

"No."

She laughed. "Is good. No man can hide from me. Pull the wool over my eyes as you say. Before a man's kiss dries upon my lips, I know his good. His evil. If he will raise his hand to caress or to slap. I have looked inside this Abraham Hayes. His heart is gold. More golden than any before him. It shines only for me. It is no matter what I did before him."

"Guess it doesn't hurt none that he's a good-looking fella either."

"Frosting on the cake."

"So, you pretended to be hurt so he could rescue you. Kinda like those knights in shining armor. Isn't that a little deceiving?"

"Oui. But of course. All is fair in love and war, is it not? Do you not feel the same for your man? Your Jackson?"

She hit a sore spot. I changed the subject.

"Does Abraham plan to stay here?"

"I cannot say. Only hope. I do not wish to see him go."

An idea popped into my head. "Thanks for the talk. Didn't understand most of it. But I gotta' git."

I ignored her shout and ran out the door. I needed to find Abraham. Where would he go? The saloon? Something told me no. The Livery? Of course. An ex-horse soldier would take care of his mount before himself. Sure enough, I found him in the barn unsaddling the ugliest strawberry roan I'd ever seen.

"I know what you're thinkin'."

His back was turned from the door. How he'd heard my footsteps on the straw-littered floor was beyond me.

"Doubt it."

He chuckled. "You's thinkin' ol' Mud here is pitiful looking. I ask ya' not to say that out loud. He's sensitive. He'll pout."

This time I chuckled. I walked over and straightened the gelding's forelock.

"Is his name really Mud?"

"Yep." He patted the horse's speckled neck. "I found him when he was a little bugger lying in the mud. His mammy just done up and left him to die. My heart damn near bust. Felt so sorry for the little thing."

"So you raised him?"

"Best thing I ever done. He's carried me loyal for many a mile."

He sounded so much like Jackson talking about Buck my heart flipped-flopped.

"Miss Dominique send you?"

"No. I came to offer you a job."

He turned to me. Astonishment turned ebony eyes round and white.

"At the White Dove?"

"Oh. No. Ya don't understand. I don't work at the White Dove. I just live there, that's all. I'm a cook for Big Finn Donovan's rail crew."

Astonishment turned to disbelief. He eyed me close. "A cook you say?"

"Well, sure. Why? Don't I look like one?"

"You any good?"

I hesitated. "Just fair."

"What I thought. Sorry about the other. I just assumed since you were at the Dove that you were one on the flock."

Jackson's worst fear.

"What sort of job you offering? I don't cotton much to railroad work."

"It's not the railroad." I dug in my pocket and showed him the deed. "I just bought a

horse ranch. Wondered if you might be interested in being my foreman. Before you answer, I have to warn ya. The place needs a lot of work before I can even think about bringing in a herd."

He leaned against the stall gate and chewed on a hay stem. "Do I look like a ranch hand to you?"

I couldn't tell right off if he was funning me or not. Decided just to lay my cards on the table and shoot straight. "You look like an honest, hardworking man. Besides, Dominique said you're golden, and that's good enough for me."

Damn. I shouldn't have said that. Dominique would skin me alive. But when he broke out into the biggest grin I'd ever seen, it didn't matter.

"She said that?"

"Yeah. But don't tell her I told ya'."

"Our secret."

"I think you should see the ranch first before answering me. It's only a few miles out of town. We could ride out tomorrow afternoon and look at it, if that'll work for you." I voiced another thought. "If you had a job, you'd have a reason to stay here."

"Reckon Miss Dominique would like that?"

Oui. But of course. "Yeah, pretty sure she would."

"Then I sees ya' tomorrow."

"Oh. By the way. My name is Dixie. Dixie Dandelion." It was my turn to study him from head to toe. "You do know how to break horses, don't ya'?"

He pushed his hat back off his head. His look turned

serious.

"Well now, Miss Dixie. Let me tells ya' what I believe concerning the horse. Ya' see, those mighty animals ain't got much but their wild, beautiful spirit. If'n ya' break their will, all you're left with is hide and hair. Nope. I don't break horses. I just bends them a little. It takes a might longer that way. But it's better for them and me. Makes them loyal to the bone. Plus, they get to keep their dignity. Leaves their unspoiled beauty intact."

In that moment, I understood exactly what Dominique had been trying to tell me.

CHAPTER 36

"Missy Dixie no cook for Chow Ling no more?"

It was bittersweet breaking the news about the ranch to Chow-Chow. Ever since the shootout at the One-Eyed Jack, the two of us had developed a special bond. I wouldn't call it a huge friendship, however. More of a mutual respect that only a secret as big as what happened to the bodies could forge. I would miss his singsong voice. On the other hand, I wasn't going to miss wrestling with flour and dough every morning one bit. Chow Ling's eyes crinkled at the corners.

"Only hope Missy Dixie better with horse than rolling pin. You tell big boss man?"

"No. I haven't seen him around lately."

"Big boss man berry busy. All time."

Sure seemed that way. Sassy said the Railroad hired the big Pinkerton detective to keep the peace between the town folk and the Chinese. Guess it worked because I never saw any hard feelings between the two. Still, I wondered if there was a deeper reason for him being around.

I finished up in the cook tent and went to saddle Joe. Abraham and Mud stood waiting for me. Dominique sat behind him in the saddle.

"I hopes you don't mind me bringing Miss Dominique along. I stopped by to check on her this morning. When I told her where we was headed, she said a ride in the country would do her mighty good."

I struggled to hide my grin. Dominique rarely went outside. In fact, her idea of the country was the tree in Della's backyard. She also claimed she wouldn't be caught dead on horseback. Now, here she was aside Mud's wide rump, arms around Abraham's waist holding tight. Too tight for just standing still. Reckon love fever burns away all thoughts of things ya swore you'd never do.

The early afternoon sun peeked through big, fluffy clouds and a breeze ticked my face as we jogged along. I listened to the small talk between Abraham and Dominique. Their voices carried more than a friendly tone. Sometimes coy. Sometimes serious. A small chuckle here. Carefree laughter there. Falling-in-love talk.

Their comfortable, easy way with one another called back memories of Jackson. I should've asked him to stay. Irritated for mooning over him like a newborn calf and tired of hearing Dominique's oohing and cooing, I spurred Joe into a lope.

When we rode through the gate of the old Double D, I studied the place with new eyes. Before, the place had belonged to some unknown rancher with hopes and dreams of turning corrals and barns into a thriving, top-notch outfit. Now, his dream was mine. Wonder if in some odd way, he'd bequeathed his vision to me in a fit of ghostly passion?

Bequeathed, my arse. I persuaded the ol' narky to move on. To stop haunting the place. That'll be my job from now on.

I heard Papa's booming laugh. Bet the floors of heaven were shaking.

We tied up at the hitching rail in front of the house. Dominique's waist disappeared in Abraham's big hands when he lifted her from Mud's back easy as picking up a bag of goose feathers. If he noticed how firm she stood on that bad ankle of hers, he never let on.

"I will see to the house while Dixcee shows you the barn. Oui? Mon Cher"

I'd wager good money an Oklahoma cyclone would have a hard time knocking Abraham to his knees, but Dominique's little French term of endearment melted him like butter in a hot skillet. Sure hoped the stars in his eyes disappeared in time for him to inspect the place.

My nose wrinkled at the smell of moldy hay and sour grain when we stepped into the barn. Cobwebs covered the rafters and waved hauntingly in the easy breeze. It was plain to see nothing but field mice and crawly spiders called the old barn home. Even still, the loft had no holes in the floor when I scampered up the ladder and tested its soundness. Same way with the stalls.

Outside, the corrals needed new wood. But the bunkhouse wasn't falling to pieces like I'd feared. Relief washed over me. All in all, the place was in pretty good shape. Of course, I hadn't seen the main house yet.

Abraham took in every detail without saying a word. His face, blank as a schoolhouse blackboard. I worried he would turn down the job.

"Miss Dixie? You got yourself a fine little ranch here."

"Does that mean you'll take the job?"

"Under one condition."

My breath caught. Couldn't imagine what he would ask. "Which is?"

"I need my own place. My own cabin. Bunkhouse won't do."

Was that all?

"Well shoot, Abraham, that isn't a problem. But may I ask why?"

I had no idea giants could turn giddy. All shy and skittish. He lowered his gaze to the ground and studied the toe of his boot until I thought it would fall off. He raised his gaze and looked at me square.

"Well, ma'am, I'm fixing on getting hitched."

Married? To who? He'd only been in Six Shooter two days. Then it dawned me. I couldn't help but shout, "To Dominique?"

He flinched at my outburst. "Shhh. I ain't asked her yet."

"When are you going to ask?"

"Well, I don't rightly know. I have to work up to poppin' the question nice and gentle like. A fine lady like her needs to be courted proper."

I could live to be old as dirt and never hear the words fine lady describe a Dove ever again. Deep down, Abraham was just an ol' romantic. But something still niggled at me.

"Abraham? How? You only saw her for the first time yesterday. How can you fall in love so fast? How do you know she's the one for you?"

"Miss Dixie, Mama had The Shine. Does you know what that is?"

Oh hell yes. I knew exactly what the Shine was. Grandmother Margaret had the gift of sight. Papa said I had the gift too. But I never saw anything. I did hear voices. All the time. But I never saw haints. Didn't want to either. Sometimes I did sense things before they happened, but not often. Truth be known, I never gave The Shine much thought.

"You mean your mama saw Dominique in a vision?"

"Seen her in a dream. Told me when I was just a little scraper, I'd grow up and marry a woman with skin the color of creamed coffee, soft doe eyes, and teeth whiter than snow. She said I'd know the minute I took hold of her hand that we was destined to be together. That it was written in the stars."

"Your mama ever wrong?"

"Mama was never wrong."

Huh. Written in the stars. I remembered Flying Eagle's story of the star lovers. About Jackson and me. Maybe there was more truth in that story than myth.

"Dixcee. Come see. The house is magnifique."

Dominique bounced across the yard like one of those strange kangaroo animals I'd seen once in a picture book. Face flushed with excitement. Bright eyes shining like new pennies. Sure-footed as a mountain goat. I saw Abraham try to stifle a grin. Right then and there, I knew Dominique's little twisted ankle ruse hadn't fooled him one bit. *Oh, the games lovers play.*

Why Dominique thought the house was magnificent was beyond me. Buckets of dirt everywhere, rat's nests in every corner, and a smell that'd make a polecat turn tail and run slapped me full in the face.

"Dominique, you're loco. I've seen inside of caves better than this."

"Is because you look with your eyes, Cheri. You must see with your heart. Here. I will show you. Take my hand."

She led me from room to room starting with the bedroom. "The rooms are full of, how you say? Possibilities? Rich curtains, a canopy bed, mirrors, and voila.. A bedchamber fit for a queen. The sitting room with soft couches, rocking chairs, pillows, and a thick rug will soften the hardwood feel. Make a comfortable home. Oh, Dixcee, you will see. We will scrub and sweep. I will help. No?"

"It does sound good, but where am I going to get frilly curtains and rugs? Not to mention all that furniture?"

"Is no problem. I am sure Della will give you what you need."

"From the White Dove? Doubt it. She needs all that stuff."

"Oh, I forget. You do not know."

I didn't like the sound of that.

"Know what?

"Dixcee, I am sorry. Della has closed the doors. The White Dove is no more."

Chapter 37

I don't know what galloped the fastest, Joe or my heart. I bust through the back door of the Dove. Caught Della at the kitchen table.

"Why didn't you tell me you sold the White Dove?"

"Why didn't you tell me you bought a ranch?"

"Well, I was headed here to tell all of ya. Then a huge Buffalo Soldier carried Dominique through the door and everything went to hell in a handbasket."

"Same here. Now settle down, and I'll explain."

I didn't wait for her explanation.

"You told me you'd never sell The White Dove."

Even I could tell my words came out too snappish. I deserved Della's irritated sigh.

"To Daggett. I told you I'd never sell to Daggett. Besides, I didn't sell The Dove. You gonna' listen now instead of acting like I strangled the neighbor's cat?"

She pulled up a chair and sunk heavily onto it. "There are two reasons why I *closed* the Dove. First. The railroad is almost finished. Folks will be moving west. Good folks who will not tolerate establishments like The White Dove. Better to quit on my terms instead of being run out of town on a rail. Second. I'm tired. Old and tired. Dixie, the type of business we Doves are in takes its toll."

Jackson had said the same thing. He had an aggravating habit of being right about a lot of things. The catch in Della's voice jarred my thoughts back to her.

"I've come to think of all my girls as family. Wayward daughters, I admit. But daughters nonetheless. I don't want to see any of them abused or sick. And I especially don't want to be responsible for burying any of them or them burying me."

I understood. I thought of Della and her girls as my family too. What was to become of them? "Does this mean you're leaving Six Shooter?"

"No. I'm not leaving. I bought a new place. The One-Eyed Jack as a matter of fact."

"What! Daggett's old stomping grounds?"

"The very same. Funny, ain't it? Got plans to turn it into an Opera House. Bring in singers and actors. Make it a top-notch, respectable place."

"But. What's going to happen with Sassy? And Abby? And..."

"I asked them to come with me, but they refused. Sassy has plans to marry Big Finn Donavon, settle down, and raise young'uns. Can you imagine?"

I gasped. "I had no idea she wanted a family. Can't you just see her? Dressed head to toe in peacock feathers, pushing a baby pram down the sidewalk? Wonder if Finn has any idea what's in store for him?"

"Oh, I hope not. It'd ruin all the fun."

We both laughed.

"I have some news about marriage as well. Abraham Hayes told me he's going to ask Dominique to be his wife."

Della leaned back in her chair and slapped her knee.

"Well, if that don't beat all. Always figured I'd lose Mary Louise and Abby to matrimony but never Sassy and Dominique. Just goes to show you how much I know."

"Abraham is going to be my foreman. He's going to

build his own cabin. Reckon he and Dominique will live at the ranch. That takes care of Sassy and Dominique, but what about the rest? What will they do?"

"Did you know Mary Louise can cipher in her head quicker than I can on paper? Numbers come easy to her. Abby cooks like she was born with a spoon in her hand. Pearl and Rosie can . . . well, I'm not sure what they can do. If they were men, they could find work as farmhands. It ain't easy for ex-Doves to find respectable jobs. They're judged before they even get a chance to prove themselves."

Sometimes ideas jump into my head from out of the blue. This was one of those times.

"Della. I just had a brainstorm. Can you round up all the girls and have them meet me here tonight?"

"Well, sure. They're still here at the Dove. I ain't thrown them out on their ear, ya know. Come by around suppertime. We'll have our last meal together."

A picture of Jesus and the Last Supper flashed through my head.

Sure hoped my idea turned out better than his.

CHAPTER 38

I glanced around the kitchen table with high hopes dancing a jig with the butterflies in my belly. My plan was a huge gamble. No one had tried it before, or I'd never heard of anyone doing it. If it succeeded, we'd be in high cotton. If not? I didn't want to think about that right now.

Abraham sat beside Dominique. So close he'd might as well been in her hip pocket. It was only fitting he'd be here as the plan would affect him almost as much as me. Every eye trained on me. Sweat tickled my armpits. Stupid to be nervous. These were my friends. My family. But my idea was wild and woolly.

"Y'all know I've bought the old Double D. I plan to turn it into a profitable horse ranch. I'll admit the place needs fixing up, but it isn't as bad as I first thought. With a lot of work, I figure I can stock it in a month. Two at the most. I've hired Abraham as my foreman. Problem is, I don't have any hands he can ramrod. That's why I wanted to talk to all of you tonight." I took a deep breath.

"I want to hire you for my ranch hands."

I expected a burst of guffaws and laughs.

I got stone-cold silence instead.

Head pounding, I rushed on, looking each square in the

eye.

"Mary Louise? Della tells me you're good with numbers, and cyphering. I was taught sums and can manage them. But I hate them something fierce. I'm going to need a good bookkeeper. Someone I can trust. I'm offering you the job.

"Abby? Ain't no secret I can't boil water and spit at the same time. How would you like to cook for the ranch?

"Pearl? Rosie? You'd work with the mares and foals. Feeding. Watering. Birthing. That sort of thing. All of us would have to work together at branding and round-up time. I can teach you to ride and rope. Abraham and I can handle the breaking and training. Sounds loco, I know. Never heard of an all-woman outfit before. But why not? We're strong. Smart. And have nothing to lose."

Plumb out of steam, I sucked in a breath and waited.

"Dixcee, I am in love with this idea. It is bold. Exciting. Just like you. But. You did not say what I can do?"

I shot Abraham a look that would melt lead. Didn't want to steal his thunder, but I needed to tell Dominique something.

"Miss Dixie, I'll answer that," Abraham said.

I knew what was fixin' to happen. My heart flopped over.

He turned toward Dominique.

"Miss Dominique? I was waiting for the right time. Guess this is it. You's gonna' help me. Stand by my side. Keep me square. Keep me loving every day because I have you in my life."

All of us stopped breathing.

"You are asking me to marry you? Oui?"

"If'n you'll have me."

I never, ever thought I'd see tough, little Dominique cry. But she did. Buckets. She threw her arms around Abraham's thick neck and dang near kissed his lips dry.

"Well. Guess that answers that," Sassy said.

Laughter made all the feelings I had bottled up inside me bust wide open. Tears. Smiles. Hugs. Congratulations. Damnation. My head spun. After the commotion settled down, Sassy lit up a cheroot and glared at me.

"Okay, Dixie girl. Where do I stand in all of this?"

"Well, Della told me you were throwing a rope over Big Finn and tying the knot. Didn't think you'd be interested."

Shouldn't have said that. All hell broke loose again. Hoops. Hollers. Congratulations and kisses.

"This calls for a drink," Della said.

A bottle of tequila made its way around the table. I didn't dare to even smell the cork.

"Dixie? Did you really mean it when you said I could help with the foals?"

"Why sure, Pearl. Is that ok?"

Tears spilled over and ran down her chubby face. My heart shriveled like a dried raisin.

"Pearl? Did I say something wrong? You don't have to take care of them. I'll find something else for you to do. Please. Don't cry."

"No. You don't understand." She downed a shot. Rosie placed a hand on her twin's shoulder and nodded like she was giving permission for something.

"Ma left Rosie and me when we was young. Our step-pa treated us bad. Real bad. Said we deserved it 'cause we ate too much. Was too big. Too ugly. That Ma runned away because she hated the sight of us. Told us over and over how God-fearing, decent men would never want us for their own. Said we was good for only thing. Reckon you can figure out what that was without any trouble. You hear things like that all your life, you start to believe it. We was soiled before we had time to be pure. We became Doves. 'Cause that's all we thought we was good for."

Della pushed back from the table and walked to the window. Her hands gripped the iron sink so hard her knuckles turned white.

"Your step-daddy still alive?" Abraham's voice oozed venom.

"No. Caught the fever and died. Suffered real bad."

"Good."

"Anyways, when we could get away from him, we'd run and hide at the neighbor's farm. We'd sneak into their barn and spend the day in the hayloft. We watched mama horses, cows, pigs, and cats take care of their babies. Them mamas didn't give two hoots and a holler about how their young'uns looked. They could be as ugly as the devil's scaly butt. Didn't matter. They loved them because they were their own flesh and blood. I know it sounds silly. But watching them love on their little ones made us feel better. Always been partial to animals. They love true. And now, because of you, we have a chance to give that comfort back."

Up until this moment, I could count the number of times Pearl spoke to me on one hand. Rosie less than that. They always stood in the background. Quiet as church mice. Tonight, the dam broke. Pearl talked a full-blown book. *What do you say after hearing something like that?* I just wanted to curl in a corner and cry. Guess everyone felt the same way. Silence threw a wet blanket over us. Mary Louise's little wren's voice broke the spell.

"What are we going to name our new ranch?"

Chapter 39

"This is so exciting," Abby squealed. "I never thought I'd be a part of something so grand. What's the ranch look like, Dixie?"

"Can we all ride out tomorrow and look at it?"

My mouth damn near hit the tabletop. Rosie's question floored me. I'd never seen her take one step away from the White Dove. Now she wanted to ride into fresh air and woods?

"Oh, I can't wait till morning," Mary Louise said. "Draw us a picture of it now, Dixie."

"I agree," Sassy said. "Let's get this table cleared."

"I'll get paper and pencil," Della said. "Then I'll put a pot of coffee on. This is shaping up to be one hell of a night."

"Oui. Is like Christmas Eve. No?"

Damnation. Plates, cups, and saucers dang near grew wings and flew from the table into soapy water. Hands moved so fast washing, drying, and stacking, it made me dizzy. Soon the aroma of fresh coffee filled the air. Excitement, joy, and anticipation bounced off the walls. I caught the fever. I pushed the paper over to Abraham.

"You draw it out, Abraham. I can't think straight right

now."

Seven heads studied the picture Abraham drew. Every breath latched on to his words. "Ya ride through this here gate. It's rusty and faded, but paint and a little grease will fix it fine. The main house sits off aways. Got a good well beside it. Over here is the barn."

"How many stalls?"

"What about the hayloft?"

"Where are you going to get the horses?"

"Can we have chickens? A barn cat?"

"Where are we going to stay?"

"You got enough money for all of this?"

Questions whizzed past my head faster than bullets. I raised my hands in mock surrender.

"Stop! Give me a chance."

They settled down. Eagerness flushed every cheek to a rosy glow.

"First of all, the horses are the least of our worries. I got them taken care of.

"Second thing. The barn. Right now, there are six stalls." I glanced over at Abraham. "If hard-pressed, we can squeeze in a few more."

He nodded in agreement.

"Third. The hayloft is sound. Tested it myself. Finally. Of course we'll have chickens. Plan on cows, maybe even a goat or two. And most definitely barn cats. Can't have mice around."

"May I have a kitten?"

Oh God. I damn near died. I watched the faces around the table. All of them blinked back tears. We knew Pearl's timid request was more than just a plea for a pet. It was a shout-out to be loved by something be it human or animal. To be accepted for who she was. Hell, I'd give her the whole damn litter if she wanted. I cleared my throat. Tried to keep my voice light.

"Sure. As many as you want."

"Dixie? How you gonna' pay for all this?"

Mary Louise was already working as the bookkeeper. I did a fast total in my head of the notes I still had tucked in my boot. Because I'd gotten the ranch so cheap, I had enough money for repairs, provisions, and payroll. Payroll? Never thought I'd be thinking about that.

"I should have enough to cover us for a while."

"Dare I ask how you got that much cash?" Della asked.

"Nope."

She smiled. "You need to start talking to the Army and Stagecoach lines now about buying horses."

"Sassy! That's it!"

"That's what?"

"Your job. You can be my go-between. My voice. Broker deals and contracts. Not only for horse sales but for feed and equipment too. Why, the way you wheel and deal, not to mention flirt and twist men around your little finger, you'd be perfect. That would free me up to concentrate on the horses. It's perfect."

"I like the sound of that. You got a deal."

"But where are we going to live?" Mary Louise interrupted.

"There's a bunkhouse."

"Bunkhouse?"

Their noses wrinkled and twitched. I felt panic crawl up my gullet. If not the bunkhouse, then where? I couldn't afford to build cabins for all of them.

"I can helps you there, Miss Dixie. I's seen the bunkhouse. It's got room for at least ten to fifteen men. I can makes rooms for y'alls."

"Won't that be a lot of work, Abraham?"

"Don't think so. I's just build some walls so each can have their own little room."

"Oh, Cheri, such a wonderful idea," Dominique chimed in. "Perhaps a small sitting room in the middle?"

"I'll give you all the furniture you want," Della said.

"Consider it my contribution to the loco notion."

I couldn't believe my ears. "Are you sure, Della?"

"Well hell yes, I'm sure. I ain't got no use for this swanky stuff no more."

"The bathtubs too?" A second passed before laughter started. Dear, sweet Abby.

"Don't see why not."

"How does all this sound?" I asked. Fingers and toes crossed.

Mary Louise spoke up. "Isn't much different than the White Dove, is it?"

"Oui. Is true. The spirit of the White Dove lives on."

"Dominique, you just named the ranch."

"What name, Cheri?"

"Spirit Dove Ranch."

Everyone shouted at once. "Yeehaw! Let's drink to Spirit Dove Ranch."

Coffee can be a toast same as tequila. Thank God.

"We need a brand."

"A white Dove. Oui?"

"Too hard to make," I said.

"Why not an olive branch?"

I gawked at Abraham.

"Hear me out now, Miss Dixie, before you say anything. Mama always told me stories from the Good Book. My favorite was Noah and his big boat, the Ark 'cause of the animals he had to round up. She said toward the end, Noah sent out Doves to scout for dry land. One day, the bird came back with an olive branch. That's when Noah made the new world. Don't ya see? That little branch was a sign. A sign of hope. New beginnings. Ain't that what Spirit Dove Ranch is? A chance for better lives? Second changes?"

I fought tears. Lost the battle. I wasn't alone.

"You're right, Abraham. The olive branch is perfect. Just perfect."

I crawled into bed only a few hours before sunup. My head whirled. Feelings had swung me like a yo-yo. Up. Down. Round the world and home again. All of this was too good to be true. Never would've guessed Doves could get so worked up over a ranch.

Right before falling into what I hoped was a deep sleep, I started to giggle. Jackson Wayne would fall off his horse when he saw all of this.

Providing, of course, he ever came back.

CHAPTER 40

For years the only thing Della's girls concerned themselves about was frilly-lace gowns, hair combs, and rouge so thick it took a shovel to hold it all and a buck knife to scrape it off. Trousers, flannel shirts, and boots were as strange to them as petticoats, camisoles, and high-heeled slippers were to me. Papa once said ranch work was too hard for a delicate rose such as Mama. I wondered if that would be the case with the Doves. I needn't have worried.

Unlike Mama, these roses had thorns.

As suspected, Pearl and Rosie took to ranch life like bees take to honey. They blossomed before our eyes. Laughing. Singing. Smiling. Talking like magpies. Between me, Abraham, and the two of them, the stalls and corrals stood brand-spanking new in no time.

Dominique surprised everyone, including herself, with her unexpected eye for color, decorating, and organizing. She, Abby, and Sassy tore through the main house. Scrubbing. Painting. Sweeping. True to her word, Della gave us all the furniture we could use. Big Finn joined in too. His men hauled wagon load after wagon load of tables, chairs, sofas, and crates full of chickens. Much to Abby's delight, Lobo came along too and stayed.

Curtains here. Rugs there. In only weeks, a dirty wood and mud cabin transformed into a soft, inviting cottage.

Working hand-in-hand with Abraham, or more like heart-to-heart, Dominique came up with a plan to remodel the bunkhouse into more of a cute doll house with separate rooms for everyone, complete with bathtubs. In the middle, a small sitting room centered around a potbelly stove big enough to keep the place nice and toasty in the winter.

Mary Louise insisted on painting a new sign, a huge white Dove carrying an olive branch. Took two days to mount it above the gate into the ranch. It was worth the effort. Printed in bold black letters, **Spirit Dove Ranch** loomed impressive.

All of us had our strengths. Separate, we were forceful. Together, we were unstoppable.

"Ye bit off a big piece to chew, lassie. That's for sure," Big Finn said. "Me boys think ye mad. Have bets for and again ya."

"How did you bet?" I asked.

Laughter shook his jelly belly. "I be no fool. I told them if anyone could make a go of an all-female ranch, it would be Dixie Dandelion." He frowned. "But, lass. The real work is yet to come. They be wagering on the horses. Most be saying ya' no can do it. That breaking and training horses coupled with procuring contracts for such horseflesh is a man's game."

"What say you?"

"Considering the fact Sassy is going to make the deals, I be daft to bet agin' ye. Still, keep your Colt and Winchesters handy. Some may not take kindly to ye proving them wrong."

The thought of rustling never entered my mind. After all, horse stealing was a hanging offense. Then again, so was killing, and that still went on.

"You joshing me? You really think they'd cause

trouble?"

"Aye, I do. Come after you, the girls, and the herd. Horses be a serious business, lass."

My temper flared. "I'll shoot every damn one of them that tries it."

"Aye. I have no doubt. Just be aware."

I made a note to stock up on ammunition and rifles. Guess I wouldn't be the only one target practicing.

"Aw, lass. Me boy, Jackson, would be proud of ya'."

Heat rushed up my back and circled my neck.

"Is that what you think? That I did all of this for Jackson Wayne's approval?"

His walrus mustache trembled. "Why, I mean nothing by it, lass. Just sayin'"

"Don't be saying it again. I couldn't give two hoots what he thinks. This ranch is all my doing. He doesn't figure into it."

"Even so, 'tis funny how just the mere mention of his name riles ya' so. Me thinks you miss the lad."

I considered punching him. Thought better of it. Ready to chew nails, I stomped off to the barn. *Stupid, damn Irishman.*

If Abraham noticed my foul mood, he said nothing. Smart man. I took Joe's bridle off the hook on the wall.

"You's headed out, Miss Dixie?"

We're headed out. Throw a saddle on Mud.

"It's time to talk horseflesh."

CHAPTER 41

We rode in silence.

Occasionally I felt Abraham's gaze on me, but he said nothing. I liked that about him. Had the feeling he could read me like a book just like Big Finn could. But, unlike Finn, Abraham had the good sense to keep his mouth shut.

I blew out a long breath. Eyes closed, I breathed in a gulp of wood-scented air. The tension in my shoulders and the pounding in my head died. Damn Irish temper had gotten the best of me yet again. I didn't mean to snap at Donovan. Besides. He was right.

I missed Jackson.

Not a day went by that I didn't think of him. Wondered if he'd found Payton. Worried if he was safe or knee-deep in snow and trouble. But most of all, did he think about me? Miss me?

And yes. More than once, I'd told myself how proud he'd be of me and the ranch. But those thoughts were private. Having them voiced out loud by another person rattled me. If my feelings were that visible, others would think me as vulnerable. I couldn't afford that. Especially now that I'd jumped whole hog into a male-dominated

business. One slip. One sign of weakness
could cost me everything.

"Miss Dixie? Just where *are* these horses?"

Couldn't help but giggle.

Wait till I told him we were heading right-smack dab
into the middle of an Indian village.

CHAPTER 42

Roaring Bear and Abraham eyed one another like two tomcats ready to square off. I understood their mistrust but was in no mood for a pissing contest.

"Roaring Bear, this man works for me and is my friend. Leave him be." I turned to Abraham. "Same goes for you."

Neither one liked being ordered around by a woman, but they backed off just the same. Abraham settled deep in the saddle. His hand was only inches away from his holster.

"Why Foxtail Woman bring Buffalo fighter to village?"

Irritated, I struggled to keep my voice calm. "I told you. He works for me. Besides. He's no longer a soldier."

"Never kilt no Indians, neither," Abraham said. "That don't means I won't."

Holy crow. He just had to throw in that last part. The hairs on Roaring Bear's neck bristled. Desperate to keep peace, I blurted out, "I need horses."

That did the trick. Roaring Bear turned his attention to me. His familiar bear cub grin brightened his dark face.

"Have many horses. What bring to trade?"

Why the sneaky, red-skinned rascal.

Accidentally, on purpose, I knocked my hat off. I knew the sun would fan the flames in my hair. "You owe me a favor. Remember?"

His grin faded.

"Foxtail Woman? Where is Big Wayne?"

Flying Eagle appeared out of nowhere. Was I ever glad to see his leathery face. Ready to hug his neck, I took a step then stopped. Maybe a hug would be stretching our friendship too far.

"He rode off." Even I heard the sadness in my voice.

"He return. No worry."

Gosh, he sounded so sure. "Promise?" I mouthed.

"Hmm. Is foretold in the heavens."

I couldn't help but smile.

"Why you want horses?"

I shifted back to Roaring Bear. "Plan on raising them. Just bought a ranch. But I need a starter herd. Thought maybe you'd give me Buck and a few mares and yearlings?"

"Come. We talk."

I motioned for Abraham to follow. Roaring Bear practically growled. Flying Eagle offered me his hand. "Come too."

I pulled him up behind me in the saddle. Roaring Bear hung back. Thank goodness young bucks respected their elders. Abraham rode up beside me and nodded at Flying Eagle. An unspoken truce formed. An uneasy one for sure, but it was better than nothing.

"Where's Snapping Turtle?" I asked as we rode.

"With ancestors."

The old man's death saddened me. "Does that mean Roaring Bear is the Medicine Man now?"

"Hmm. That is so." He placed my hat back on my head. Hadn't even seen him pick it up. "Fox hair has much power."

Red hair had power. Silly notion. Or was it? Didn't we give power to words chiseled on two stone tablets? Was this really any different?

Joe let out a whinny and pulled at the reins.

In the distance came a high-pitched answer.

The sight of Buck standing lean and muscled against a backdrop of waving grass and blue skies gave me gooseflesh. I wanted to think the big-barreled stallion recognized me. But I knew it was his ol' pal Joe what made the buckskin come on the run.

Only a few feet from us, Buck slowed. I dropped the reins to Joe's neck. Cautious and skittish, the two walked toward one another. One whiff was all it took. Nuzzles. Nips. Small nickers. The two were one again. Had to admit, seeing Jackson's faithful buddy sparked tears to my eyes. Flying Eagle pressed something in my hand.

Persimmons.

I dismounted and offered the treat. Buck plucked the fruit from my hand. Joe crowded in, hunting for his share. I threw my arms around the stallion's gold shoulders and took a good whiff of horse. Buck was so much a part of Jackson I felt like I was hugging a piece of him. Silly. But nevertheless the truth.

The ground rumbled. Buck pulled away. Gave a shrill cry.

His harem of mares circled. Frisky colts pawed the ground. Bucked and kicked in excitement. Abraham's low whistle sounded behind me.

"Miss Dixie. Them's prime horseflesh."

I walked over to Roaring Bear and glanced up. "Tall Warrior has much love for this horse. Thank you for taking good care of him."

Face beaming, Roaring Bear grunted. "Tall Warrior's buckskin make much trouble. Fight with other stallions. Steal mares. I give to Foxtail Woman. Not sad for him to go."

"And the mares?"

A muscle twitched in his jaw. He raised his gaze. Stared off into the distance. I knew I was asking a lot. Horses were valuable to Indians.

But so was my hair.

I could almost hear the arguments in his head. Feel the conflict in his heart. One of those out-of-the-blue thoughts hit me upside the head. I grabbed his reins and led him out of earshot from Abraham and Flying Eagle. Surprise raced across his strong face.

"I need six tame horses as well."

"Foxtail Woman push favor too far."

"Winter must be hard on your people."

Confusion replaced surprise. "Roaring Bear no understand. What is winter to horses?"

"Hear me out. Hunting for food is a big problem in winter, isn't it?"

He nodded.

"You give me Buck and his mares to honor my favor. In exchange for the six tame horses, I'll give you the same number of steers come winter. Their meat and hides should be enough to get your people through the worst part."

He hesitated but only for a moment. "Foxtail Woman half coyote. We have deal."

I marched back to Joe, pretty damned proud of myself. I untied the lariat from my saddle and looped it around Buck's neck. I handed the rope to Abraham.

"The mares will follow Buck back to the ranch. Doubt you'll have any trouble. I'll catch up with you."

"Where's you going?"

"Got to pick up six more horses. Won't take long."

He shook his head. "Miss Dixie. There be times I's think you is the smartest, bravest little woman I's ever knowed. Then there be times I's think you plumb loco. Not sure what I's think right now."

"Want to know a secret, Abraham? At times I think the same thing."

Laughter trailed behind him as he led the horses away.

On the way back to the village, I asked Flying Eagle,

"What did Roaring Bear mean when he said I was half coyote?"

He chuckled. "Coyote is the trickster. Mean you sly. Good trader."

Sure hoped that was true.

I no more had six head of cattle than the man in the moon.

CHAPTER 44

Papa claimed girls and horses went together like corned beef and cabbage.

While it was true a man and his horse were inseparable, a girl and her horse were born with a magical bond no man would ever obtain, let alone understand. Joe and I had this bond. Couldn't put it in words, but it was true, nonetheless. Overnight, this magic touched the Doves and worked its charm. Come morning, every horse had a name.

Sassy's showy gelding was Dancer because, "He prances and dances with every step."

Mary Louise's bay was Jewel. Sounded more like a filly's name to me, but she insisted it was the only one that fit.

Dominique named her dark chestnut Poe after some writer fella who wrote spooky tales.

Pearl and Rosie kept it plain and simple. Bill and Bob. Don't ask which was which.

Last but not least, Abby called her spotted-butt horse Prince Charming —Prince for short. Typical.

Every morning after breakfast was over and done, Abraham worked a few of the wild horses in the catch pen while I taught riding lessons in the big corral. I started with the basics, like feeding, grooming, and how to stop screaming when stepped on. Funny thing. No matter how careful, a horse will eventually stomp on your foot. It's just the nature of things. Just like being thrown off. More than once, Papa said, "If ye nar fall off a horse, it be because ye nar climbed on top of one."

How to saddle up and ride came next. Countless hours of riding in circles taught balance and feel for the horse. First a walk. Not much of a problem.

Then a trot. Butts hit saddles so hard I could hear the slap. Feel the pain.

Finally, a slow lope. Hands tight on the saddle horn. Stirrups lost.

Laughter and cussing.

I had to hand it to them. They were quick learners. Tickled the fire out of me when at last they left sore butts, chafed thighs, and the safety of the round pen behind to gallop, hell-bent for leather.

Flushed and breathless, eyes shining like diamonds, Dominique summed up the feeling.

"Is so exhilarating. Like flying. Is it not, Dixcee?"

Roping was a whole other can of worms. At best, I was only fair. Pearl and Rosie showed us all up. They could shake out and throw a loop after only a few tries. Not really a big surprise there. Much to our amusement, the only thing Abby could rope was herself. She'd twirl and twirl only to have the lariat collapse, twist, and curl around her body like a hemp snake. Abraham laughed till he cried.

Confident enough that none would fall ass-over-teakettle and be trampled to death, Abraham started the branding. It was backbreaking, hot, smelly work. Mary Louise tied a neckerchief around her nose and mouth to keep from gagging from the smell of burnt hair. Dominique's sleek hair curled like lamb's wool from the heat of the fire and branding iron. Abby cried. "You're hurting them poor babies, Dixie."

"Abby, I assure you the brand only stings for a few minutes."

"Says who?"

Good question.

"I just can't watch this, Dixie. It's cruel."

I banished her to the kitchen.

Beat the hell out of me how she could wring the neck off a chicken, cut it up, and fry its ass and liver without blinking an eye, but slap a brand on a horse's rump, and she'd damn near fell into convulsions.

CHAPTER 43

Six women.

Six horses.

Six minutes before I realized teaching flowery-perfumed greenhorns how to rope and ride would be about as easy as teaching pigs to sing. Abraham had it right. Sometimes I was plumb loco.

"They stink, Dixie."

"Well of course they do, Abby. They're wild beasts."

"They're not wild, Mary Louise," I said. "And they're horses. Not beasts."

Six pairs of eyes rolled at the same time.

"If this ranch is going to work, y'all need to at least know what end of a horse eats and what end craps."

"Well, trust me, Dixie gal," Sassy said as she tiptoed around a steaming green pile. "That ain't gonna' be a problem."

Six peals of laughter.

"I went to great lengths matching each horse with your traits," I continued.

"Are they girls or boys?"

Six deep breaths.

"They're boys . . .geldings, Abby."

"Because we are so good at handling men. Oui?"

Six heartbeats before all of us doubled over. My ribs hurt so bad from laughing, I hugged myself to keep them from breaking in half.

"Did God really make one of them just for me?"

Bless Rosie's heart. Her innocent question changed everything. Now each horse was rare. Special. Like a custom-made ring or necklace. No fancy girl can resist having a one-of-a-kind.

"Let's see how good you did with matching us up," Sassy challenged.

I handed her the lead rope tied to a blazed-face sorrel with four white stockings. "I picked this fella for you 'cause he's flashy. Bold. High-spirited."

Her smile told me I'd hit the mark.

"Mary Louise, I chose the little bay for you because he has a gentle soul and kind eyes. Dominique, you get this one." I walked a lanky chestnut over to her. "He's dark as ebony wood and just as mysterious. Like you."

Two blue roans stood side by side, the spitting image of each other. "Pearl? Rosie? These big boys are for you. Both are solid. Dependable. Loyal to the bone. From far away, they mirror each other. But up close, each has a special beauty all their own."

One horse left. A striking Appaloosa with black spots covering his white rump. Earlier, he'd come within a frog's hair of sticking his nose in a hornet's nest instead of his feedbag. Beautiful to look at but a might slow on the uptake.

"Abby, this beauty is for you."

"Because he's so pretty?"

"Well, of course. Why else?"

"Can I give him a bath?"

"You can wash all those black spots off his white ass for all I care."

"Oh, Dixie, I won't scrub him that hard. Promise."

Sixth time that morning I'd counted to ten.

CHAPTER 45

Most afternoons, I took over for Abraham in the catch pen gentling the wildness out of the mares. With winter knocking on the door, Abraham wanted to finish his cabin before the snow flew. Couldn't fault him. He'd been sleeping in the tack room and had reached his limit smelling leather and saddle soap all night. Besides, the quicker he got his home finished, the sooner he and Dominique could be together. Winter hung low over my head too. I still had no cattle for Roaring Bear.

From sunup to sundown, I was too busy to think of Jackson. There were times, however, when I caught Abraham and Dominique walking hand in hand. On good days, I didn't give it a second thought. On fair days, I envied their closeness. On bad days, it made me hornet-buzzing mad. A team of plow mules couldn't pull that confession out of me, but I wasn't fooling Sassy. She'd cock that damn eyebrow of hers and shoot me an all-knowing look. Nine times out of ten, I could shake off the feeling and chalk it up to foolishness. I didn't need a man to complicate my life.

Nighttime called me a liar.

Dog-tired, I'd crawl into bed only to have Jackson Wayne ride through my dreams. Sometimes he'd linger for only a hazy moment. Other times, all night long. I'd wake up grumpy and out of sorts for hours remembering the vision of his cursed dimples waltzing through my head.

It was his fault. He never should've gone. Oh hell. Who was I fooling? I was to blame. One word. I only had to say one word. But for some reason *stay* lodged in my gullet and strangled me.

Della surprised us one morning with a basket of kittens, courtesy of Big Finn's barn cat, Sylvester. As promised, Pearl got first pick of the four. Her heart went out to the runt of the litter, a little calico she named Patches. Scrawny and rib-thin, I prayed the tiny gal would make it. If she died, it would break Pearl's heart. Mine too.

"She needs lots of good milk. Dixie. Get a cow. Now. Today."

"Pearl is right, Dixie," Mary Louise chimed in. "Got plenty of chickens but it's time we got at least one milk cow. A few hogs wouldn't hurt none either. Maybe even a goat."

"Don't forget about them steers neither, Miss Dixie. Don't want Roaring Bear going on the warpath."

"What? You didn't make another deal with that Injun, did you? Ain't it enough you chopped off all your hair for him?"

I wanted to wring Sassy's neck. Yes. Sir. I surely did.

Only two others besides Jackson and Flying Eagle knew the real story behind my short hair. Dominique and Sassy. Didn't have any notion of telling them. The secret just slipped out. 'Course that shot of tequila I had while Dominique tried to style the ragged mess might've had something to do with that. Now, thanks to Sassy's loudmouth, everyone knew. All of them gawked at me like I'd grown mule ears.

"I didn't cut it for the *Injun* and you know it, Sassy. But even if I had, what right do you, of all people, have to judge me?"

I never understood why they were called Doves. These women were tough as boot leather. Hawks or Eagles would've been a better name. Yet, for all their independence and grit, they willingly sold themselves. They allowed slobbering, whiskey-breathed, sweat-drenched strangers to kiss, fondle, pinch, and slap. I told myself what happened behind closed doors was none of my business. They had their reasons. Mainly money. But I'd just as soon clean spittoons for pennies a day than lower myself to such ruin. But here again. That was me. Not them.

I'd never thrown the White Dove in their faces. It hurt me to do so now. I cringed yet stood defiantly. Hard as year-old jerky, Sassy glared at me with smoldering eyes. Then as quickly as the fire had flamed, it went out.

"None. I ain't got none."

I saddled Joe and rode off.

If anyone had the guts to ask me where I was going, I would've claimed target practice. Truth was, I was fed up with the whole situation. I needed to get away. Clear my head. Maybe I stepped over the line. They might all walk out on me. So be it. That was a bluff. I'd be hard-pressed if they left. But the loss of their friendship would trouble me more than having no ranch hands.

Chow Ling tripped over his feet when he saw me.

"Missy Dixie. Missy Dixie. You come see Chow Ling?" His eyes narrowed. "You not come to cook again."

"Not in a hundred years." I laughed. "Big Finn around?"

"Boss man with horses. You drink tea with Chow Ling?"

I really didn't like tea. But I did like Chow Ling. One cup wouldn't hurt. When I got up to leave, he handed me a covered basket.

"You give to Missy Abby. You come again. I have more vegetables."

I missed Chow-Chow more than I wanted to admit.

CHAPTER 46

Big Finn jumped when I called his name.

"What be on your mind, lassie?"

"Can't I just come to town to visit old friends?"

"Aye, ye can. But 'tis not the case today. Ye wear the look of a troubled soul."

I didn't mean for it to happen. Everything tumbled out of my mouth before I could stop them. "Sassy and I got crossways this morning. I'm worried about Jackson. I promised six head of cattle to Roaring Bear that I don't have. Pearl will pound me to dust if I don't come back without a milk cow. And I need some pigs and a goat."

"That be all of it?"

Well hell. Wasn't that enough? Something else was gnawing on me, but nothing I was willing to share.

"Not quite. But it's all I'm gonna' talk about."

"Well then. Work here is nearly done. Take me cow, Matilda. I can acquire your pigs and the goat with little trouble, but the beeves be trickier. Will have to study on that. Jackson is a strapping lad. Can take care of himself. As for Sassy? She be a headstrong lass for sure. Had heated words with her a few times me self. But no worries, lass. She be a good woman. She holds nar a grudge."

"She plans on marrying you."

"Oh, does she now?"

"Yes. Don't let on I told you."

"Not a word, lass."

"Would you?"

"Would I what?"

"Marry her?"

"Aye. That I might. Providing she lets me do the askin'."

"I'll drop a hint."

"Would'cha now? Well then, in that case, I'll throw in that worthless tomcat Sylvester with the cow."

I loved Big Finn.

Sylvester rode curious but content in my saddlebags. Every now and then, he'd poke his scarred head out just to make sure things were on the up and up. Matilda, the cow, was a different story. She balked at every twist and turn. I was in a hurry to get back. To see the shock on everyone's face. Turned out, however, it was me who got the surprise.

Lips pulled back. Teeth barred. Lobo had a white-faced, short-legged cowboy pinned against the corral gate.

The cowboy's horse ran wild.

Mary Louise cussed a blue streak.

Abby screamed back at her.

Steers milled about ready to stampede at the drop of a hat.

Abraham and the others were nowhere in sight.

Sylvester hissed and growled.

Matilda bawled.

Joe goose-stepped.

What the hell did I ride into?

CHAPTER 47

"Lobo! Back! Abby, shut up."

"Good thang you come along when ya did. I was jest getting ready to give that dawg a good ass-whupping."

I hated the cowboy right off. Shot him a look that would melt stone. "I beg your pardon?"

Abby rushed over. "Dixie, this is my friend, Dakota. I have no idea why Lobo attacked him like that."

The cowpoke put his arm around Abby's shoulders. Pulled her tight to his side.

"That's right. He jumped me for no good reason."

"Liar."

I glanced over at Mary Louise. Always composed, and neat as a pin, she was anything but. Looked like she'd run a mile. Sweat trickled down the side of her blotchy-red face.

 Dark stains circled her armpits. Straggly hair flew about her head. She brushed the wild locks back with a trembling hand.

"What's going on?" I asked. "Where did these steers come from?"

"From me." The cowpoke squeezed Abby harder to his side. "Ain't that right, darling?"

"What's he talking about, Abby?"

She ducked her head. Made tiny circles in the dirt with the toe of her boot.

"I just wanted to help, Dixie. I knew you needed cows. Dakota visited me a lot at the Dove. Told me more than once what a big cattle ranch he had, so I went to see him. We . . . we . . . made a deal."

"What kind of deal? Did you buy them?"

"Well, no. More like traded for them."

I let that sink in for a moment. Didn't like the sounds of it one bit.

"Traded what?"

No answer.

"Abby. Answer me. What did you trade?"

"Her soul. She traded her soul, Dixie."

Mary Louise's outburst severed my last nerve. I jerked Abby away from Dakota. Made her look me square in the eye.

"Tell me the truth, Abby. What did you trade?"

"Git your hands of her! It ain't none of your business no how. The deal is between me and her. One night for each cow. Yes siree. Ten long days and nights of good loving. Whenever, wherever, and however I want. Come over here today to hold up my side of the bargain. Now it's her turn. For the next ten days, she belongs to me."

I didn't know what to do next. Puke. Or shoot the bastard's face off.

"I tried to stop him, Dixie," Mary Louise said. "He pushed me down. Got rough. That's when Lobo grabbed him."

"Why are you making such a big fuss, Dixie?" Abby yelled. "I get so sick and tired of your uppity ways. Maybe I want to go with him. Ever think about that? Maybe I like the deal. Agreed to it, didn't I? And let me tell you something, Mary Louise. A leopard don't change his spots no matter how many horses they wrangle. Once a Dove. Always a Dove."

All the blood drained out of me. Stunned, I watched Abby climb up behind Dakota and ride off. Numb, all Mary Louise and I could do was stare at one another. I didn't understand. Couldn't even feel Mary Louise's hand on my arm when she pulled me to the house.

"Come on, Dixie. We both need a drink. Where do you keep the whiskey?"

"Kitchen," I mumbled. "In the cupboard. Behind the plates."

I sank onto the kitchen chair and watched her pour two shots. I downed the first one like water. She refilled the glass. "Sip this one. You know how you get."

The sharp whiskey burned away my stupor. "Am I that righteous?"

Mary Louise scoffed. "Pfff. You? Not hardly."

She poured another round. "Are folks always gonna' think me tainted?"

"No."

"Think I'll ever find a man who'll love me no matter my past? Like Abraham does Dominique?"

"He sure does moon over her, that's for certain."

"I'll say. Sometimes he's so sweet it gives me a belly ache."

Maybe it was time to put the bottle away.

"Where'd you get the cow?"

Shoot! I done forgot all about Matilda. Sylvester too. "Got her from Big Finn. Guess I better get her in the barn. Gotta round up those steers too. Where is everyone?"

"They all went to help Abraham and Dominique at the cabin. Left me and Abby behind to hold down the fort. I made a mess of that, didn't I?"

"Not your fault. You ever hear her talk that hateful before?"

"Never. Think she'll come back?"

I shrugged. "Can't say."

"What are you going to do if she does?"

I shrugged again. "Got no idea. Feel like a fool. Thought we were like sisters. Guess not."

"Well, don't fret too long about it. Sisters fight all the time, ya' know. Especially about men. Come on. I'll help you with the cows."

"Mary Louise? Can you cook?"

CHAPTER 48

It was late when I sank into bed. Abraham and the girls got back in time to help pen the steers in the corral. Overjoyed at Matilda, Pearl threw her arms around me. Gave me a big kiss on the cheek. "Bless you, Dixie, for the milk cow." Everyone listened in shock when Mary Louise and I filled them in about Abby.

"Don't sound like her at all," Sassy said. "I know Dakota. He's a cocky little son of a bitch. It's his daddy's ranch, not his. Causes trouble wherever he goes. You should've let Lobo gnaw on him awhile."

A tiny meow interrupted my thoughts. I reached over and put the tiny fur ball beside me. Pearl wasn't the only one who was a sucker for kittens. I fell in love with the little dickens the first time I saw him. Not content to stay by my side, he wobbled up my leg and snuggled all comfy-cozy on the pillow. So small. So innocent. So trusting. Just like Abby.

Abby.

The day crashed down on top of me. I broke into tears.

I cried for Mama.

I cried for Papa.

For Jackson

For Abby.
But most of all, I sobbed for me.
Today was my birthday.
Only the kitten knew.

CHAPTER 49

The girl in the looking glass stared at me with red-rimmed eyes. What a fool. I wasted a good night wallowing in self-pity. Mama and Papa were gone. Couldn't change that. Jackson was gone too. My fault. I pushed him away. No one knew of my birthday because I never told them.

I studied my reflection. Seventeen. I was seventeen.

I giggled. Most girls my age would be married and have young'uns by now. Bet ol' buck-toothed Ima Jean was trapped in a tedious life depending on some dull, bald, round-bellied, store clerk for money and a roof over her head.

Not me.

I owned a ranch. Seventeen years old, and I had my own place.

My best friends were rough and tough Doves who bowed to no man. I was Foxtail Woman who rode into Indian camps without fear and made deals with Medicine Men and chiefs. I'd stabbed a man who tried to ruin me. Stole a lawman's horse. I drank whiskey. Granted not very well but still. Smoked sometimes too. I could rope and ride. And, when push came to shove, I could whip up a batch of biscuits as soft and fluffy as clouds. I looked mighty pretty in green too.

I was Dixie Dandelion and by God, I wasn't going to let any sawed-off buckaroo ride onto my property, shove my friends in the dirt, threaten my dog, and take my sister away without a fight.

So much for perfect hair, ironed skirts, and manners.

I strapped on my Colt and grabbed the Winchester on my way out the door.

"Just where do you think you're going?"

Sassy caught me halfway to the barn. I whirled on her.

"After Abby."

Pearl and Rosie walked up beside her.

"Been doing some thinking on things," I said. "We all agreed. Abby would never act or talk that way to us without a good reason. I think Dakota forced her to go." I eyed Sassy. "Don't try and stop me. My mind's made up."

"Stop ya'? Hell, I'm coming with ya'."

"Us too," the twins said.

"Not without me," Mary Louise joined in. "I got a score to settle with that bowlegged runt."

"Dixcee? You should not go without Abraham. He is at the cabin. I will go for him."

I'd purposely waited till Abraham rode away. I didn't want him mixed up in this. "You can go fetch him if you want, Dominique. I can't stop you. But I'm not waiting."

"Ah, Dixcee. Always full of fire. I will get him all the same."

"Suit yourself."

Horses saddled. Pistols and rifles loaded. Lobo by my side. We mounted up and rode.

CHAPTER 50

I stopped at the ranch gate and stared at the sign: **Rutherford's Rocking R.** Where had I heard that name before? No. Couldn't be. I twisted in the saddle and glanced at Sassy.

"Don't tell me this ranch belongs to Hubert Rutherford the land bank president?"

"Yep. One in the same."

"Dakota is his foreman?"

"Son. Now ya know why he thinks he's God's gift to the world. After his mother passed away, Dakota went wild. Spends his daddy's money like water. Whiskey. Women. Cards. Hubert thinks he hung the moon. Can't do no wrong. Thought you knew."

"Nope. I had no idea."

"That change your mind any about Abby?"

"No. Makes it all the sweeter. I didn't like that pompous jackass the first time I dealt with him. He's uppity and probably a lying swindler. Talked down to me like I didn't have enough sense to come in out of the rain."

"He talks to all women that way."

"Not today."

I had to admit. The Rocking R was quite the outfit. A barn so big you could stable a herd of buffalo inside stood surrounded by corrals large enough to hold the woolly beasts. At least a half-dozen long-legged, fast-looking horses stood tied to the hitching rail. They snorted and pawed the ground, ready to run. Good-looking and flashy but a far cry from working cow ponies.

The two-story main house, painted an eye-squinting dazzling white, sported columns and even had two stone lions at its entrance. The place mirrored its owner. Big and showy. Abby sat on the porch. When she caught sight of us, she hurried down the steps.

"Dixie. Get outta' here. Dakota will throw a fit ifn' he sees y'all. Why are you here anyway?"

"We came to fetch you," Mary Louise said before I could swallow.

"Maybe . . . maybe I don't want to go back."

"Oh, Abby, you can't lie worth spit," Sassy said. "I've known you since you was knee-high. You couldn't fib when you was little and you can't all grown up neither. I don't know what hold Dakota has over you, but it don't matter. Come on home where you belong."

"Well, well. What do we have here, boys?"

Dakota's mocking tone cut through me slicker than a knife. The little grin on his face made me want to slap him just 'cause I could. Surrounded by four of his men who looked more like gunfighters than cowpunchers, he stepped to Abby's side. Lobo growled.

"Dakota," I said just as sweet as maple syrup. "I came for Abby. I need my cook back."

"She ain't fulfilled all her bargain yet."

"About that bargain, I continued. "May I see the signed contract?"

A dull, stupid look replaced his sneer. "Huh?"

"What I mean is, you *claim* you and Abby entered into an agreement." I glanced at Abby. "You sign any paperwork?"

"No."

"Didn't think so." I turned back to Dakota. "Without a written, signed contract, how do I know a deal was even offered?"

Flustered, Cody stammered. "You . . . you calling me a liar?"

"If she ain't, I am," Sassy interrupted.

Dakota's back straightened. The smirks on his men's faces disappeared. Behind me, I heard the smooth slide of Winchesters being pulled from scabbards. Things were heating up fast.

"Weren't no call for no contract," Dakota insisted. "It was a verbal agreement."

"Dakota? What's going on here?"

All three hundred pounds of Hubert Rutherford waddled out the front door. He fixed me with a beady-eyed stare. "Miss Dandelion?" He gawked at the rifles in the girls hands. Rifles aimed at his only son's head. "May I ask what business brings you to the Rocking R that necessitates the use of gunplay?"

"Mr. Rutherford. How nice to see you again," I gushed. "I assure you I'm not looking for trouble today. I just came to get my sister."

"I was not aware you had a sister, Miss Dandelion."

"Oh, I wager there are a lot of things about me you're not aware of, sir." I heard Mary Louise snort. "Did you know your son traded ten head of cattle for ten days *and* nights for the company of a young woman?"

"I was told this woman agreed to the arrangement, Miss Dandelion. What reason would I have to doubt it? After all, she's nothing but a two-bit whore . . . "

The cold, hard sound of rifle hammers being pulled back stopped him mid-sentence. Ready to beat him to a pulp, I dismounted and stormed up the porch steps to stand face-to-face with the fat banker.

"Just this once, I'm going to overlook that slip-of-the-tongue, Mr. Rutherford. I'm also going to pretend you had no knowledge of your son's wickedness and deceit."

I dug in my jacket pocket for the bills I'd taken from my boot stash. "It's my understanding cattle in Texas are going for $5.00 a head. Since we're a long way from Texas, I'm paying you twice that amount." I pushed the money into his hand.

"I'll need a receipt if you don't mind. Nothing personal, just good business. I'm sure you understand."

All puffed up like a Rhode Island Red, Hubert shot Dakota a scowl so poisonous I almost felt sorry for the fella. Rutherford turned on his heel and stomped into the house.

I backed off the porch and took Abby by the hand. "It's all up to you, Abby. Do you want to come home?"

She glanced over at Dakota. I tipped her head back to me. "Never mind him. Do you? Or don't you?"

I struggled to hear her whisper, "I do."

Mary Louise brought up Prince Charming. I held his bridle until Abby got into the saddle.

"Miss Dandelion." Hubert cleared his throat. "Your receipt."

I handed the paper to Mary Louise who read every word with a hawk eye. Satisfied, she nodded. I put on my best smile. "Mr. Rutherford, as always, it's been a pleasure doing business with you."

I didn't blow out the breath I'd been holding until we rode through the gate.

Dominique and Abraham met us halfway home. We stopped to let the horses blow. Abraham pushed his hat back off his forehead.

"Miss Dixie. A word of advice. Never go into battle without guarding your flank. Next time you go off half-cocked and don't let me know, I's riding out for good. Brave is brave. Stupid is stupid. Savvy?"

"Yes, Abraham. I give you my word."

Chapter 51

By the time we got back to the ranch, I felt like I'd been rode hard and put up wet. All I wanted to do was sit down and glue my nerves back together, but there was something I had to do first. I put my arm around Abby and walked her into the house. We sat at the kitchen table and drank warmed-over morning coffee. I sighed. "I gotta'. know. Tell me square. Why did you do this?"

She twirled her hair and wouldn't look at me. "I didn't mean no harm."

"Not good enough, Abby. That's the second time you said that. Try again. Did you mean those rude things you said to me and Mary Louise?"

Ramrod straight, she finally quit fidgeting and met my gaze. "Lord, no. Dixie. I just said those things to get Dakota away from here. I didn't want anyone to get hurt."

"Did you want to go with him?"

"Not really. But I did agree to the bargain."

"Why?"

She got up and paced the kitchen. Back and forth. I put out my hand and stopped her.

"You don't understand, Dixie. I wanted to do something to help. I don't feel like I pull my weight around here. Oh, I can cook but cooks are a dime a dozen."

Really? I opened my mouth to disagree. She interrupted.

"I ride good enough. But the only thing I can rope is me. Branding makes me sick. I feel useless. I overheard Abraham saying you were in a real bind about the cows. I knew Dakota from the White Dove. Knew I could persuade him. Because he said. I thought. Well."

"Let me guess. He said he loved you?"

She nodded.

"So you sold yourself to help me out."

"It's the only thing I'm good at."

She might as well have thrown a rope around my heart and jerked it from my chest. Tears stung my eyes. I blinked them back.

"Abby, listen to me." I took a deep breath. Wasn't sure where I was headed with this.

"I wish there was a way I could make you understand how special you are. Just because you have a hard time roping and branding doesn't mean you're not doing your fair share. A cook is the most important person on a ranch. Or anywhere for that matter. Do you really think Big Finn's men could build a railroad eating only beans three times a day?"

She giggled.

"Don't try to be someone you're not, Abby. Don't make excuses for who you are. You're smart. You can read and write. Play the piano. Got a heart so full of love it spills over and touches everyone. Heals their sadness. That's what angels do."

"Oh, Dixie. You calling me an angel?"

Her little-girl voice and wide-eyed innocence about flattened me. I hugged her to my chest.

"About as close to one as I can imagine. Angels don't sell themselves to any man. Don't you either."

She pulled away from me. Couldn't tell if it was her tears or mine that dampened my collar.

"Ain't no one ever talked to me this way before, except maybe Mama. This is the second time you saved me, Dixie. There won't be need of another. I promise. Besides, you might not come the third time."

"I always come, Abby. That's just what sisters do."

After Abby left to fix what she claimed would be "the best supper I ever ate." I eased into the rocking chair. Little dickens kitten bounded across the room and jumped into my lap. I patted his head and let his kitten purrs ease the tightness in my chest.

Seventeen. But right now, I felt older than the hills.

This time, I not only heard Papa's voice but felt his hand on my shoulder as well.

You be one hell of a woman, Margaret Katelyn O'Shea.

CHAPTER 52

Our first foal came into the world with oohs, ahhs, and happy tears filling the barn to the brim. Abraham had kept a close eye on the mama horse all day and woke us in time to witness the little fella's first breath.

"Let's name him Morning Star because he was born at dawn."

Abraham shook his head and whispered in my ear. "If Miss Abby's gonna' name every colt born on this ranch, she gonna' run out of names. It ain't good. Putting a name on something makes it yours. When it comes time to sell this little bugger, she'll be mighty sad."

I didn't say a word. Deep in my heart, I knew Abby wouldn't be the only one feeling low the day someone bought him. I would too. However, Abraham made a good point. It was a bad idea to get attached to any of the foals. After all, I *was* in the horse business. But I could no more stop Abby from falling in love with every baby colt than cook. If she wanted to name them, so be it.

Our second birth took place two weeks later. Another colt. Abby called him Sticks because of his thin legs. A week after, during the full moon, our black mare threw a little filly. Abby dubbed her Moonbeam. I had to hand it to her, Abby sure could pick good names. My horse ranch was in full swing.

"Pretty proud of yourself, ain't ya'?" Sassy asked one morning.

"Is that a bad thing?" I asked.

"Nope. You got a right. You've come a long way in a short time."

"Couldn't have done it without you and the girls."

"Wildest notion I ever heard of; Doves trading in silk stockings and lace corsets for boots and chaps, but it's worked out so far. Never thought any of us, except maybe the twins, would like ranch life, but it isn't that bad. It's hard work. But it's got its rewards."

"Big Finn said most of the town is betting against us."

"Told me the same thing. We ain't out of the woods by no means. Of course, you leaving a trail of enemies behind ya doesn't help matters none."

"What enemies?"

"Hubert Rutherford and son. You embarrassed Dakota in front of his men. Made him look like a fool. Daddy didn't take kindly to writing out that receipt neither. I have no doubt the two of them had words over the whole deal. Ain't the first time Rutherford's had to bail Dakota out of a mess. Won't be the last time neither. Even still, blood is thicker than water. Besides, I think Hubert wants this ranch all to himself."

"Then he should've bought it. Place was vacant for months."

"Maybe being the president of the land bank had something to do with that. Maybe not. Just a guess. All I'm saying is trouble has a way of finding you. Don't get too comfortable."

She was right.

That "trouble" damn near broke down my door one Sunday afternoon.

"Missy Dixie! Missy Dixie!"

Chow Ling?

It wasn't Chow Ling who stood on the other side of the door. It was Mae Ling, his daughter. Tears streamed down her delicate face and choked her words. Had a hard enough time understanding her when she was calm; being so worked up made it double hard to figure out what she jabbered. I helped her inside and tried to calm her down.

"Mae Ling, what's wrong?"

"Father. Bad men take Father away."

Face pale as milk, she gulped air. From the looks of things, she'd runned all the way from town. Exhausted, she collapsed in a heap at my boots. I pressed a wet neckerchief to the back of her neck. I wouldn't let her talk again until her little bird chest quit heaving.

"Talk slow. Tell me what happened."

A little calmer now, she turned her teary face to mine. "Men come, take Father. They say Father kill another."

This time, it was *my* heart that tore loose and stampeded. The One-Eyed Jack had just raised its ugly head and bit me.

"They hang Father."

Where the hell was Donovan in all of this? He wouldn't let them take Chow Ling without a fight.

"Mae Ling? Where is Big Finn?"

"I look. Cannot find."

She clung to my hand. "Please, Missy Dixie. Hurry."

My mind raced. No way would I let them hang Chow Ling. Not if I could help it, but without help, I wasn't sure I could stop them. Everyone, except Abby, had gone with Abraham and Dominique to help finish up at the cabin. Abraham. Damnation. I'd promised him I wouldn't go on a rampage without telling him first. Surely, he wouldn't ride away. It was a bluff. But not a bluff I was willing to call.

"Missy Dixie." Mae Ling jerked my sleeve. "Don't let them kill Father."

Oh hell. I'd worry about Abraham later.

"Mae Ling, you stay put. Do not go back into town. Understand?"

She nodded.

I buckled on my six gun, grabbed my backup revolver, and a handful of preloaded cylinders. I raced to the bunk doll house and shook Abby awake.

"Abby, I need your help. They're going to lynch Chow Ling if I don't stop it. I need you to ride out to the cabin and tell Abraham."

For once, Abby had her wits about her. She nodded. No hysterics. No tears. Just tight-lipped determination.

Saddle blankets flew onto wide backs. Saddles cinched. Bridles fastened. We stepped up in the stirrups.

Prince tore out of the barn like his tail was on fire. Abby held tight, riding fast and wild.

I spurred Joe into town.

CHAPTER 53

Not wanting to be seen, I checked Joe down to a walk and rode into town the back way. I checked the cook tent for Big Finn. Nothing. The stable was next. The heavy wood doors were shut. My heart broke into a trot. The doors always stood open. I drew my Colt, cracked the door a few inches, and slithered in. Nothing. Gun holstered, I turned to leave when my foot hit something hard. A shovel. A bloody shovel. I gawked at the thing like it was the devil's cloven hoof and forked tail lying at my feet. A low groan came from one of the stalls.

Finn, tussled up neater than a Christmas goose, lay sprawled out on the straw. The copper scent of fresh blood wrinkled my nose. Forget the trot, my heart tore into a full-out gallop.

Several deep breaths settled my panic. I kneeled beside him. From the looks of the blood and the cut on his scalp, some coward had smacked him good in the back of the head with the shovel. Wouldn't want to be in the boots of that low-down yellow belly if Finn ever found out who he was. Still out cold, there was nothing I could do but cut him loose and let him wake up on his own.

I swallowed hard. Once again, I'd have to face danger alone.

Before mounting up and riding into a hornet's nest, I stopped to think. Something I didn't usually do in situations like this. Abraham would be proud. Jackson too. I sure could use that dimpled Pinkerton right about now.

"Papa, what should I do?" I whispered.

Stampede.

There were three horses in the barn. Two more tied up outside. If I could run them through the mob, I could grab Chow Ling before they knew what hit them.

At the edge of town stood a huge tree. I have no idea what kind of tree, but it was strong enough to hold a man four times the size of Chow Ling. I reasoned that's where they dragged him. I paused a few yards off. Sure enough, there was Chow Ling meekly letting his hands be tied. What was wrong with him? If someone was about to hang me, I'd be damn if I would go down without a fight. I'd be a screaming, biting, kicking demon from hell.

With pistol drawn, one deep slug of air, and a prayer on my lips, I shot into the air.

The horses spooked and ran full bore down the hill. The lynch mob's horses caught stampede fever. Reared. Bucked. Kicked. Joined in the chaos. Rocks and dirt flew and surrounded the crowd in an eye-burning haze. I gave out a rebel yell. Then another. One after another. Loud. Fierce.

The Colt bucked in my hands. The bitter smell of gun smoke circled my head. Shot after shot. Empty. I grabbed my backup revolver and kept right on shooting. The gritty taste of gunpowder coated my lips. Confused and scared, the mob around Chow Ling ducked for cover. Without breaking stride, I reached for my friend and hauled him up behind me in the saddle.

Everything moved at neck-breaking speed and slow motion all at the same time. I felt Chow Ling's breath on the back of my neck. Smelled his fear and sweat. Even saw the face of one of the folks in the mob and heard his scream when a bullet ripped through his shoulder. Micky Doogan. Big Finn's trusted foreman. Bet he was the one who clobbered Finn. Glad I shot him. Hope the cockroach bled to death.

Out of bullets, I settled deep in the saddle and concentrated on riding hard and fast.

"Anyone following us?" I shouted at Chow Ling.

I felt him twist and turn. "See nothing."

I pushed Joe hard. Had to get back to the ranch before they regrouped and came after me.

Abraham had just swung in the saddle when we came racing in.

"I's sorry, Miss Dixie. We took the buckboard to the cabin. Had to come and get Mud before heading your way." He glanced over at Chow Ling sitting behind me. "Don't look like you needed my help anyways."

Blood roared in my ears. Made it hard to understand Abraham. Didn't matter. I was more curious about the Chinese woman standing in the middle of the yard. Chow Ling bailed off Joe and hurried to her side. Wrapped in his arms, the woman sobbed. Abraham followed my gaze.

"That's the Chinaman's wife. Showed up here a while after you lit out. Reckon she walked from town."

Sassy and all the girls came out of the house with Mae Ling in tow. At the sight of her father all safe and sound, she broke down crying as well.

"What's you gonna' do now, Miss Dixie?"

Huh. Good question.

"Before I do anything, I gotta' cool Joe down."

"I'll take care of him," Rosie said. "You stay here and fix things."

Fix things?

Every eye trained on me. Guess it was only fitting, seeing how I was the one who tore off and rescued Chow Ling, but that didn't mean I had a plan.

"Did you find Finn?"

"Yeah. Micky Doogan cold-cocked him. Tied him up in the barn." The worry on Sassy's face made me rush on. "He's ok. Gonna' have a whopper of a headache when he wakes up that's all."

"I'm going to town."

"No."

She bowed up ready to pitch a fit.

"Not yet. It isn't safe. That mob may be riding our way right now. You don't need to run into them on the trail."

"Miss Dixie, I'll ride out a ways and stand guard. If I see hide or hair of them, I'll let you know in plenty of time to get ready."

"Be careful, Cheri.

I walked over to Chow Ling. He pressed his palms together and bowed so low he could lick dirt. "Missy Dixie save Chow Ling. Can never repay."

"No need for that, I'm just glad I got you out of there in time." I motioned to Mary Louise. "Why don't you take Chow Ling and his family into the house? There should be some tea stashed in the cupboard." As soon as the door closed, I turned to the girls.

"They cannot stay here, Dixcee. You know this."

"Dominique's right," Mary Lousie said. "They can't go back to town neither."

"I know." I paced. Back and forth. "What bothers me is how did those galoots find out about the One-Eyed Jack in the first place?" I stared all of them in the eye. "We swore to take that night to our graves."

"Dixie? Hmm, I might have accidentally let that slip."

All of us whirled on Abby.

"What the hell does that mean?" Sassy asked.

"Dakota bad-mouthed Dixie. Said she was too yellow to come after me. I couldn't let him get away with saying that." Her voice trailed off to a whisper. "So, I might have mentioned how Dixie rescued me from Daggett and that Chow Ling shot him."

I thought the big vein in Sassy's neck was gonna' pop.

"Abby, I swear to God, I'd slap you silly but it would be a waste of time."

I stepped between them.

"I didn't mean no harm."

"Mother of God, how many times are you going to say that? Dammit. You weren't even there. You don't know what happened that night." Sassy took a long breath.

"I killed Daggett. Not Chow Ling. He just got rid of the evidence. Why can't you keep your little mouth shut? All a fella has to say is, I love you and you spill your guts. When are you going to get it through your head? They don't love you, Abby. They're only using you. We've pulled your butt out of the fire twice now and every time, you promise it will be the last. You've been saying, I don't mean no harm all your life. I'm sick of hearing it." She turned to me.

"I'm going into town to take care of my man. You can't stop me so don't even try. Doubt I'll be back any time soon."

"You running out on me?"

"'Course not. But I ain't going to sleep under the same roof with a nitwit who'll probably end up getting us all killed."

Abby broke into sobs and ran to the bunkhouse.

I'd never seen this side of Sassy. She was so angry. Dominique stood rooted to the spot, brown eyes bigger than walnuts. Bewildered, Pearl and Rosie watched her stomp past them.

Thing was, there was a part of me that agreed with everything Sassy said. I was getting weary of handling Abby with kid gloves. Was she that naïve? Tears and feigning innocence was a darn good way to get out of trouble.

"Dixcee? Chow Ling and his family? Where are we to hide them?"

One of those out-of-the-blue ideas popped into my head.

I grinned.

Flying Eagle and Roaring Bear were going to kill me.

CHAPTER 54

Sassy pushed Dancer hard, partly from concern over Big Finn and partly from anger. Abby could piss off the Pope with her fake innocence. Men ate up her poor-little-lamb act with a spoon, often paying more than the regular price. Guess her cute babydoll pout and childlike voice made them feel protective or some such nonsense. But that's all it was—an act, a performance. She didn't blame Dixie for believing it, however. After all, Dixie didn't know the ways of their business. Doves were a lot of things, but innocent wasn't one of them.

All the girls understood the pretense. Money was money, but spilling the beans about the One-Eyed Jack was taking the forgive-and-forget part too far. The man she loved almost got killed.

Keeping an eye peeled for Doogan and his pack of jackals, she slowed to a jogtrot and patted Dancer's lathered withers. She rode to The White Dove and eased through the back door. She hoped Della knew about the ruckus and where Finn was. No need to worry. The big Irishman sat at Della's kitchen table, with a glass of whiskey in his hand. Della dabbed at his head wound and fought to keep him still. The pungent odor of turpentine circled the room.

"Saints preserve, woman! What manner of nasty be in that bottle?"

"Horse liniment."

"It burns like banshee tears, it do."

"Quit your squirming." Della laughed. "Ya don't want this cut to get infected, do ya?"

"If I ever find out who the no-good bastard was who busted me head, I'll nail his hide to the barn door."

"That would be Micky Doogan."

Both Finn and Della jumped at Sassy's voice. Finn took a gulp of whiskey to hide his grin.

"How do you know?" Della asked.

Sassy crossed the room and settled upon a chair across from them. "Dixie told me."

"Aye. That makes sense. Doogan is a tool if ever they be one."

Della wrapped a white bandage around Finn's head and gathered up the wash pan and liniment. "Well, that's the best I can do for now."

"Della?" Sassy asked. "I need to stay here for a while ifn' ya' don't mind. Things at the ranch are tense right now."

Della cocked her eyebrow. "With Dixie?"

"No."

"Ah, I see. Then it's Abby, I wager. Wouldn't be the first time you and her had words.

Of course, you can stay. I'll get your room ready."

After Della left the room, Sassy grabbed Finn's hand. "Are you ok?"

A confused look crossed his face and his voice came low.

"Ye be concerned about me welfare, would'cha now?"

"Almost rode Dancer's legs off getting here."

His voice took on a teasing tone.

"Why be that?"

Suddenly shy, she avoided his gaze and toyed with the lace tablecloth. Finn patted his lap. "Come here, me bonnie lass."

Sassy hurried to sit on his lap and put her arms around his neck.

"Would ye miss me much ifn' I wasn't here?"

"Life wouldn't be worth living without you in it, ya big galoot."

"Well, now. What's a man to say when he hears such as that?"

"Marry me?"

"Aye, me love. Those be the words."

CHAPTER 55

I didn't sleep for several nights, worrying over payback from the lynch mob. No retaliation came.

Maybe the confusion, rocks, and dust of the stampede masked my identity. However, Joe's brown-patched rump was pretty hard to miss, and who else but me would risk their neck for a Chinaman?

True to her word, Sassy didn't return to the ranch. I missed her. On several occasions, she rode out to check in but returned to town before nightfall. She never spoke to Abby.

"How long are you going to ignore Abby?" I asked one afternoon.

"Not sure. Kinda' hard to be friendly when she almost got Finn and Chow Ling killed. All because she's got bad taste in men and silly notions about love."

"How *is* Big Finn?"

"He's fine. Good thing he's got a hard head. When I told him Doogan bushwacked him, he was roaring mad. He's looked everywhere but can't find that yellow egg-suckin' dog anywhere. God help him when he does."

"I've been wondering. Why would Micky Doogan, a railroad man, care about Daggett and the One-Eyed Jack?"

"It goes deeper than that, Dixie, but I can't tell you why."

"Has it got something to do with Finn being a Pinkerton?"

"You're too smart for your own britches, you know that? I ain't saying one way or the other. Let it die. You got enough on your plate to worry about."

I didn't want to let it die.

She changed the subject.

"He asked me to marry him."

I about swallowed my tongue. "What? Oh, Sassy, that's great news."

"Mum's the word for now. Keeping it under our hats until his business here is done. By the way, what those Indians say when you showed up with Chow Ling?"

I laughed. "Roaring Bear refused to talk to me. Flying Eagle said plenty. I smoothed it over with the cattle. I'd promised six head but thanks to the generosity of Dakota Rutherford, they ended up with ten."

She snorted. "It was more lust than generosity."

"I thought for sure that mob would try something, but it's been weeks and nothing. Think they've forgotten?"

"Keep your eyes peeled. I heard rumors Dakota was behind the lynching. You can be sure he hasn't forgotten anything."

That made me feel about as comfortable as a treed ringtail coon.

"None of my business but where are you living? With Finn?"

"No, Miss Noisy. I'm not. Staying with Della. Which reminds me, and you're going to be mighty interested in this. Della is going to Santa Fe next week on some kind of Opera House business. I'm tagging along. There's a certain Army captain there I plan to see about a horse. Or horses as the case may be."

My heart leaped. "My horses? Do you think you can get

a contract? How do you know this captain?"

"Of course, your horses. Who else's? And let's just say I know the captain from a previous relationship."

I didn't ask any more questions. If Sassy could get a contract from the Army captain for a shipment of future horses, I could care less how she met him.

Excitement for a possible deal with the Army overrode caution. I should've known Dakota wouldn't give up.

CHAPTER 56

Lobo's howling and the smell of smoke jolted me from sleep. The thunder of hoofbeats and gunshots greeted me when I threw open the cabin door. A blanket of red flames covered the barn's roof. Whinnies of frightened horses cut through my sleepy daze straight into the pit of my belly.

Oh God no. Not the horses.

I grabbed my jacket and raced outside. The wind caught the embers from the barn and carried them to the pasture. The threat of a full-blown prairie fire loomed large. Without hesitation, I ran toward the struggling flames. My mind whirled. *Take the jacket off. The leather won't burn and will be heavy enough to smother the fire.*

The cursed wind wouldn't stop. It whipped the sparks into a frenzy. Flames took on a life of their own. Like growling beasts, they surrounded me, evil and mocking. They snapped at my boots. Dodged and weaved around my pant legs. Snarled at my desperate attempts to quash them.

I flogged the beast with my coat. Behind me, the barn twisted and screamed for help in the grips of a fiery-death struggle.

My lips dried and cracked. Eyes burned and itched from

the smoke. All around me, the scent of burning grass and wood stung my nose. I gasped for breath. Unwillingly, I drank in the smell. Throat raspy and rough, I fought for a deep breath of cool air. I was going to die. Burned alive trying to save my horses and ranch. Deep down panic ate its way up into my gullet.

"Oh God. Help me!"

A shadow loomed beside me, stomping out the flames. Who? Didn't matter. I wasn't fighting this battle alone. Two could kill the fiery beast.

Abraham's booming voice roared in my ears. "They's free, Miss Dixie. They's free!"

The geldings and mares tore past me. The terrified squeals of colts right behind them.

Safe. All safe.

Relief weakened my legs. The threat of a raging grass fire died as quickly as it had started, but the barn still burned. I headed toward it. Heat laughed. Slapped me in the face. The shadow grabbed my arm and pulled me back. No! I fought against the steel band that held me in its grasp.

"'Tis too late, lassie."

I kicked and screamed. Battled against Finn's meaty arms when he pinned me against his whiskey-barrel chest. Helpless, I watched the hungry beast gorge itself full of wood, nails, straw, and hay. One last death rattle and the barn's charred shoulders folded and collapsed to the dirt.

Dead.

Anger gave strength back to my shaking legs. With one mighty shove, I broke away and stormed the cabin. Hands trembled when I notched the Colt around my waist and grabbed the Winchester.

Those son of bitches! I'd shoot every last one of them.

Big Finn caught my arm as I ran past. "Ya can't kill them all, girl. Let it go."

I whirled and gawked at his ruddy face.

"Let it go? Are you loco? They burned down my damn

barn. Tried to kill my horses."

"Let me and Jackson handle it, lass."

I sputtered. "Jackson ain't here, remember? He rode away. Just like that day on the wagon train. Rode away and left me there to fight Payton. All alone. Always alone."

"Dixie!"

And there he was.

Bigger than life.

Jackson Wayne.

He stepped down from his magnificent black stallion like a knight returning from some far-off crusade. Long legs ate up the ground between us. He grabbed my shoulders and gave me a shake. My breath caught as the look of worry and concern inched across his square face.

"Damn it, Dixie. Why didn't you say the word?"

He dropped his arms. The heat from his stare blazed hotter than the hissing, spitting brimstones of hell and scorched the edges of my heart.

"I waited, Dixie. But you never said it. Ya never once said, 'Stay.'"

I heard the plea, the hurt in his deep southern drawl. Saw the pain in his chestnut eyes.

Sweet Jesus, daughter. Say something. Explain to the boyo how it would be weakness if you asked him to stay. Tell him how dreary the days be without the hope of seeing him again.

How hollow the nights without his laugher to fill them up. He deserves an answer, lass. Just tell him.

No.

I ran.

I dashed around his solid frame, caught Thunder's dangling reins, stepped up into the saddle, and heeled the black toward town and away from Jackson Wayne.

CHAPTER 57

"**A** wee bit harsh on the lass, weren't ya' lad?"

Jackson tore his gaze away from Thunder's disappearing rump to stare Donovan square in the eye but said nothing. He couldn't talk, not yet. Feelings of anger, confusion, hurt, and relief swam too strong in his head. A minute passed then two. His voice came rough.

"What caused this?"

The big man's chuckle irked him. His eyebrow cocked.

"Ah well, ye know Dixie. Always in the thick of things. 'Tis a long story."

A figure loomed large out of the smoke. Wayne's hand tightened around his gun butt.

"Easy now, son," Donovan said and put his hand on Jackson's wrist. "That be Abraham Hayes. He'll do ye no harm."

"Who's Abraham Hayes?"

"Dixie's foreman."

"A Negro?" Jackson stared at the grizzly bear of a man striding toward them.

"Told ye it was a long story. He's an ex-Buffalo Soldier. Rode into town a couple of months back. Took up with Della's girl, Dominique."

"Mr. Finn, all the horses, Matilda, and pigs are safe. I'm gonna' corral them up for the night. Just wanted you to know."

"Aye. Abraham? Meet Jackson Wayne. He's—

"I knows who he is." Abraham extended his hand. "Miss Dominique told me all about you, Mr. Wayne. Glad to meet you at last. Just wish it was a better time."

Jackson shook hands with the man. He could tell a lot about a fella by his handshake. Abraham's was strong, firm, and direct. A gentle giant he reasoned. Slow to anger but a force to be reckoned with if pushed. "So do I, Mr. Hayes."

"Abraham."

"Jackson to you, then."

"You's going after Miss Dixie, or should I?"

A frown crossed Jackson's face. "Let her run. Town's a long ride from here. I wager she'll cool down and start thinking straight before she gets there."

"You don't think she'll go through with it?" Abraham asked. "'Cause if you think Miss Dixie won't shoot the low-down polecats that did this, you got another think coming. Miss Dixie don't back down from nothing or no one."

"Oh, I have no doubt she'll shoot the varmints." His laugh held no humor. "But not tonight." He turned to Donovan. "I need to hear this long story."

"Aye. But we be needing whiskey. Wager there be a bottle in the house. I'll fetch it. Better sit outside and talk, keep an eye out for any unwelcomed guests."

"I's got to tend to the horses." Abraham nodded.

Weary, Jackson sank to the porch steps and leaned against the railing. The whiskey Donovan handled him slid smoothly down his gullet. He sat the Mason jar down beside him and waited for his cohort to plop his beefy butt on the willow rocking chair. Stray wisps of smoke from the smoldering mound of the barn floated across the yard in an eerie frost. The scent of scorched wood surrounded him. Burning down someone's barn was the greatest sin since Eve gave the apple to Adam. Whoever did this had a big ax to grind. What could Dixie have possibly done to bring on such madness? He glanced at Big Finn.

"Well?"

"Hold ye horses, lad. First things first." He took a big swig and smacked his lips. "Ah, better now." A deep breath. "Remember the donnybrook at the One-Eyed Jack a few months back?"

"Of course I do. Dixie shot the place up and Sassy killed Daggett. The way I heard it, Chow Ling took care of the bodies."

"Aye. That be the long and short of it. Someone let slip the details about the whole mess and how the evidence got disposed of."

"Who would be stupid enough to do such a thing?"

The big Irishman squirmed. The rocker creaked. He ran his hand through his carrot-orange hair and refused to meet his friend's intense gaze.

"Donovan."

A huge sigh lifted Finn's shoulders. "Keep in mind it weren't done on purpose. Bedroom talk. 'Twas all it was. She meant no harm."

Understanding crossed Wayne's face. He clicked his tongue. "Abby?"

"Aye."

"Go on."

"As ye know, there be no love toward the Chinese. The hooligans of Six Shooter saw this as a chance to rid the town of one of the slanty-eyed bastards. Their words, lad. Not mine. Dixie's made some enemies here, which is another long story. A mob hauled Chow Ling out of bed. Dragged him to that mammoth oak outside of town. They intended to lynch him sure as the sun shines down on the Emerald Isle itself."

"Did they?"

"Chow Ling's snip of a daughter, Mae Ling, slipped out her back door and ran straight to Dixie's front door. I got bushwhacked by one of me own men. Knocked senseless and tied up in the barn. Well, it don't take much imagination to know what Dixie done."

Jackson sighed. "Oh, I have no doubt."

Donovan leaned back in the rocker and took another drink. He grinned. "Ah, lad, you'd been proud of the lass. As I heard it, she started a stampede and rode like a banshee straight out of hell, guns blazing."

"She hit anything?"

"A few branches. William Cockran's fat arse. And a bullet through Micky Doogan's
shoulder."

"She's getting better."

"Aye that she is. Now this next part of the story will be hard to swallow. But I be tellin' ye the God's honest truth."

Jackson extended his empty Mason jar. "Better hit me again."

Donovan chuckled. He filled his own cup as well and took a massive gulp. A huge belch followed. "After Dixie rescued Chow Ling, she had no place safe to hide him and his family. So she did the next logical thing. Well, logical to Dixie anyway."

"Where did she take them?"

"Think, lad. Have ye no idea?"

"I ain't got time for guessing games. Just tell me."

"Flying Eagle."

The jar slipped from his hand and crashed on the wood porch. Whiskey trickled down the steps and wet the dirt in front of him. "You're joshing! She took Chow Ling to live with the Indians?"

Donovan slapped his leg. "Aye. That she did."

The rocker bucked and pitched with each huge belly laugh. "I never heard of Indians and Chinese living together. Would bet a good pint it wouldn't work. But what do I know? It had never been tried before. Last I heard, they be living nice and peaceful together."

Jackson joined in with Donovan's laughter. "Only Dixie could get away with such a thing. So, to get even for her spoiling a perfectly good neck-tie party and hiding Chow Ling, they burned down her barn."

"Aye. 'Tis no secret the lass loves her horses. Most folks know the best way to hurt her is to harm what she loves the most."

"Bastards."

"Aye."

"When I got wind of their plan, I rode out quick as I could. Got here in time to stop a full-blown prairie fire but was too late to save the barn. Glory to the saints, Abraham didn't go with the girls to his cabin tonight. He got the mares and their babies out before the roof fell in."

"The girls?"

"Aye. The Doves. All of them, except Della, are her ranch hands. Can ye imagine such a thing?"

"Good God no. Are you serious? Women?" He shook his head. "Looks like a lot of things have changed since I've been gone."

"Aye. Dixie hired Abraham as her foreman."

"Hayes seems like a nice enough fella."

"Aye. That he is. Natural around horses." Donavan took another snort. "Now tell me, lad. How be it you came ridin' in after being gone for months? Did ye nail Payton's hide to the barn door?"

"Nope. When I got back to the train, he was gone. Doc Webster thought he'd heal faster in a bed that didn't bounce. Dropped him off in a little town along the trail called Tumbleweed."

"They be wondering what took ye so long getting back?"

"At first. But when I lied and told them Buck went lame

and I had to find another horse, they backed off. Especially when they caught sight of Thunder. I didn't think Morgan would pull any shenanigans without his partner to back him up, but I had to stay with the wagons until they cleared the mountains to make sure.

"I doubled back to Tumbleweed, but the yellow-bellied cur had left by then. The town's sawbones said Payton talked nonstop about finding, the 'red-headed whelp' who crippled him. Since I'd been gone for so long, I thought he'd come back this way thinking Dixie was here. I lit out as fast as I could. Heard in town about her ranch. When I saw the smoke, my heart stopped."

He ducked his head.

"Thought Payton had found the lass, did ye?"

"I expected the worst. Thought I see her lying face down in the dirt covered with ash and soot." Eyes squeezed tight, his voice turned to a whisper.

"Just like Kansas."

"Instead, I saw her screaming and kicking you." He grinned. "Prettiest sight I'd ever seen. I started to breathe normal again until I heard what she was hollerin'. I didn't want to leave her, Finn. But she acted like she didn't want me to stick around. I don't understand."

"Ah, lad, for all her fire and passion, Dixie is still a young girl on the verge of womanhood all alone in the Wild West. And that scares her."

"She's so determined and stubborn that sometimes I forget all she's been through. Payton may not have ruined her, but his actions left a scar just the same." He gazed at his boot and toyed with his spur. "But I hoped . . ."

"She'd feel different about you?"

"Yeah, something like that."

Donovan heaved his big frame out of the rocker and hitched up his pants. "She's proud. It isn't easy for her to say what's in her heart. But I've seen the way the lass looks at ye. She worried over ye. Be patient, laddie." He winked.

"She'll come around. Now, I think it be time to go fetch the little stick of dynamite back home, don't ye?"

"Need a favor first."

"Anything, lad. What be it?"

"Can I borrow a horse from ya'? Dixie's done rode off with mine . . . again."

CHAPTER 58

I was almost to town when I came to my senses. Well, halfway to my senses. Fire still raged in my belly, but my chest ached from the thrashing of my heart. Dizzy, my head pounded from the blood thundering in my ears. I had to stop. Get my feelings under control. Surprise had been on my side when I rescued Chow Ling. This was different. They'd be expecting me this time. For sure, I'd be riding into an ambush.

High in the night sky, the full moon bathed the night in ice-crystal brilliance. I dismounted and led Thunder through the brush to the bubbling stream that ran alongside the trail. With long, deep slurps, he drank deep. I pulled him back. Not too much at first. His coat shimmered with sweat. Like me, he needed to cool down. I leaned against rough tree bark and slid to the ground.

I'd done it again. Pushed Jackson from me. Lord, what a hypocrite. One minute, longing to see his face, the next, angry that he was around. Yearning for his arms yet rejecting his embrace. Relief damn near dropped me to my knees when he rode up tonight. Seeing his face made my heart soar. Still, despite all of that, I ignored his concern. Pity. That's all it was. Pity. Didn't need that. I'd made it this far without him, hadn't I?

No.

I argued with myself.

If Jackson hadn't left Joe, you would've never escaped Payton.

Not true. Dozens of horses were tied to that picket line.

He rode ahead. Warned Big Finn. Paved the way for your welfare.

I didn't ask him to. I had money. Could've made my own way. Got my own job.

Doing what? Working for Della at the White Dove?

Shut up.

Jackson put the idea of the ranch in your head.

I would've gotten around to the notion sooner or later.

He loves you.

No argument there.

What is wrong with you?

Nothing.

I picked up a flat rock and threw it. The sound of the splash echoed loudly in the moonlight.

Thunder's soft nicker told me I wasn't alone. I stood but didn't turn around. Didn't need to. I knew who was walking toward me. I smiled. He was late. Expected him a lot sooner.

Heat warmed my back when he walked up behind me. Eyes closed, I waited for his familiar scent of shaving soap, wind, and rain to engulf me. Strong arms reached around and hugged my back to his chest.

This time I didn't pull away. This time I surrendered. Revealed in the rhythm of his easy drawl.

"Howdy, darlin'."

Two words. These two words turned my knees weak, made me smile, and tear up all at the same time.

I swallowed the lump in my throat. I needed to explain.

"I saw trusting and depending on others buried in a hole in the middle of nowhere with only the four strong winds to sing hymns. Hard to forget that. To let it go."

It wasn't much of an apology, but it was all I could manage.

His hold tightened.

We stood together surrounded by moonlight and singing water. Bullfrogs grunted. Crickets chirped. The wind touched the moonbeam water with gentle fingertips and stirred the ripples into silver ribbons. Wrapped in his warmth, the tight band around my chest loosened. The itching to keep fighting, to keep running eased. I wanted to freeze that moment in time. Never move. Never step away.

His soft sigh tickled my ears.

"When I saw the smoke, I thought I'd find you dead."

"Not quite. They want me to suffer first."

"They?"

"Dakota Rutherford, his daddy, Micky Doogan, and probably every horse rancher
from here to Santa Fe."

"Dang, darlin', what did you do to piss them off?"

"I had the guts to beat them at their own game. Proved I could breed top-notch stock with only the help of a Negro and a handful of women."

"What about Chow Ling and the One-Eyed Jack?"

I grinned. "Sounds like you've been talking to Finn. Yeah, that little bruhaha lit the fuse."

"You did wonders with the ranch. Never would've thought of using Della's gals for ranch hands. Smart thinking, darlin.'"

"Should've seen it before sneaking coyotes burned the barn."

In a whisper, the magic spell of harmony Jackson had woven shattered. I could taste the burning wood and grass on the tip of my tongue, hear the colt's terrified whinnies. My breath quickened. Anger returned. I squirmed in his arms. "Let me go."

He turned me loose without a word. Surprised at his

quick release, I stumbled a few steps then turned to him.

"I didn't come here to fight with you, Dixie."

"What did you come for?"

"Payton is on the prowl. Thought maybe he doubled back to Six Shooter."

"Is that the only reason?"

"No."

I waited. He said nothing, just kept simmering my blood with his chestnut-eyed stare.

I'd forgotten how good-looking he was. His strength and charm. His little-boy smile and white teeth. The smooth glide of his walk. His catlike grace and speed. Wide shoulders. Flat chest. His overall masculinity he wore like armor, unaware of its allure. But not his dimples.

Those I would always remember. Till the day I died.

I walked back to him. Stopped within a whisker of his solid frame.

"You come back for me, Lawman?"

God Almighty. That was bold.

The heat that passed between us could burn down a hundred barns.

"You *are* damn hard to forget."

Good enough . . . for now.

Guess our fever scorched the tail feathers of an owl. The night bird swooped down from the tree standing beside us. Let out a screech that made my toes curl and the horses spook. The scream dissolved the moment and brought me back to the present. I marched toward the horses, intent on making Dakota and his bunch pay. Jackson caught my arm and whirled me around.

"You can't fight them alone."

"The hell I can't."

"What? Ya' gonna' ride in there and shoot every man that walks? Ya got no proof who was responsible."

"I know who they are. Don't need no proof."

"Well, ya' need a plan. Got one of those?"

Damn the man. He had me there.

"No. But I'm not going to roll over and play dead. Forget the whole thing happened."

"I'm not asking you to. Let me and Finn poke around. He's had his eye on Micky Doogan for a while now. Followed him here from back East."

"Why?"

"Has something to do with the Molly McGuire's."

"Who are they?"

"More like *what* are they. They're a secret society come over from Ireland. Bad bunch of hombres. They're Irish American coal miners mostly. They've been known to kill and maim. Destroy property. New Mexico has a lot of coal mines, and the trains will be hauling cars of it back East which means big money. The Railroad hired the Pinkerton Agency to make sure the gang wouldn't get a foothold here. Up until now, they haven't shown their hand. Burning down your barn may be the break Donovan's been looking for."

"What am I supposed to do in the meantime?"

"Build a new barn."

"You offerin' to help?"

"Are you asking me to stay?"

"I can always use an extra hand."

He chuckled.

"Good enough . . . for now."

CHAPTER 59

Jackson and Abraham wasted little time getting the barn framed. Big Finn even sent a few of his railroad crew to help. I asked how the Railroad would react if they knew their labor was building my barn.

"'Tis not your concern, lass. Take the help and be grateful. Besides, I owed ye one for shooting Micky Doogan."

The Doves flocked to Jackson like . . . well, like Doves. They flirted, laughed, and teased. Couldn't blame them. His easy laugh and laid-back manner, not to mention the way he filled out a pair of breeches, could melt even a Saint's resolve. Jealously would've been a big problem on my part, except for one thing. He never flirted back. He'd laugh and joke. Help out if necessary but would take it no further. As Dominique put it, "He only has eyes for you, Cheri."

I didn't know if that was true or not.

Concerned for our safety, Abraham offered to move back into the tack room. But with a Pinkerton standing guard, he was free to go home to his cabin at night without fear of leaving us unprotected. He needn't have worried. All of us were armed to the teeth.

Having a Pinkerton detective only yards from my door

should've made me sleep better. It didn't. If the lawman had been some other fella', things would've been different. But we were talking about Jackson Wayne. Like it or not, I had a hard time not thinking about him every hour of the day and night. It didn't help matters none when after tossing and turning one night, I finally gave up on sleep and stepped outside onto the porch. I caught him washing up at the well.

Naked from the waist up, wet hair slicked back, he stood as a statue chiseled out of moonstone and starlight. Lean. Muscular. My breath caught. I sank onto the rocker, not daring to breathe, captivated by his beauty. Never thought a man could be beautiful, but I knew of no other word. A peacemaker. A warrior. A kindred spirit to this wild, untamed land birthed by earth, wind, rain, and fire.

And I was his woman.

His woman.

What did that mean?

His partner? His equal? Or his property? Like his horse or gun?

I felt my muscles tighten. My lips flattened into a straight line. The moonlight had bewitched me.

I was no one's possession. No one's blue ribbon.

I was my own woman. I belonged only to me.

If Jackson wasn't man enough to realize this, if he'd try and tame me, bend me to his will, be his property, then all the love in the world wouldn't be enough to hold me.

CHAPTER 60

Wide shoulders leaned against the barn door. Lost in shadows, Jackson never took his gaze off her. Moonlight had reached out and captured a firefly in its beam. He watched her slip back into the house. Willowy. Graceful. Silent as dandelion wisps in the wind. He smiled at that. Seemed like years had passed since he'd called her a wild, prairie dandelion. Proud. Independent. Vulnerable. A child. But not anymore. The child had given way to a woman. Still just as noble and wild. And in many ways, just as vulnerable.

He sensed the passion simmering under the cover of indifference, her façade of self-reliance. Took all the strength he could muster not to storm her door. To kiss those pouting lips. Fan that passion into a raging fire and burn in its essence.

Did she know how her unyielding mistrust made him? The mask had almost slipped. That night he held her by the water when she confessed how hard it was to let go. But the moment only lasted as long as a sigh. Did she have any idea how frustrating it was to be so close yet so far away from her? Big Finn said to be patient. He would. But not a lifetime.

He loved her. Heart and soul. Always had. Always would.

But a man could only take so much.

CHAPTER 61

I said it before. Doves are tough women. But even the strongest women cry. Maybe that is the secret behind our strength. Next to Sassy, Dominique was the sturdiest woman I'd ever known. She spit in the face of danger. Threw thin-bladed knives at its threat. When I found her sobbing in the barn the next morning. I couldn't believe it.

"Dominique? What's wrong?"

Her tearstained face wrenched my heart. I knelt and put my arm around her shoulders. Her fragrant perfume filled my nose. Brushing horses or mucking stalls, Dominique always wore some flowery scent.

"Oh, Dixee. I cannot marry Abraham."

"Why? Don't you love him anymore?"

"I love him more than my own life.

"Did he change his mind?"

"He would die for me."

I eased my butt down on the straw. "Then what's the problem?"

"The priest refused. Is not important to me. My God cares more for the love in your heart than a union sanctioned by a man dressed in robes spouting store-bought religion. But to Abraham, this is not so. He insists on a priestly blessing."

"Why won't the priest marry you?"

"We are both dark. My soul is not pure. Abraham is not white."

Holy crow. So much for love your neighbor and do unto others.

This wouldn't do. Love was too hard to find on its own. When found, nothing should tear it apart. A pang of guilt brushed past me. Love stared me right in the face, and I pushed it away more than once. I jumped up and brushed the straw off my bottom. This wasn't about me. I reached out a hand to Dominique.

"Come on. There's got to be a way around this. We'll get the rest of the girls together. I'm sure we can come up with something. Oui?"

Tears finished, she smiled. "Oui."

Maybe I spoke too soon. All of us, including Sassy who was back from Santa Fe with a promise from the Captain to inspect our stock, sat around my kitchen table. After explaining the problem, there was a lot of outrage and sympathy but no suggestions on what to do.

Sassy lit up a cheroot. I'd forgotten how heady the vanilla tobacco made me. I could taste the sweetness on the tip of my tongue. She blew out a lung full and cocked that eyebrow of hers.

"Maybe we need to look at this another way."

Excitement and blue smoke circled the table. I could feel an idea in the making.

She gazed over at Dominique. "Would any man of God fit the bill?"

"What are you getting at?" Mary Louise asked.

"Just saying, there's more than one way to skin a cat."

"Tell me about this cat," Dominique said.

"Chow Ling."

"What's he got to do with this?" I asked.

"Chow Ling is an interesting and educated little fella.

He and I talked about things when he dropped off vegetables at the White Dove." She glanced around the table. "Don't y'all look so shocked. I have you know beneath all this makeup and beauty, I have a mind that is curious about other notions and people."

Well, whaddya know? Sassy revealed yet another side. Always full of surprises.

"Chow Ling is a Buddhist. It's a long story, but basically a Buddhist monk is very pure in heart and about as close to God as a body can get. Of course, they don't call Him God. But what's in a name? A cougar is just a big cat, but I don't call him kitty, and I don't want him lapping up cream in my kitchen."

Coffee squirted out my nose. We laughed till our sides ached. Sassy just kept right on smoking without a hint of a grin, which made us laugh that much harder.

"When y'all are finished hee-hawing, I'll go on."

We settled down.

"According to Chow Ling, the Buddhist pretty much think marriage is a private thing between two people. They don't stand on ceremony that much. All that is important is love. But. A Buddhist monk will bless a marriage if so desired."

I knew where she was headed. "Is Chow Ling a Buddhist monk by any chance?" I asked.

"No. But he knows of one in Six Shooter Siding."

All eyes turned to Dominique.

"Would being blessed by a monk satisfy Abraham?"

This time, Dominique cried happy tears. "Oui. I am sure of it."

I took a deep breath.

"Well, it's settled, then. Let's go see a Chin-ee Indian."

CHAPTER 62

Jackson rode with us to visit with Flying Eagle while we talked with Chow Ling.

"Flying Eagle sees me coming, he might duck and run," I said. "Last time we saw one another, he ended up with houseguests."

Jackson grinned. "Only you would try something that wild but this scheme is even wilder."

"I had nothing to do with this. Blame Sassy."

"You do realize it's dangerous? Someone will have to talk to the monk. If it's Chow Ling, you'll have to smuggle him into town and pray no one sees him. Then you'll have to get this monk fella to wherever the wedding is going to be." He cocked his head at me. "By the way, where *is* it going to be?"

Hell if I knew. First things first.

Flying Eagle greeted his blood brother with a toothy grin. "Big Wayne, has been many moons. You come. We smoke." He shot me a suspicious look. "What favor you ask this time?"

"Nothing for you."

"Hmm. This is good."

Dominique's eyes nearly popped out of her head.

"Dixcee? So many Indians."

"We're safe."

I'm not at all sure she believed me.

Something about sitting cross-legged in a teepee drinking ginseng tea didn't ring true. Yet Chow Ling and his family seemed content.

"Chow Ling berry happy see Missy Dixie and Missy Dominique."

I took the teacup from his wife and smiled. "How are things here? Any problems?"

"No problems. Red skin. Yellow skin. Same, same but different. All want peace. We together but apart. Redman stay on other side of stream. We share vegetables and tobacco. Why you come?"

I glanced at Dominique. After all, this was her rodeo. She explained her idea. I expected reluctance. What I got was quite different.

"Chow Ling most honored to do this for Missy Dominique. To repay for life. Indeed, there is a monk who lives in the village by the railroad. My most honored friend, Chen Ping. You say I send. He will know is true."

"You and your family must come to the ceremony," Dominique said.

Chow Ling nodded, but his wife knelt by Dominique and took her hand.

"This most kind. Wedding is happy day. But have no gift."

"Oh, Cheri. No gift is required."

"For me, is. You have a ceremonial gown?"

"A wedding dress? No. Not yet."

Chow Ling's wife rose and scurried over to an old chest in the corner. I looked at him. He shrugged.

"Jiao berry serious."

"Jiao?"

"My wife. It means delicate, tender, and most beautiful."

She returned and placed a square package in

Dominique's hands.

"For you. You like?"

We glanced at one another. With long, delicate fingers, Dominique unwrapped the package, careful not to tear the delicate paper. With a gasp, she held up the gown and pressed the dress against her.

"It called, Kimono," Chow Ling said.

Kimono. Ever so much more regal sounding than a robe. But then again, it was only fitting seeing how the gown must have been sewed by angels.

How do you explain beauty? Mere words never quite get the job done. Freed from its cage of paper and string, bold fire-red silk burst alive and wrapped Dominique in a living, breathing cocoon of gentle, sweeping elegance. Long sleeves trimmed in gold thread cascaded to her waist. Deep sky-blue, peacock-green, and tiger-lily butterflies adorned the back and sides, so brilliant and real I expected them to flit away. The gown dripped its magic onto Dominique's black hair and transformed her locks into a halo of sleek, liquid onyx.

Jiao clapped her hands together. "Daiyu."

I turned to Chow Ling.

"Mean. Black Jade."

Abraham would be struck deaf and dumb.

Dominique blinked back tears and turned to Jiao. "This was your wedding dress, wasn't it?"

"*Shi.* Yes."

Papa claimed women were the biggest mystery in life. Maybe that was true to men but not to other women. Surrounded by the simplicity of tanned hide and wood, silence loud as thunder passed between the three of us. There were no words powerful enough to explain how golden this moment was. Dominique handed the silk robe to me, pressed her hands together, and bowed to Jiao.

"I would be honored to wear this."

"Where wedding be?" Chow Ling broke the spell.

I laughed. "Not sure yet. But you and your family must come. It'll be somewhere safe, I promise. I'll let you know."

Dominique and I rode in reverent silence back to the ranch. Jackson was at a loss to explain our mood but said nothing. It would've been easy to explain, but the plain truth was neither Dominique nor I wanted to speak. Words would muddy the water, taint the deep feeling of sacrifice, gratitude, and love that was the essence of Jiao.

CHAPTER 63

The old Spanish Mission slept in the sun, a hollow shell of what it used to be. But where I could only see crumbling stones and weeds, Dominique saw a grand cathedral.

"Dixicee, do not look with your eyes. Feel with your heart. This is holy ground. I feel God and all his wonders seeping through the wood and stone."

I tried. I truly did. I glanced over at Della and shook my head.

"This is all your doings, ya' know," I scolded. "Ever since you heard about this wedding, you've filled her head plumb full of dreams and crazy ideas."

"I've done what? Pardon me, missy, but I'm just riding on Sassy's coattails with this one. Monks. Silk gowns. Why, this old broken-down church is the only thing sane about the whole shebang."

"Hey, don't blame me," Sassy grumbled. "I was just trying to find a solution to this mess."

"My wedding is no mess," Dominique shot back.

"Y'all calm down," Mary Louise said. "Quit squabbling and accept the beauty of this place. The tall trees stand like guardian angels. Smell the marigolds and chicory. Look at the old mission tucked in and nestled against the stone cliff smothered by purple, blue, and white wildflowers and green grass. You wanted a safe place? A hidden spot? What better paradise than this? Just think of all the baptisms and weddings that happened here. This church was beautiful once. We can make it that way again."

"How?" I asked.

Mary Louise flitted around like a little Jenny Wren songbird. "Lanterns. We'll hang lanterns from the trees. Put candles in the stone's nooks and crannies." She darted over to the side of the church where a peaceful stream wove through the woods. "Oh my God. Come see."

Expecting to find a coiled rattler the size of my leg, I drew in a sharp breath when Mary Louise grabbed Dominique and squealed.

"Look at this old vine-covered bridge!" She clapped her hands together. "Dominique, I have a wonderful idea. We'll line the path leading from the bridge to church with lanterns too. Instead of walking down the aisle, you'll walk over the bridge and up the lighted pathway." Unable to control her excitement, she jumped up and down. "You'll look like a fairy princess stepping out of the mist. It'll be so romantic."

Dominique caught Mary Louise's fever. "Oui, Cheri. Magnifique."

"Who's going to give the bride away?"

"I am. Who else?" Della laughed. "After the ceremony, we'll head to the ranch for the reception."

"Reception?"

"Well, hell yeah. Mother of God, Dixie, ain't you ever seen anyone tie the knot? There's always a big shindig afterward."

Della didn't mean anything by it, but her words hurt. Yes. I'd seen a wedding—Mama's.

That day still left a bitter taste in my mouth. I swallowed hard. Dominique's marriage would be different. Joyous.

Loving.

"I'm bringing my china and crystal I bought in Santa Fe to use at the Opera House," Della continued. "Already talked with Abby. She's all excited. Gonna' cook up a fest and I hear a big cake too. Jackson's gonna' build a large bonfire. We'll set up a long table outside, sit by the firelight, eat, drink, and be merry. Maybe even dance ifn' I can find someone to play the fiddle."

"I talked to the monk," Sassy said. "He's more than willing to bless the happy couple and see his old friend, Chow Ling, again. Finn and I will smuggle him out of town." She glanced my way. "Think you can fetch Chow Ling and his family?"

I nodded. Dumbfounded. Everything was moving fast. When had they planned all of this?

"Well, that settles it, then," Della said. "All we need now is the date."

All of us turned toward Dominique.

"Next Saturday? Oui?"

"Oui!"

CHAPTER 64

When things are right, everything runs smoothly. Saturday dawned a perfect day. Not too hot. Not too cold.

Mary Louise was up at sunrise gathering enough lanterns and candles to light the whole forest. She rode out to the church leading a packhorse loaded with boxes and packages before I'd even washed the sleep from my eyes. Abby cooked up a storm all week and was busy making sugar flowers to put on the wedding cake. Jackson was gathering wood. Everyone scampered around like ants. I headed out to the Indian village for Chow Ling.

The ceremony took place right before twilight. Everyone was decked out in their Sunday go-to-meeting best. I even shed my breeches and spurs for a mint-green dress. Big Finn wore a new vest and bowler hat.

As grand as Mary Louise's vision had been, we weren't ready for the satin and lace happy-ever-after- land she created for Dominique and Abraham. Lanterns hung from tree branches threw a softening glow over the scene, relaxing the sharp edges of rock and wood. Dozens of pink and white satin ribbons cascaded from the branches as well. Waving long and delicate in the gentle breeze, they reminded me of feathered angel wings in flight. Candles hid in the cracks of the old church walls. Some melted, and warm wax inched between the stones to freeze like lacy lady fingers on the cold rock. To add to the dreamy feeling, Mae Ling placed small wooden boats with lit candles upstream on the creek. The lazy current floated them downstream and under the bridge. Flickering candlelight reflected off the water to hold hands with the star points and moonbeams skipping along the surface. Magical. A fantasy land straight out of a storybook.

"Ah, surely there be wee folk peeking out from under every leaf and flower petal." Big Finn sighed.

Dominique glided over the ivy bridge and up the lightened pathway. So beautiful in her fiery red and gold that even Mother Nature held her breath to watch. Dressed in a new starched-white shirt and tie, Abraham never took his eyes off her.

Chen Ping stood where the wooden mission door had been. A tiny man, with wire spectacles and a tranquil spirit whose warm smile charmed everyone into peace and harmony.

East meets West.

Abraham and Dominique exchanged traditional vows.

"In sickness and health."

"For better or worse."

"Till death do us part."

Rings slipped onto fingers.

Chen Ping's hands joined theirs and his singsong blessing rang out smooth and clear. None of us understood one word. Didn't matter. Love surrounded us and spoke its own language. Finn had his arm around Sassy.

Chow Ling and Jiao held hands.

All the Doves stood side-by-side, teary-eyed and grinning like possums.

Jackson stood next to Della.

I stood alone and tried to breathe.

It wasn't fair. The groom should be the best-looking man at a wedding. Hands down, Jackson Wayne shamed every man there, or anywhere for that matter. He stole my air. All I could do was gawk at him.

Buckskin and fringe gave way to black trousers, a white shirt, and a dark cutaway coat that accented his wide shoulders and slim waist. If that wasn't enough to make my mouth water, he added a black western bow tie and Stetson. Candlelight bounced off his dress boots. If he were a peppermint stick, I would've licked him till my tongue fell off.

"Cuts a fine figure of a lad, doesn't he, lass?"

Oh, God. Shoot me now. It was bad enough to be caught ogling Jackson by the Doves, but by another man was downright humiliating, especially when the other fella' was Big Finn.

"'Tis his going-to-court suit. Intimidates the prosecuting attorneys, turns them into blithering idiots."

I managed a weak smile and resisted the urge to crawl under a rock.

Vows said.

Blessing received.

A kiss to seal the deal.

We gathered the lanterns and headed back to the ranch. Reluctant to ruin the fairy tale and almost sacrilegious to blow the candles out and take down the ribbons, we left them there to throw twinkling light into the night and guide wandering spirits home.

Jackson rode ahead and had the fire started when we arrived. Abby placed dish after dish of food fit for a king on the lace-tablecloth table. Here again, Mary Louise's taste was evident. Candles in canning jars sparkled against bone-thin china. Firelight touched the crystal and made red wine shimmer like liquid rubies in a glass. Chow Ling brought his own drink. A rice wine called Baijiu.

"Tastes like kerosene and kicks like a mule, it does,"

Finn claimed. "Any brave enough to partake might see Jesus himself sitting beside him."

Sometimes I fall out of myself, step back, and watch the world as if in a dream. Doesn't happen too often. Don't know the how or why of it. I just do. This was one of those times. Good food. Good drink. Close friends. Lovers. Each of us different yet the same. All sat around one common table, laughing, joking, and sharing in a love that had been labeled taboo. As if mortal man had the right to brand anything so divine as pure love.

"Della, me darling. Did ye find a fiddle player?"

"Sorry, not a one."

"Pity. Would like to dance a jig, I would."

"No worry, Big Bossman. Chow Ling and Chen Ping bring music."

An ear-splitting tinny twang jarred me out of my reverie and dropped me back at the table with a thud. What was that? Sounded like a cat being strangled in a tin can. Made the hairs on my arm stick straight up. Every coyote in the county wailed and howled.

"Saints alive, Chow. What manner of beasty be that?"

"You no worry. You wait. You see. Berry pretty."

Yeah, well. Maybe. Beauty was in the eye of the beholder.

I shouldn't have doubted Chow Ling. When tuned, the strange three-stringed banjo produced soulful music. Even more so when Chen Ping played along on his bamboo flute. Of course, most of the tunes were from China with only a few American songs thrown in, but that didn't matter to any of us. I leaned back in my chair, listened, and watched Finn whirl and twirl Sassy and the girls. About fell over backward when Jackson pulled out a harmonica and joined in. Who knew?

Somewhere along the line, Dominique and Abraham slipped off into the night. The fire died down. Mae Ling fell asleep. Jiao carried her inside, and I tucked her in on my couch. Dickens kitten curled beside her. We cleared the table and packed Della's precious dishes and crystal.

Big Finn and Sassy loaded Della and Chen Ping in their wagon and headed back to town even though I begged them to stay until morning. "Nay, lass. Will be better for all to bring the monk back under cover of darkness."

I gave Chow Ling and Jiao my bed for the night. I would take them back to the village in the morning. I'd sleep in the bunkhouse instead.

Just like that, the party was over. The clock chimed midnight. The magic spell ended.

I felt empty inside. Let down somehow.

I'd drank just enough wine to blur the line between reality and dreams. When Jackson strolled toward me and eased beside the campfire, it wouldn't have surprised me to see him vanish in a hazy mist.

"You sure look handsome tonight, Lawman."

He tipped his hat. "Well, thank ya', darlin'."

I giggled. "Didn't know you could play the harmonica."

"Just full of surprises, aren't I?"

He pulled makings from his pocket and rolled a cigarette. Another surprise.

"I didn't know you smoked."

"Not very often."

"Why tonight?"

"Seems a fitting end to a special day."

I sighed. Slipped from the chair to join him by the fire. "It was a grand day, wasn't it? Dominique was beautiful."

He removed the black Stetson and put it on the log behind him. "Couldn't say. Too busy admiring the girl in the green dress."

I watched the tip of his cigarette glow orange and pitch tiny sparks into the autumn air. We sat quietly, listened to the night, and the crackling of the fire. He flicked the smoke into the embers and reached out a hand to me.

"Let's dance."

"Dance? With no music?"

"Yep."

Long legs uncurled and he helped to my feet.

"I don't dance that well," I said.

"I got you. You'll do fine."

A strong arm cinched me up tight to his muscled body. Had I been sober, I would've been stiff as cardboard, more concerned about my feet than the man who held me tight. But drink and his musky scent chased away any thought of dance steps. I melted into him. Closed my eyes. Felt the deep rumble in his chest as he hummed a tune and waltzed me into deep night.

I remembered Mama saying how Papa danced like liquid silk. If Papa was silk, then Jackson Wayne was quicksilver on ice.

Firelight. Twinkling stars. Dancing in the moonlight. It was perfect.

I kissed him.

Not a small peck on the cheek, but full on the lips that tasted of sweet bourbon and tobacco.

He kissed back.

Fevered. Hungry. Powerful.

My head swam.

A low groan.

He pushed away.

I stood stupid. "What's wrong? What did I do?"

A low growl. "Nothing."

"Then what? I thought you…" A deep gulp. "I thought you wanted me."

"I do. More than day yearns for light. But not tonight. Not this way."

"What way?"

"You're burning up in wedding fever, and you're drunk."

"I certainly am not. A little light-headed maybe. But I know full well what I'm doing."

"Do you?"

His crooked smile wasn't so cute this time. Pissed me off good. Here I was throwing my heart out to him and he'd thrown it back. Felt betrayed. Foolish.

"Go to hell."

One step put him square in my face. He grabbed me. Pulled me rough to him. Kissed me so hard, so demanding and wild it scared the liver out of me.

He turned me loose. Dark eyes, smoky and deep flamed my fire. His voice came husky.

"You're a wild prairie dandelion, Dixie gal. But I don't pick flowers until they're ready."

He turned on his heel and faded into the dark.

CHAPTER 65

Short room and long legs didn't fit. Jackson paced a few steps one way, a few the other in the small tack room.

It wasn't right. The bride should be the prettiest woman at a wedding. While Dominique's red gown and honey skin had indeed been striking, hands down, Dixie stood head and shoulders above them all.

That green dress wrapped around her like a second skin. Hugged her curves and willowy frame. And tonight? Sister to the fire's golden embers, her copper hair danced hand-in-hand with its flame. The candlelight flickering in her blue eyes put every twinkling star to shame. Upturned nose. A bridge of freckles. Face glowing with excitement. Lips sweeter than the wine she'd drank made his blood boil. It was enough to drive a man to his knees.

But it was her unbridled spirit that set her apart from all others and made him struggle to hold himself in check. Took all he had to push her away. Hell yes, he wanted her. Had from the first time she'd swung a fist at him that day on the wagon train. White-hot passion. Grit. An untamed daring as impossible to contain as a whirlwind in a bottle. That was Dixie's true beauty. Her soul.

But a soul was a delicate thing. One false move, one

careless moment could bruise and shatter, never to be whole again. A prairie dandelion grew wild and strong. Yet for all its strength could wither and die if handled wrong, its beauty destroyed. That was the reason for his tight rein. The kid gloves he wore around her. Contrary to her notion, she wasn't ready for his love tonight. He wanted to be more than a regret the next morning. True, he'd embarrassed and confused her by stepping away. He could live with that.

But to break her soul, kill the spirit he so desperately loved would be a sin he could never forgive himself or atone for.

He rolled another smoke. Took in a deep draw.

Yep. No doubt about it. Sleep wouldn't come easy tonight.

She sure did look pretty in green.

Chapter 66

Neither Big Finn nor Jackson had any luck finding Micky Doogan.

"'Tis like Mother Earth herself opened up and swallowed him whole," Finn said.

"I wager he left the county," Jackson replied.

"Bet he's laying low at the Rocking R waiting for his shoulder to heal," I said. "I know he and Dakota are in cahoots, plotting and planning their next move against me."

"Aye. Could be so. But we have no call to go and search."

Jackson pointed a finger at me. "Neither do you. Stay away from the Rocking R."

Maybe I would. Maybe I wouldn't.

The barn was finished. Good thing. Fall was on its last legs, and winter frothed at the bit

waiting to run full bore. I dreaded the cold and damp and took full advantage of the dwindling warm days every chance I got. Since coming to the ranch, Jackson had been too busy to see his faithful buckskin. One sunny afternoon, we saddled up and headed out to find the golden stallion and his herd.

"Better leave Thunder here," Jackson said. "Don't think

Buck would take too kindly to him."

"Ride Poe. Dominique won't mind."

I'd forgotten the thrill of the ride. The wind in my face. Blood roaring in my ears. The total surrender of all thought, all control. To just feel the power and speed of the horse. Joe was in fine form, racing both the wind and Poe. Running beside us, the long-legged chestnut chewed up the ground and spit it out. We let both horses take the bit before checking down into a nice, comfortable jogtrot.

I'd never ridden the whole fifty acres that was Spirit Dove Ranch. Even though it was fall, lush grass still covered the land, and tall, leafy trees dotted the landscape. I glanced over at Jackson.

"I have no idea where Buck and his mares would be."

"Good bet he'd be close to water."

We followed the creek bed. A slight breeze rustled the treetops. Clear water bubbled alongside. The crisp, fresh smell of wood and crunchy leaves swirled around us. I had no reason to feel uneasy. But I did. Queasy and nervous, I slowed to a walk. Jackson noticed the change in me right off.

"What's wrong?"

"Don't know. Can't put my finger on it."

We stopped. He turned in the saddle. Hawk eyes swept the terrain looking for anything out of place.

"Anything?" I asked.

"Nothing."

Silly. I was just being silly. Even still, I couldn't shake the feeling of being watched.

I rode on slightly ahead.

Joe's ears pricked.

Poe whinnied.

The side of my head burned something fierce.

I saw Jackson reach for me.

I pitched from the saddle and smacked the ground hard.

Blackness.

CHAPTER 67

Your mother is a banshee witch and is not welcomed in his house!"

Papa stood solid, naming me after his mother, but he gave in to Mama that day. I was heartbroken.

Grandma Margeret had the gift of sight. She knew things before they happened. Wild animals were putty in her hands, a trait Papa inherited and bequeathed to me, especially horses.

Gram healed my skinned knees just by putting her hands over the wound. Helped deliver many babies. She grew herbs. Brewed remedies and could read people like a book.

I loved her with all my heart. She loved me more than that.

Often, she would speak to me of the wee folk and taught me how to look for them in the woods and fairy rings. But the best thing, as well as the spookiest, she could see and talk to dead people.

"Death is not the end," she'd tell me. "Ye only step over into a different world."

Papa took her abilities for granted, and never questioned her beliefs.

Mama was scared to death of her, which I found

amusing.

In the darkness, she came to me and touched my cheek.

"A leanbh, my child, 'tis not time to fly with the fairies and walk in spirit.

Wake!"

I refused.

Chapter 68

Payton's face shot before me. Changed into Dakota's. Then Micky Doogan's.

"Leave me alone!"

Black again.

"Papa?"

Aye, daughter. I be right here.

Here? Where was here?

No colors. No smells. No sounds. Just snowy, hushed whiteness all around.

"Am I dead?"

A soft chuckle. *Ye not be at the pearly gates just yet if that be what ye mean.*

That's exactly what I meant.

You be in Saint Peter's backyard for sure. But the living or dying part, he's leaving up to you.

Holy crow. Even dying was complicated.

"Where are the angels? There's nothing here but white. Thought heaven would be prettier."

Oh, heaven be a grand sight, child. But 'tis like I say. You're not quite there yet. Ye be on the borderline.

"I'm tired. Think I'll sleep some more."

Nay, lass. Been napping too long. Make a decision. Get

busy living or get busy dying.

That was harsh even for a ghost.

"Don't you want me to stay here with you?"

Aye, would be grand, but I've lived my life. 'Tis yours we be discussing. What of that boyo of yours?

"Jackson?"

He's a fine lad, girl. Loves ye more than his own life. Would break his spirit to see you leave.

"Oh sure. Loves me so much, he pushed me away."

For your own good, daughter. And ye have no right to cast stones. How many times have ye pushed back?

Good point.

"You like him, don't you."

Aye that I do. 'Tis the only lad I know man enough to let ye run, lass. That be rare.

"I'm kinda hungry."

Then open your eyes, girl.

Wake up!

CHAPTER 69

Like a lantern in the fog, Della's voice guided me out of the whiteness.

"She's waking up! Everyone. She's awake."

I heard shuffling of feet and chairs being scooted back. Still groggy, I fought the urge to fall back into sleep. Someone grabbed my hand. That did it. I opened my eyes.

"Mother of God, Dixie. It's about time."

Sassy. Good ol' Sassy. Out of all the Doves, she was the most steadfast. Should've guessed she'd be the one to take my hand and jerk me back into the land of the living.

Throat dry as sawdust, I tried to croak out a word or two, but a fit of coughing stopped the words cold.

"Easy does it there, gal. Sip this."

Della held a cup to my lips. Water never tasted so good. She eased me back. "What happened?"

"You got shot," Della said.

"In the head," Sassy added.

I must've looked at them goofier than a city slicker wearing a bow tie with spurs.

"We ain't joshing. Someone bushwhacked you and Jackson."

My heart flipped over and threw me upright. Woozy,

my head swam.

"Good God, Dixie. Take it easy." Della propped me up against the pillows. "Your cowboy is fine. Well, physically, at least. Ain't got his head on too straight right at the moment. He was worried plumb sick about you."

"Oui. He never left your side."

"How long have I been out?"

"Today makes three days," Della said. "The bullet only grazed you, but Jackson said when you fell, the ground punched you in the head with a sickening thud. Doc said you'd either wake up or . . . well, that don't matter none now. What Dominique said about Jackson is true. He damn near rode Poe's legs off getting you back here. Had blood all over him. Looked like he'd wrestled a bear. Practically had to take a crowbar and pry you out of his arms. He just kept hugging you to his chest. Mumbling over and over how it was his fault."

"Where is he now?"

"When you started jabbering in your sleep and saying you were hungry, he figured the worst was over and you'd be coming out of it. So, he and Donovan rode out yesterday morning headed to the Rocking R. Donovan came back last night for supplies. Said when there was no sign of Mickey or Dakota, Jackson took off toward Santa Fe, vowing he'd track down those two varmints and some yahoo named Payton or die trying. Big Finn left at dawn to catch up with him."

"Did you say Payton?"

"Yep. Both of them suspect that this hombre, Payton, has been behind all your troubles from the very beginning. The attempted lynching, the barn, and now you being shot. Heard you mumble his name in your sleep. Who is he?"

Just hearing the slimy weasel's name made me sick to my stomach. Wondered if I'd ever get rid of him and the memories that haunted me. Hoped Jackson drilled him full of holes. If Doogan and Dakota were riding with Payton, he needed to take extra care. One-on-one, Jackson could snap Payton in half easier than a twig, but three-on-one was a different story.

"He's my stepfather. Killed my mother. Tried to rape me on the wagon train. I stabbed him. Stole Jackson's horse and rode to Six Shooter."

You could've heard a pin drop. Mary Louise's tiny voice broke the silence.

"You never told us that, Dixie."

"Isn't something I like to talk about."

"So that's the connection between you and Wayne," Sassy said. "Always thought the two of you had a past. Now I know. You should've told me, Dixie."

Just a little put out, I snapped back. "And Finn should've made Jackson wait to ride to Santa Fe until he got back with the supplies."

"Shoot, not even Archangel Michael and all his Legions could've stopped Wayne. The man was on fire."

"I'm going after him."

I swung my legs over the bed only to kiss the floor and fall on my butt. Clicking her tongue, Sassy rushed to my side and helped me back into bed.

"Land sakes, Dixie. Did all your common sense leak out that hole in your head? You ain't going nowhere. Not yet. Gotta build your strength back first."

The room bucked and pitched. Maybe she was right.

"Yet? Does that mean when I'm back to normal, you'll let me go?"

She grinned. "Only if I ride beside ya."

"Deal."

CHAPTER 70

Jackson scowled at the rain. He turned his anger on Finn.
"How can you be so calm? While you suck on that pipe, Doogan and Rutheford are getting further away. We're wasting time and daylight."

"Don't bark at me, lad. 'Tis Mother Nature holding ye up, not me. Besides, in this downpour, those two will he holed up same as us."

"We could catch up with them if we keep going."

Thunder cracked bullwhip sharp. Lightning forked the sky. Uneasy, the horses snorted and threw their heads. "Me thinks the Grand Lady be trying to tell ye something, lad."

Jackson watched the rain bounce off the cliff. They'd barely found the shallow cave before the skies opened up. He settled down on the dirt floor, leaned his back against the rock, and closed his eyes.

"Yeah, like what?"

Finn pulled the corncob pipe from his mouth and knocked it against his boot. Sharp tobacco smoke circled the thin niche before vanishing into the cracks and creases. He pulled a pouch from his vest pocket and refilled the bowl.

"Slow down for one. Ye been pushing yourself and the

horses too hard. Not to mention me self. Me arse be sore as a boil."

Jackson opened one eye. "You got plenty of padding in that area. Surprised you felt anything."

Frowning, Finn clamped down hard on the stem. "No need to be insulting."

A deep sigh. "Sorry. I'm worn out and frustrated. This rain will wash away any sign of tracks and make it double hard to find them."

"Have ye not noticed we've been riding blind for days?"

"I've noticed. But I can't give up. I owe it to Dixie to keep pushing."

"Ye owe the lass nothing."

His short fuse exploded. "Damn it, Donovan. How can you say such a thing? It's my fault she got shot."

"Oh, is it now? How could ye have known?"

"She did. She told me something felt wrong. I looked. Couldn't see anything out of place. Thought she was being skittish. We had a misunderstanding the night of the wedding. I should've trusted her. If I'd just looked harder, I could've —

"Could've what? Stopped the bullet?"

"You don't understand. If she's dead—

"She isn't. No dying person asks for food."

He found that funny and chuckled.

"Guess not."

"You're being too hard on yourself. Ye be so wrapped up in guilt and worry riding both of us into the ground, that ye missed the mark."

"What mark?"

"Think, lad. For one thing, why haven't we found any tracks? Two men riding hard would leave some sort of evidence behind. Second, Dixie was shot on her own land. Which—"

"Which means someone's been watching and following her."

"Aye. Now ye be thinking."

"Micky Doogan?"

"Would explain why we never found him. He be camped out right under Dixie's nose just waiting for the right time to strike. But, we have no proof of that. He may not be behind any of this."

"Dakota?"

"Possible. But why?"

"Dixie made him look like a jackass."

"She wasn't the first, lad. If the stupid arse shot everyone who made him look that way, he'd run out of ammunition."

"What about Daddy Hubert?"

"Aye. But for what reason?"

"The ranch?"

"Could be. Sassy's always suspected him of that. But, here again, for what purpose?"

"That only leaves Payton."

"Aye."

Jackson's face blanched. He swallowed hard. "Dixie and I were sitting ducks yet the bullet only creased her. It was her head bouncing off the ground that did all the harm."

"Where ye going with this?"

"Even Dixie isn't that bad of a shot. What if I was the target and she just happened to get in the way? Or . . ."

"Or what?"

"What if the ambush was a diversion to get us out of town? Payton would know we'd assume that Dakota and Doogan were guilty. He'd figure we'd ride out looking for them."

"Aye. Dixie and the Doves would think all danger be gone. Their guard would be down."

Realization dawned on both of them at the same time. Jackson scrambled from the ground and hit the saddle a split second before Finn cut the supplies from the pack mule. Jackson tossed the reins on Donovan's big dun to him. He caught them midair and found the stirrup.

Supplies. Rain. Sore butts. Wind and lightning be damned.

They raced toward Spirit Dove Ranch and Six Shooter Siding.

CHAPTER 71

It took a week before I started to feel my oats again. Sassy moved back to the ranch to make sure I didn't try to sneak out and follow Jackson. She knew me too well. Would never admit it, but I tried to ride out the day before. Made it as far as the front door before my head spun and ears buzzed. I managed to stumble back to bed without hitting the floor. At least she and Abby were talking again. Still not bosom-buddy pals, but at least they'd started to mend fences.

"It's been a week. Do you think they're ok?"

Not wanting to admit worry, Sassy made light of my concern. "Of course they are. Finn and Wayne are the best lawmen ever to pin on a star. Going to take more than the likes of that brainless Dakota Rutherford to get the drop on them."

"What about Micky Doogan?"

"Him too."

Didn't have the guts to remind her Doogan had clobbered Big Finn once already.

"Miss Dixie, you better come see this."

Most folks would think I was lying if I told them a black man's face could turn pale, but I'm here to tell you, it can.

Something awful had to be wrong to rattle Abraham so. My breath
stopped. Dominique!

Abby sat in the dirt by the corral, rocking back and forth, sobbing like there was no tomorrow. Lobo lay in her arms. My first reaction was relief. Dominique was all right. A split second later, the air left my chest again.

"He's dead, Dixie. Someone shot him. My little Gumdrop is dead."

No. Couldn't be. Too scared to gaze into lifeless eyes, I stood flat-footed. I glanced over at Abraham who shook his head.

"That ain't so, Miss Dixie."

By this time, all the girls had come running. We surrounded Abby who hung onto Lobo tighter than a cocklebur.

"Abby, we can't help him if you don't let go," I said.

She clutched him tighter. "No!"

"Mother of God." I heard Sassy mumble. "He ain't dead, Abby. But if you don't stop blubbering and smothering him, he soon will be."

Holy crow. So much for those mended fences.

In the end, Lobo decided his own fate. A slight thump of this tail convinced Abby he was alive. She let Abraham take him to the barn.

"Abby, honey? Why don't you and me boil some water to help clean up Lobo," Mary Louise said.

Back ramrod straight. With a scalding look thrown at Sassy, Abby stomped off.

Abraham eased Lobo onto the straw. Gentle hands found the bullet hole. "Good thing he's got thick fur. Probably saved his life."

I sat back on my heels. "He's going to be all right?"

A wide smile. "Sure." He patted the dog's large head. "Lobo here be half dog half warrior. Gonna' take more than one shot to put him down."

"Who would've done this? And why?"

Dark color had returned to the big man's face, but it didn't hide the worry lines around his eyes.

"Miss Dixie. If'n' Mama was here, she'd say you be cursed."

"What do you say?"

"I think they wants you to suffer before—"

"Before what?"

"They move in for the kill."

That made my heart shiver and shake. "If that's true, why did they shoot me?"

"I don't think that bullet was meant for you."

"You mean they were after Jackson?"

"Yessum" Heard him say you was uneasy that day, like you knew something was fixin' to happen. That right before the shot, you nudged Joe ahead of him. I think you took his bullet. I wager whoever fired the shot wasn't happy. You got the luck of the Irish for sure."

I laughed. "What do you know of Irish luck?"

"I've seen ya. Heard ya too. Talkin' to your pappy."

Hell and damnation. Heat raced up my neck.

"Don't worry none. I ain't tellin' nobody your secret."

"Reckon you think I'm crazy."

"No, ma'am. I believe in such things. I think your pappy is keeping you safe. Bet whoever it is that's after you is scratching their head trying to figure out why their schemes always fall short."

"It's not them, Abraham. It's only one man."

He ducked his head. "I know. Dominique told me all about the troubles with your step-daddy. She said you don't like to talk about it. and for sure it's a mighty private matter, so I wasn't going to let on I knew."

"Don't worry about it."

"Took guts to fight him off like you did and make a new life all on your own."

"I'm not courageous. Payton scares the spit out of me."

"Never said brave folks don't get afraid now and again. That's what I admire about you, Miss Dixie. You might be shaking so hard your boots fall off, but that don't stop you none. You never back down."

"Some might call me foolhardy."

"Was saving yourself from ruin a fool thing to do?"

"No."

"Was it loco to save Chow Ling's life?"

"No."

"Stupid to fight for this ranch?"

"No."

"Silly to watch over and care for Miss Abby?"

"No."

"Well, then. I reckon them folks don't know the meaning of the word foolhardy."

That made me smile. "Payton doesn't back down either. What am I going to do about him?"

"Mama always told me never to go looking for trouble. She also said to get rid of rats. The sooner the better."

"A showdown?"

"Yep. Take the fight to him. Get shuck of him once and for all."

"You mean, kill him."

He looked me square in the eye. "I do."

"I have no idea where he is. How do I find him?"

A wide grin split his face.

"Oh, I wouldn't fret none about that, Miss Dixie. Trouble has a way of always finding you."

Pretty sure when I died, those words would be chiseled on my tombstone.

CHAPTER 72

Nightmares of Payton jumping out from behind every tree and bush tormented me all night. I crawled out of bed before dawn. Might as well help Abby with breakfast.

Mornings should ease a body into the day with pink sunrises, birdsongs, and lots of steaming mugs full of Arbuckle's. Mine seldom worked that way, however. I get thrown into life on the run. My mind, still fuzzy from lack of sleep, balked at making sense of why Prince Charming stood in the middle of the yard.

"Prince?"

My voice spooked the Appaloosa. I eased toward him. "Easy, boy." Head down, he surrendered to my touch. On the way to the barn, Abraham caught sight of us and walked over.

"Miss Dixie?"

"I'm just as confused as you are."

Big hands ran down Prince's shoulders and legs. The blotched gelding gave out a soft nicker. "He ain't hurt none. Judging from all that dried sweat on his chest, he's run for miles. Poor fella' is plumb tuckered out." He pushed his hat back and scratched his head. "Ain't like Miss Abby to ride so hard."

"Isn't like her to ride at all."

"There's blood on the saddle."

Well, there were five words you didn't hear every day.

Legs shaking, I stormed the barn. Busy doing morning chores, the girls didn't pay me any mind until I yelled. "Any of you seen Abby?"

The high shrill of my voice surprised everyone, including me. All of them, except Dominique, shook their heads.

"Dominique?"

"Abby is not here, Dixcee." Dark cat eyes darted in Sassy's direction. "She was angry over Lobo. She rode out late yesterday to spend the night in town with Della."

"Why didn't you tell me?"

"She knew you would stop her. Made me promise not to say anything."

Dandy. Just dandy. All the Doves knew Abby was simple as a child in a lot of ways. Knew her tantrums lasted about as long as snow in water. Why Dominique let her leave when darkness was just around the bend was a mystery.

"What's the little twit done this time?"

Sometimes the itch to slap the fire out of Sassy burned my hand.

"Prince came back without her. Found blood on the saddle."

"Oh God. Dixie, I'm so sorry."

It gave me little satisfaction to see the color drain from her face.

"Maybe Prince threw her," Pearl said.

"Maybe the reins cut her hand," Rosie added. "Maybe it's not her blood at all."

And this was supposed to make me feel better? Panic teetered on the edge of reason. I swallowed hard. "Payton's grabbed her."

"No. Is not possible."

Mary Louise reached for my hand. "Dominique's right. Bet there's a simple explanation for all of this. I'll ride into town. I'm sure I'll find her nestled deep in one of Della's fluffy pillows."

"Oui. I will go with you, Cheri.

"No. That's just what he's counting on," I said. "It's a trap. No one's going anywhere."

"Then why are you saddling Joe?"

I ignored Sassy and tightened the cinch.

"Dixie? Answer me."

I brushed past her and led Joe out into daylight. One by one, the girls followed me like a line of baby ducks. Sassy stepped in front of me.

"I ain't asking again. What are you doing?"

I glanced over at Abraham. "Killing rats."

That drew a slight smile from the Buffalo Soldier.

While the girls fumbled for words of reason, I went into the house for my pistol and rifle. Sassy trotted behind me, followed me from room to room, and back outside.

"No. You are not doing this, Dixie. You've had some hairbrained notions before. Usually, I'm right there in your hip pocket. But not this time."

"What about Abby?"

"Payton won't hurt her."

"Really? I'm his stepdaughter and he abused and tried to destroy me. Abby is nothing to him. He'll beat the life out of her then throw her to the wolves when he's done."

Hand on the saddle horn, I lifted my foot for the stirrup.

"Damn it, Dixie! This is a man's job. Wait for Wayne. Let him take care of this."

I lowered my leg. Hesitated. I had all intentions of remaining calm. Really, I did. But the more I thought about it, the more pissed I got. I whirled on her.

"I am sick and tired of everyone telling me to wait for Jackson Wayne."

My voice started out low and steely cold. That lasted

about as long as my first breath. I yelled. "Why do y'all think a man is the answer to everything? Get this straight once and for all, I do not need Wayne or any other man to help clean up my messes. Payton is an evil demon from *my* past, not Jackson's. It was *my* mother he murdered. It was *me* he tried to rip the innocence from. *My* barn he burned. *My* friends he kidnapped and *my* dog he shot. I've been scared and hiding from him far too long." I pointed at each one of them.

"None of you can stop me from taking care of him once and for all."

I gathered the reins and settled in the saddle. "If Jackson happens to show up, tell him any damn thing you please. Abraham, please stay at the ranch. It'd be just like Payton to try and sneak up on y'all and you're the best shot here."

"Mother of God, Dixie. What are you fixin' to do?"

I pulled my Stetson down low.

"Shoot the bastard. I'm finished running."

CHAPTER 73

My head shouted, "Slow down. Think."
My heart yelled, "Act first. Think later."
Logic? Instinct? Which one?

One thing I knew outright, blood raced through my veins hotter than lava. Yes, some sort of plan would be good. On the other hand, plans had a way of backfiring, especially mine. My head often lied. My gut told the truth. Besides, I didn't want to calm down. Lose my nerve if I did.

I rode to the Rocking R. Something deep down told me Rutherford, Doogan, and Payton were thicker than the Father, the Son, and the Holy Ghost. Payton's reasons for destroying me were crystal. I could even understand Dakota's motive. But why Hubert Rutherford wanted me out of the picture wasn't clear.

If Sassy was to be believed, it was my ranch he was after. Why? Had to be the unlimited water supply and prime pastureland. His men, what with their fast horses and low-slung gun belts, were no more ranch hands than the Doves were. Gunslingers. Pure and simple. Range-war hombres. Bet anything Hubert Lee Rutherford dreamed of adding "Cattle Baron" to his bank president title.

Over my dead body.

I winced. Poor choice of words.

Even though riled up, I wasn't stupid. I reined in a few yards from the house and studied the terrain. No long-legged horses tied to the hitching rail. No shifty-eyed gunfighters milled around either. The only thing moving was a slow breeze. Quiet. Too quiet? A trap? Only one way to find out. I cued Joe forward.

Wait.

Movement caught the corner of my eye.

Several Chinese girls hung washing on the line. I moved slowly. None of them looked up but one spoke low.

"I friend of Chow Ling. You save him."

Leery, my gaze traveled the yard. "Where is everyone?"

"All leave. You come for pretty lady?"

"Abby. Yes! Is she here?"

"She in big house. But not alone."

"How many?"

"One man."

I was no more going to dismount and walk inside that house then walk over hot coals barefooted. Like hair was to Samson, Joe was to me.

To hell with it.

I nudged the gelding past the stone lions and up the porch steps. I leaned over and pushed the door open. We burst into the sitting room. Iron shoes clattered on the floor and echoed up the stairs. Eyes wide as dinner plates, Micky Doogan reached for his pistol. Before the .45 cleared the holster, Abby busted a porcelain oil lamp over his head. The skunky odor of kerosene flooded the room. He hit the floor like a sack of potatoes.

"Is he dead?" Abby asked, voice cool and calm.

I steadied Joe and stepped down. I paid no mind to the heap on the floor. Abby's bruised face and split lip tore my heart to shreds.

"Abby? Are you ok?"

"It looks worse than what it is."

"Did they?" A slow breath. "Did they hurt you any other way?"

"No. Dakota wouldn't let them."

Well, I'll be damned. Guess instead of killing the goof, I'd just shoot his pinkie toe off.

"I knew you would come, Dixie. Because . . . because that's what sisters do. Right?"

The catch in her voice and tears crawling down her black-and-blue cheek about did me in.

"That's right."

Back stiff, she walked over to Micky and toed him with her boot. He grunted. "Damn. I hoped I'd killed him."

"Abby, was there another man here? Tall, whip-thin? Face like a weasel?"

"Crooked nose. Walks with a bad limp?"

I swallowed hard. "Yeah. That's him."

"He busted my lip."

I took the lariat off my saddle. "Let's get this yahoo tied up. Big Finn can deal with him later."

Tying up a man who was nothing but dead weight was about as easy as hog-tieing Goliath. By the time we'd tugged, pulled, and wrestled Doogan around, sweat rolled off us. Satisfied he wouldn't be going anywhere if or when he woke up, we sat back on our heels and panted.

"I need a snort," Abby said.

She was different. No longer sugar and spice. More like bitter, rock-hard candy. The simple naïve light that shined in her eyes had hardened to an icy glaze. True, she needed to grow up and stop acting like a spoiled child, but not this way. Not forced by a man as vile and wicked as Nathanial Payton. It saddened me. Yet again, innocence had died at the hands of that scum-sucking varmint.

While Abby slugged down whiskey directly from an elegant crystal decanter, I stewed. Too easy. All of this had been too easy. They had to know I'd come after her. Why not hide and wait for me to literally walk into the lion's den and say howdy?

"Nice touch. Riding Joe into the parlor. Hope he shits all over Rutherford's shiny floor."

The smirk on her face and the smart-ass way she'd said the remark pitched me into a fit of giggles. They were short-lived. Sickness washed over me. Abby was bait to lure me away from the ranch while they shot up the place.

"Abby, we have to get back to Spirit Dove. Now. Can you ride?"

"Well of course I can ride. I'm not helpless, ya' know." A deep breath.

"I'm done being used, Dixie. Done crying and acting childish all the time too. I'll take one of the horses from the barn." She pointed to the next room. "Grab me a rifle and bullets from the gun case. A shotgun too."

She yelled on her way out the door. "Bound to hit Rutherford's fat ass with that."

Well, I'll be damned.

CHAPTER 74

I heard gunshots before we topped the hill, which was saying a lot since my heart beat louder than hail on a tin bucket. Tight-lipped and pasty-faced, Abby threw me a look of pure dread. I took a bite of air. "You still with me?"

The easy sound of a rifle sliding from its scabbard was her answer.

"You realize we might have to kill someone, right? Or worse. *We* could end up dead. You don't owe me anything, Abby. You can ride away."

"Not true. I owe you everything, three times over. Besides, I ain't running no more. Remember? Let's get close. See where everyone is."

We inched forward just enough not to be seen. I pointed at the shootout below. "Rutherford's gunslingers are grouped by the corral."

"Yeah, looks like the girls and Abraham are holed up in the house."

Something Abraham once said niggled me. What was it? Something about watching your flank. I smiled. Payton's flank was unprotected and wide open.

"Abby, think you can hit something from this distance?"

"Pretty sure. Why?"

"Keep them busy trying to figure out who's shooting at them from up here. I'll sneak up beside them. Use the barn as cover."

"Good plan. Bullets be popping from every direction, the barn, here, the house. They won't know straight up from sic'em." She grabbed my wrist. "Don't get killed, Dixie. Promise."

"You either."

I worked my way down to the barn praying to everything that wore a halo. The barn's side door stood only a few feet away. I laughed at Wayne when he built that door. Told him I'd never use a side entry. If he were here now, I'd hug his neck. Did that make me a liar for saying I didn't need him? No. A lawman trained in this kind of thing would just be a big help right about now, that's all. I scooted inside and waited for my eyes to adjust to the dim light.

I slapped both hands across my mouth to keep from gasping out loud.

Back turned to me, Payton stood not more than six feet away. A lit match in one hand and a torch in the other.

Son of a bitch was going to burn down my barn! Again!

Not this time, you lousy bushwhacker.

Could I shoot a man in the back? No. But I could a monster.

I shot.

CHAPTER 75

I hurried my shot. The bullet went wide and splintered one of the stall gates. Thank God no horses were in the barn.

Payton jumped.

The match flamed out.

He dropped the torch. Reached for his gun and wheeled. Nothing.

I'd scampered up the ladder to the hayloft before he saw me.

I willed my breath to slow. Steadied my gun hand. Ok. What now? It would be only a matter of seconds before he figured out where I was and came looking. Well, let him come. I'd shoot him dead before he placed a boot on the second rung.

I cocked the Colt and waited.

Taut nerves burned. Sweat popped on my forehead.

A scream broke the tension.

Heart slamming against my ribs, I peeked over the loft's edge.

Payton had Dominique in a choke hold. Her thin knife pressed against her throat. A

crimson trail of blood tricked down her neck.

He laughed. Cruel. Feral.

Payton was loonier than a bedbug.

"Let her go, Payton before I—

"Before you what? Shoot me?" Another taunting laugh. "Dare ya'."

The knife's sharp point nicked Dominique's tender skin right below the ear. A thin red line appeared. Eyes squeezed tight, she whimpered.

"Drop your gun. Get down here." His hold tightened. "Before I peel the skin off her pretty little face one inch at a time."

The urge to kill him burned hot and deep.

Pretty sure I could do it. Put a bullet right between his beady eyes. Only problem was pretty sure wasn't good enough. I'd never forgive myself if I shot Dominique. Or worse. Missed all together. No doubt Payton would skin her alive.

Outside, sounds of gunfire, cussing, yelling, and horses' screams roared. Sounded like all the demons from hell had escaped and descended on Spirit Dove Ranch.

"Don't you count on those whores busting in here and saving your hide. My boys have big plans for them. And forget about that big buck too. Left him flat out in a pool of blood."

The sour taste of vomit crawled up the back of my gullet.

I dropped the gun to the ground below and climbed down. Stopped just short of him.

"Ok. You got me. Now let her go."

A sneer so vile the devil would've cringed crossed his thin face.

"Maybe I will. Maybe I won't. Or maybe I'll jam this knife up and under her ribs and fling her to the dirt to bleed to death like you did me. I knew that wagon scout was lying. Knew all the time you were hiding out in Six Shooter. No other place you could've gone. Yes sir, I've had eyes on you for a long time."

"Dakota Rutherford and Micky Doogan?"

"Daddy Rutherford too. Idiots all three of them. Told Papa Daggett to burn you out. Made a mess of that. His addle-headed son couldn't even manage to shoot a dog. Doogan botched the lynching and killing of the wagon train scout too. Ah, well. You know the saying. If you want something done right, do it yourself."

"Bet that pissed you off good." My voice sounded so sure. So calm. Don't know how. I was about ready to pee my pants. "Oh, and by the way . . . that *scout* is a Pinkerton Detective. Knows all about you and Morgan's little scheme. Knows you murdered Mama too. He's gonna' put the noose around your neck personally."

"Don't count on that. By the time he and that big Irish Mick get back from the wild goose chase I sent them on, I'll be long gone. And you'll be long dead."

Before I could blink, he whirled Dominique around and punched her square in the jaw. She dropped like a stone and didn't move.

Red. All I could see was red.

Fists flying, I charged at him. Raked my nails down his face.

He threw me off.

My back hit the barn wall. Hard. Knocked the breath out of me. He was on me like stink on a skunk.. Pinned my arms over my head. The back of my hands were skinned and burned from the rough wood. He stood so close I could smell his sweat. See the spit on his lips.

I kneed his groin.

He was too close to do any real damage, but I got enough of him that I tore loose from his grasp. A thin haze of dust, straw, and dirt swirled in the air. Gasping, and coughing, I grabbed a pitchfork and jabbed at him.

He whirled. Headed for the door.

I threw the fork. The four-prong spear missed his back by inches and clattered to the ground.

Quick as a snake, he turned back. Grabbed me up by the

collar.

I spit in his face.

He backhanded the injured side of my head so hard my teeth rattled. That did it. All the fight drained out of my bones.

The barn spun. Eyes blurred. Vomit and blood marched up my gullet. He dropped me. I sank to my knees and retched.

He would kill me now for sure.

Underneath the humming in my ears, I heard a fierce growl.

Lobo!

The half-wolf/half-dog shot across the barn and hit Payton square in the chest. Knocked him flat on his back. He kicked. Lobo caught his boot. Shook it like a rat. Sharp teeth pierced leather and went straight to the bone. Snapping. Tearing. Ripping. The savage wolf inside Lobo broke free.

Payton yelled. Kicked. Cussed. His hand latched onto the pitchfork. He smacked the fire out of Lobo. Rolling ass-over-teakettle, the dog gave a sickening yip and went silent.

Payton crawled toward the nearest stall. Pulling himself up by the gate slates, he managed to stand. Ears ringing, I lunged for my Colt. Shouldn't have moved so fast. Dizzy,

gagging on the oily taste of bile sloshing back and forth in my belly, I struggled to sit up. Flat on my butt, legs sprawled out in front of me, I gripped the Peacemaker with both hands and took the shot.

I hit his arm.

I pulled the hammer back.

He hobbled out the door.

Crab-like, I made it to the entrance in time to see him jump on a horse and tear off. Other riders trailed behind him.

He was getting away!

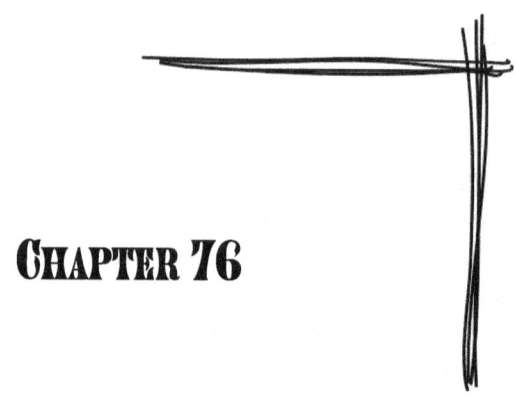

CHAPTER 76

Joe! Joe could outrun the wind. I could still catch him. If only the room would quit spinning. Staggering better than any rum-guzzler, I made it to the side of the barn and Joe. I reached for the stirrup. Hell, which one? Three floated before me. I guessed. Picked the middle one. Wrong. I hit the ground. I sat in the dirt and cradled my pounding head with my arms. Just needed a minute. Then I'd try again.

"Dixie?"

Abby knelt beside me. I blinked at her. "Payton. He's getting away."

"Let him go."

"No!" I rolled to my knees. She helped me to my feet. "I can still catch him."

"Not today you can't. Not in the shape you're in."

She was right. I knew it. But it hurt so bad to fail.

I gave up and leaned against her shoulder. Arm in arm, we walked to the front of the house. The girls met us halfway. I found the porch steps. My breath caught.

"Dominique! Oh my God. In the barn. Payton punched her good."

"I am ok, Dixcee."

With Pearl on one side and Rosie on the other, Dominique wobbled our way and eased down beside me.

The bruise on her chin would be black by morning.

"Dominique. I am so sorry."

"Is nothing. He did not cut me deep. No scars. No broken bones. The bruise will fade."

"No. Not that." My voice cracked. "Abraham. I'm so sorry Payton killed him."

"I ain't dead."

Abraham's voice never sounded so good.

"The bastard shot me in the thigh. The bullet went straight through. Mary Louise stopped the bleeding. Got me bandaged up and all taken care of."

Sassy laid her hand on my shoulder. "All of us are fine. Bruised and battered. A little shot up. But we'll all good. Which is more than I say for you. Looks like you went a couple of rounds with Beelzebub himself."

"I was holding my own until he hit me upside my bruised spot. Hurt like hell." I grinned. "But he paid for it, believe me. He'll limp twice as bad now. Lobo . . . oh God."

"Lobo is all right too, Dixie," Rosie said. "Banged up some but with a lot of rest, he'll be up and running in no time."

"Good advice for both you and Dominique." Mary Louise clicked her tongue. "Let's get you two cleaned up."

"But Payton."

"He ain't gonna' bother you for a long time, Dixie, if ever. Not after the reception we gave him and Rutherford's men today. Reckon he thought a bunch of women would be easy pickings. Guess he found out different, didn't he, gals?"

Like I said. Doves were hawks with velvet wings.

My gaze traveled the yard to the corral. A couple of men lay face down in the dirt.

"What are we going to do about those bodies?" I asked.

Sassy let out a low chuckle and winked.

"Choppy? Choppy?"

CHAPTER 77

I slept until late afternoon the next day. The room closed in around me. I needed fresh air. A ride was just the ticket. Joe paced the corral. Guess he needed to run too. I'd just buckled his bridle on when I heard hoof beats.

Jackson!

He reined in but didn't dismount.

My heart flipped and flopped. Overjoyed at seeing him, knowing he was safe, I slammed the corral gate shut and raced to the house only to stop short. Something was wrong. He sat stiff and cold in the saddle. I walked past him to the porch steps. Puzzled, I turned back to him.

"Jackson?"

"Damn it, Dixie. Why? Why didn't you let me handle Payton?"

"Well, it's nice seeing you all safe and sound too."

He ignored my sarcasm. I'd never seen him so angry. Not at me anyway. It scared me.

He stepped down. Brushed past me to stand by the rail.

"If you had only waited, Payton would be behind bars. Abraham wouldn't be shot full of holes. Dominique's face wouldn't look like a punching bag, and you would never have to look over your shoulder again. But no. You wouldn't hand over the reins. You refused to trust me . . . again."

My temper flared. I shot back at him. "What was I supposed to do? Let Payton kill Abby? What makes you so cock-sure you could've caught him anyway? And Abraham wasn't shot full of holes either."

Dark storm clouds swirled in the sky and across his face. I waited, afraid to know what he was thinking.

"You're the talk of the town. Do you know that? All of Six Shooter is buzzing over the shootout. Wild and woolly Dixie Dandelion. She don't need nobody telling her what to do. No one fools with her. Guess you feel pretty good about that, don't ya'?"

Well, yeah. I did. Was that so bad?

He drew a deep breath. "Want to know how I feel? All the way back, with wind and rain beating my face and my heart pounding so hard it hurt, I kept picturing you at the mercy of Payton. Kept seeing you broken and dead. Do you know what your death would do to me?"

He didn't wait for an answer.

"Put me six feet under too." His voice softened. "Dammit, gal. I love you. Always have. Always will."

In all my life I never thought a man would say those words to me with so much fire and passion burning in his eyes. Especially a man so gallant, so steadfast, and strong.

I stepped toward him.

He backed away.

My heart fell.

"No other woman will ever take your place, Dixie. Not in my heart or in my life. But. I can't do this anymore, darlin'."

He gathered his reins and mounted up.

Panic froze me to the spot. "Where are you going?"

"After Payton. I'll find him too even if I have to track him halfway around the world. I'll catch him because that's what I do. That's who I am. And because I once made a promise to a desperate young woman trapped on a wagon train that he'd hang for killing her mama. And I always keep my promises." He threw a mock salute. "Congratulations, darlin'. You made it more than plain you don't need anyone or anything. Even me." His smile held no humor.

"I won't be riding back this time, Dixie."

He waited for the words to come. Waited for me to deny it. To say, stay.

I didn't believe him.

I said nothing.

"You'll always be my wild prairie dandelion, Dixie gal." He touched the brim of his Stetson. "Take care of yourself, darlin'."

With a touch of his spur, Thunder wheeled.

Jackson Wayne was gone.

CHAPTER 78

Stunned, I stumbled back into the house and sank onto a kitchen chair.

He's bluffing.

He'll come back. Always has.

But. What if he wasn't fooling?

What if I never see that chiseled face again? Feel his strong arms around me? Smell his shaving soap? Never hear darlin' ever again? Could I live without him to lean on?

Damn it. Even if I didn't want to admit it. Even if he doubted. I did need him. In the back of my mind, I knew no matter what happened, what foolish mess I got myself into, Jackson Wayne would be there to back me up. Be there to love me no matter what and never cast judgment. His strength fed my own. Gave me the courage to keep on fighting. To pick myself up no matter how many times I fell.

But it was more than that. Crooks like Payton, Rutherford, and Doogan were yellow-bellied cowards. To make up for their lack of courage and confidence, they abused and destroyed. But Jackson was cut from a different cloth. He knew who he was. Stood firm in what he believed in. He was man enough to let his woman be who she was, even if that meant she was a wild and woolly horse rancher.

Did ye ever tell the boyo that, lass?

Even though I couldn't see him, Papa's presence filled the room. Gooseflesh popped along my arms. I spoke out loud.

"No."

Why be that?

"I didn't want him to think me weak, depending. I didn't want to be like Mama."

Daughter. That notion be only in your head. Ye ridden that horse into the ground. Ye can't keep blaming your sainted mother for your stubborn Irish pride any longer. Love as deep as Wayne's comes around only once in a lifetime, lass. Don't be a fool. Ride after the boyo or regret it the rest of ye life.

I tore out the door like the hounds of hell were nipping at my heels. Didn't have time to slap a saddle on Joe or fool with corrals or gates. Without missing a beat, I leaped onto the fence and jumped onto the gelding's back.

Spooked, Joe reared. Pawed at the air. He broke into a gallop. Circled the round pin and headed for open pasture. He cleared the top rail with inches to spare.

I clung to him tighter than a prickly pear. Tears filled my eyes. But not from the wind that whistled past. I cried for Jackson. At the thought of losing him. For being so selfish.

"Jackson!"

I screamed his name and kicked Joe to go faster. Muscled legs chewed up the ground. A dust cloud came into view. Joe caught Thunder's scent. Bit in his teeth, he lengthened his stride.

I let him run.

"Jackson!"

The wind stole my cry and threw it back in my face.

"Jackson Wayne!"

He heard me. Stopped. Turned in the saddle and watched Joe barrel toward him.

I didn't check the little Mustang with even one click. Closer and closer.

With only a few feet to spare, I pulled back on the reins. Joe tucked his nose, gathered his hind legs under him, and slid to a sliding stop so perfect and smooth, every cowpony in Texas would be jealous.

I baled off his back. Stomped toward Thunder.

"Jackson Wayne! I got something to say to you."

His jaw dropped. Gave me time to catch my breath. I lit into him with everything I'd kept bottled up inside for so long.

"You're damn right I'm your wild prairie dandelion." My throat tightened. New tears threatened. My voice came low but rang clear. "But even the wildest flower needs the sun and rain to grow, to bloom beautiful. Needs strong, rich soil to hold roots deep enough to weather any storm."

I paused. Gulped for air. I put my hand on his leg. His eyes, deep and wickedly dark, reached out and roped mine, hog-tieing me with a stare so intense my knees shook. I wanted to crawl into his skin, his soul, and brand my words forever in his heart.

"Don't you understand? *You* are my sun and rain. Without you, I'd wither and die on the vine with nothing to anchor me . . . just an empty wisp blowing in the wind."

He shifted in the saddle. Was he leaving? I grabbed the reins and tore them from his hands.

"We were destined to be together from the beginning of time. Flying Eagle told me that once. I believe it. And if you think I'm just going to let you ride off into the sunset, you got another think coming."

He threw a long leg over Thunder's neck and slid to the ground. We stood so close I had to step back to see his face.

"And just how do you plan on stopping me?"

My heart quickened at the teasing tone in his soft, southern drawl. I drew myself up tall and fired back.

"I'm not. I'm going with you."

A crooked grin pulled his lips. "What?"

"You heard me. If you aren't ever riding back, then I'm coming with you. Always by your side. Forever."

"What about the ranch? Those precious horses of yours?"

Oh, if he thought I didn't have an answer for that one, he was sadly mistaken.

"I'll make Abraham a partner. Be a nice wedding present for him and Dominique."

His dimples deepened. Those damn cute dimples that made me wilt.

"I'll become a Pinkerton Detective." I rushed on. "We'll be the first man and wife Pinkerton team. Together, we'll track down all the outlaws in this wild territory. Bring them to justice."

"Whoa! Slow down. Man and wife?"

"You got a problem with that, Lawman?"

He pulled me tight to his side.

"Nope. Just like the way it sounds."

"We'll be famous."

"Famous, huh?" He chuckled. "Think someday some author fella will write one of those dime novels about us?"

"Yep. I can see the title now." I snuggled closer into him.

"The Legend of Dixie Dandelion and the Pinkerton."

He spun me around to gaze up at him. Every bone in my body melted, but I knew I wouldn't fall. Knew I could trust him to always be there to catch me.

"And every man for years and years to come will read the words and say, "That Dixie was one hell of a woman!""

"And every woman will fall in love with Jackson Wayne," I added.

He laughed. Deep and rich.

"What" I grinned. "You don't think folks will remember our names?"

"Oh, darlin'."

He lowered his lips to claim mine.

"Of that, I have no doubt."

ABOUT THE AUTHOR

R.H. Burkett, aka Ruth Weeks, is an international tarot card reader who draws from her deep Cherokee and Cajun roots to write riveting tales of the paranormal. From her travels to ancient stone circles in rural Ireland to her explorations in the French Quarters of New Orleans, she tells stories that encompass her love of all things mystical.

Her latest release *Broom Flyers Tales and Spells* is a compilation of her short stories, one of which was nominated for a 2023 Spur Award (Western Writers of America). Her first novel, *Soldiers in the Mist*, was voted Ozark Writers League (OWL) 2012 Best Book of the Year. Her second novel, *Daughter of the Howling Moon*, was the Oklahoma Writers Federation (OWFI) 2015 Book of the Year.

As a child, Ruth was fascinated by stories about her Grandmother Ely, who was part Cherokee and part Cajun. That was the inspiration for her adopting the handle Witchy Woman. She currently lives in Springdale, Arkansas, with her familiar, Fred. Check out her website RHBurkett.com and follow her author's Facebook page, where you can watch videos of the author talking about her travels, her heritage, and the people she meets both from this world and the next.